Ian Wild is a writer living in t numerous literary awards, incl award in 2015 for Mrs. Shake Short Story Prize 2012 and the *Fish International Short Story Prize* 2009. His broadcast work includes *Way Out West* – a comedy series for RTE Radio One; and over twenty children's stories for RTE's *Fiction Fifteen*. Four of his musical comedies appeared in Cork Midsummer Festivals between 1998 and 2003.

'One of the most truly original writers in Ireland today.' *Irish Examiner*

'Highly entertaining.' *Ed Handyside*

'Extraordinary!' *Anne Caldwell*

'Pushes the limits of how much fun a novel can be.' *Clem Cairns*

Other praise for Ian Wild's work.
'Funny, clever and inspiring.' *Broadway Baby*
'Hilarious from start to finish….you won't be able to stop laughing'. *SF Crowsnest*
'Masterfully written by Ian Wild, demonstrating his quick-witted flair for combining literary accuracy with psychological unravelling.' *Female Arts Magazine*
'A writer of simply astonishing stories.' *Aidan Stanley RTE*

ALSO BY IAN WILD

Novels
The Naked Umbrella Thieves
The Celtic Tyger Hunt
My Fourth Dimensional Friend
The Woman Who Swallowed the Book of Kells
(Short Stories)
Plays
Homage to an American in Paris
Spaghetti Western
Marco Polo's Toilet Brush
The Milk of Human Kindness
Somebody and Nobody
The Pirates in Short Pants
Mrs Shakespeare
Rachmaninov's Maid
Poetry
Intercourse With Cacti

The Girl with Two Heads

A Romantic Comedy

Ian Wild

Green Room Books

Published in 2025 by Green Room Books.
Copyright © 2025 by Ian Wild.
Ian Wild has asserted his moral right under the Copyright, Designs and Patents Act 1998 to be identified as the author of this work.

All rights reserved No part of this publication may be reproduced, distributed, or transmitted in any form or by any means, including photocopying, recording, or other electronic or mechanical methods, without the prior written permission of the publisher, except as permitted by copyright law. For permission requests, contact Green Room Books, notmorestories@gmail.com.

The story, all names, characters, and incidents portrayed in this production are fictitious. No identification with actual persons (living or deceased), places, buildings, and products is intended or should be inferred.

first edition 2025

Book Cover design and illustration by Willow Liao

ISBN 9798298138734

For Fun

One   *Kite*

My heartfelt advice to doting parents at a font, is this: *be careful what you say.* From an early age, I yearned to be ordinary, an ambition one might assume, well within the grasp of anyone who likes a bar set low. Unfortunately, my name was Alphonso Blink. Now I defy anyone to grow up ordinary with such a label etched on their christening cup. If a birth certificate has John Smith scribbled across it, that person—especially if he is a boy—has a very solid foundation on which to build a humdrum existence. John as a name is almost as off-the-shelf and standardised as a number. The same goes for a plethora of boy's names such as Alan, Dave, Ben, Rob and so on, all of which have a foggy, indistinct identity because they are shared by multitudes. There's nothing weird or unusual about being a Tom, Dick or Harry, because the names are quite commonplace and therefore the suspicion must be, deep in the psyche of their owners, that so are they. To grow up with such appellations is to feel that there is nothing outré or unusual about your life otherwise you would have been called Alphonso Blink. It is quite an unfair advantage these people have when it comes to achieving an existence that is comfortable, unremarkable and well, sane.

From the very beginning then, my name was an impediment and I had none of the privileges enjoyed by those with a conventional signature, like fitting in with society. What made it worse was that my parents were phobic to the point of weirdness about weirdness. My father once stood at a bus stop beside a man who was wearing different coloured socks and fretted about it over breakfast for weeks. One sock was grey, the other navy blue. Had the man done it deliberately? Should my father have chastised him for the sartorial solecism his ankles were committing? My mother had a neurosis about a couple from a nearby village who rode a tandem and would pedal along our street on it, smiling and waving to those who stared. She would run indoors at the sight of them cresting the hill on which we lived, dragging me with her and muttering, "Don't look, don't look." Then she would peer through net curtains as the cheerful pair went by. "Why can't they buy two *separate* bicycles?" When I got into trouble at school for painting a landscape with a green sky and red fields, she put my paints in the bin.

So why then, I hear you thinking, did my parents call me Alphonso? And why not alter their surname from Blink to something like Jones? Yes. Why? *WHY?* Fair enough, changing a name from Blink to Jones would mean signing a deed poll, an act that might well be on the weirdness scale, though not so very far along it. But why Alphonso for your only child? Ronnie, Kevin or Sam would all have passed completely unnoticed.

I only discovered the truth from my Aunt Esmeralda.

On her rare and uninvited visitations, Aunt Essie would blow in like the West Wind—it would not have surprised me had blustered drifts of leaves accompanied her entrance into the house. On this occasion she appeared at the front parlour door in a large feathered hat and voluminous scarlet coat to find my father and mother painting the room beige.

"Oh there you are."

"Essie." My father looked uncomfortable. Drips fell from his brush onto the floor. "This is unexpected. But then I suppose it always is."

She looked around the half-decorated room critically. "Thought I'd drop by to see if either of you had become less dull. But I see you haven't."

My Mother flinched and gave my father a pleading look.

"No need to be rude, Essie."

"Forthright, Jonathon. Forthright means knowing where we stand. And as Alphonso's Aunt I have a duty to pop in now and then to liven things up for the boy. I daresay he doesn't want to grow up as beige as his surroundings."

Well actually Aunt Esmeralda ... I wanted to say but didn't dare.

"What would his grandfather make of the boy being brought up on an estate where all the houses look the same?"

"Would you like a cup of tea Esmeralda?" my mother asked with trembling politeness.

"Not if it's tepid and weak like the last offering I drank here. But otherwise yes. I can't stay long. I have a meeting somewhere north of here. This place was on the way so I thought I'd put in an appearance."

"Well, it's nice to see you Essie," my father lied.

"Oh don't be ridiculous, of course it isn't. Now, Alphonso..."

Unbelievably it had only just dawned that my parents had parents—for they had never been spoken of before.

As if from a dream I said, "Why would my grandfather not like me being brought up where all the houses were the same?"

"Your grandfather Alphonso..."

"*Alphonso...?*" I stuttered.

"You must know you were named after your grandfather? In fact, I seem to remember I insisted on it."

"But ... why Auntie?"

She looked at me in surprise, as if the answer were obvious. "Well, you don't want to grow up *ordinary* do you?"

I wasn't forthright.

"Your grandfather would rather have hated that."

At which, unable to control some writhing sensation inside me, I ran out of the room.

I knew it. I had long suspected that my name and the odd events that stalked my every waking moment were connected. It was bad enough that on being introduced to someone, whether adult or child, they would repeat my name as if tasting something slightly unpleasant. Then however, they would experience one of the events that seemed to stick to me like bluebottles to flypaper and which grew ever more extraordinary. I had managed to get through the first few years of school without the teachers or other children being overly suspicious. Unfortunately at the age of eight, my desk began to move of its own accord. At the end of the school day it would be correctly positioned, half-way back and beside a window. Next morning it would be across the room and upside down on the floor. Or on top of the teacher's desk or outside on the lawn. It would not have mattered if this poltergeist activity had also happened to the desks of others. But only mine moved and it was nothing to do with me except that it was obviously EVERYTHING to do with me, even though I never touched it. I was sternly quizzed by several teachers and the caretaker eventually glued the legs down only for the furniture antics to spread to my chair. One morning this was discovered in the passenger seat of the headmaster's car. By which time my schoolfellows had begun avoiding me in the playground, whispering in distant huddles and pointing in my direction. When my parents heard of the misbehaviour of my table and chair, they stopped my pocket money and mother refused to speak to me for a week.

The chair was taken away, broken up and used to fuel the school boiler, at which point the classroom furniture went still. Some weeks of orderliness followed, before a number of further incidents occurred, too many in fact to adumbrate here. They all however eroded my communal standing.

I did try to find out more about my Grandfather Alphonso.

"Is he still alive?" I asked my father.

"No. He ..."

"Yes?"

"... isn't."

The final straw, with regard to my social non-acceptance, came when Aunt Esmeralda visited on my birthday, which was unprecedented. She came with a gift—also unprecedented. It was furthermore without precedent that she gave my parents a day's forewarning of her arrival.

My mother sat on the sofa twisting and untwisting a handkerchief. "Not again, not after the last time."

"It can't be helped," my father said in exasperation, possibly with both my mother and aunt, "I dare say she won't stay long".

"She threw my butterfly cakes into the garden and laughed when they didn't fly."

"She's just going to drop in a present for Alphonso. She'll be less than an hour. Essie's always rushing off to some meeting or another."

"Something dreadful will happen. You know it will. It always does."

The following morning I unwrapped my presents, two pairs of grey socks and matching sweater, a comb, and a set of junior golf clubs. Aunt Esmeralda burst in as Mother was laying the table for lunch which caused my place setting to have two forks either side of the plate. My Aunt looked younger than the previous times I'd seen her, perhaps because she was dressed so casually: in jeans, a floppy straw hat and a t-shirt printed with *Happy Birthday Alphonso* on the front. She dropped a large package onto the table.

"Many happy returns."

Never having received a birthday gift from my Aunt before, I could only stare at the package, feeling it must have momentous contents. My parents gazed at the parcel wrapped in brown paper and sellotape with fascinated horror. What had my strange and astounding relative bought me?

"Thank you, Aunt Esmeralda."

I lifted and squeezed the package which felt like it contained pieces of kindling. Clumsily I tore off a layer of brown paper to find swathes of tissue paper underneath. Then the moment of truth: yellow cloth; wooden struts; purple ribbons tied on a string. It was an unassembled kite.

"I used to adore flying one when I was a child," my aunt enthused. "The tug of it on the string. The sight of it swooping on the wind."

My parents relaxed.

"A lovely present Esmeralda," my father beamed.

"Running with it across the downs. Running and running and looking back at a diamond with its sinuous tail climbing higher and higher."

I ponderously assembled the pieces. It was decided that my aunt and I should go out into the meadow behind the house to fly the kite whilst lunch was being prepared and my father fixed the gate-leg of our dining table.

The housing estate on which we lived was set beside a piece of undeveloped land and here my aunt and I unravelled a length of string and galloped through a field in an attempt to persuade the kite to fly. Thrown into the air the yellow rhombus crashed cartwheeling to earth like an early 19th century aviator.

After several attempts my aunt stopped, looked up at the sky and murmured, "Hmmm. There's no wind." She picked a few grass stalks and tossed them upwards. They landed at her feet. "Disappointing."

Undaunted, she spotted a ladder in our yard and dragged it into the field. She then disappeared into the garden shed, emerging with a claw hammer and six-inch nail. Leaning the ladder against the sky and taking the kite, she climbed to the topmost rungs and hammered the kite into the blue firmament. The kite hung motionless, with more a semblance of hovering than flight. When I tried to run over the field with it, the string snapped. Momentarily dismayed, I turned to apologise to my aunt, but having clambered down the ladder she was welcoming my father who had come to call us into lunch.

"We got it airborne," Esmeralda said triumphantly to my father.

He spluttered at the sight of many neighbours peering over fence after garden fence at the sky.

"And now," my aunt continued, "I must go as I am late for a meeting. Happy birthday Alphonso."

She swept out of the field, past my father and out of my family life. At the same time, a throng of children arrived in the field to goggle at my present adorning the heavens.

"Auntie nailed it up and so the string broke when I ran with it," I explained.

Aghast, my father marched into the meadow, picked up the hammer and in full view of a growing audience of neighbours, climbed the ladder to remove the six-inch nail. The kite dropped and landed beside me. Speechless with mortification and fury my father descended, toppled his ladder onto the grass and dragged me inside the house. There he snapped the kite over his knee several times and shoved it at my chest.

Hearing what had happened, my mother sobbed and insisted we would have to move house. I was sent to my room and my birthday cake incinerated with the broken kite, though I kept the beribboned tail hidden in a box under my bed. Esmeralda was forbidden to visit again. Ever.

After this phantasmagorical episode, people would cross to the other side of the road if I went walking in the village. None of my schoolfellows would sit beside me in class nor the canteen, regarding me with a mixture of awe and revulsion. I was probably too strange to bully. I think my classmates were frightened that if they surrounded me and started chanting 'weirdo' I might do something really terrifying like agree with them and not cry.

All this went on depressingly into my teens. Every now and then some minor surrealism would visit to remind the world, as with a firework display, to keep well back. Leaving school therefore was a relief—I couldn't wait to bin the uniform. And also fail my exams. It wouldn't have helped my parents to learn that even when I'd known the answers, my pen had scrawled the wrong ones down. Without qualifications, I found unsuitable employment in a local cafeteria washing dishes. This lasted two weeks before the inevitable occurred. One morning the proprietor discovered every plate in the kitchen smashed—not whilst I had been there. Overnight. But it was enough that I had been the current *plongeur*.

After which, I was too scared to seek another job. I found that nothing weird happened if I merely sat alone in my room. My parents let me, wanting no further social embarrassments. It didn't affect my social life as I'd never had one. I'd been to school with most of the girls from my village who regarded me as too freakish for words, never mind anything else. And the boys were sullen, not daring to befriend me for fear of becoming social outcasts themselves.

My one consolation in all of this, was the weekly visit to our village of a mobile library. After borrowing the maximum of four books, I would retire to my room, part a cover and meet worlds undreamed of. Fictional beings became dear friends.

I was a close acquaintance of Raskolnikov and Elizabeth Bennet, though never introduced them to each other. Atticus Finch sat on a porch rocking-chair in my room. Hamlet and Rosalind were a surrogate brother and sister. For two years I did little more than read the bus. Twenty buses.

There *was* an uncanny occurrence in the mobile library during this time. I found a book written by my grandfather. Browsing the shelves one morning, my own name leapt out at me from a spine: *Alphonso Blink*. It seemed fantastical, like a slice of magic. I immediately tugged the book out and looked at the cover. It was a clothbound, hardback book, in plain green. The title in black and gold said,

Let Them Have It. *A Farewell to Socialism*

I stared at the cover, as if fearing it would vanish in a puff of smoke. It had to be written by my grandfather. There couldn't be three Alphonso Blinks. I looked at the dedication inside: *For Imogen.*

After it was stamped (nobody had taken it out for three years), I raced home, concealing the book up my jumper, mounting the stairs to my room. It was read, cover to cover. Then cover to cover again and cover to cover once more. Not because it was a good story—it was in fact a polemic—but because it contained my grandfather's innermost thoughts, and therefore, in some way I had met him, shaken his hand, and by the third reading, given him a hug. Not least, the contents of my amazing grandfather's book were contrary in the extreme to my parents' way of life.

That was fascinating and oddly heart-warming, though the pages did not seem to relate to my own life in the slightest.

He argued over many chapters that material wealth impoverished those who touched it and that the only riches worth having were within a person's own being and these could be nurtured easily for free. There were compelling thoughts about how those suffering from material poverty do not notice the holes in their pockets nor care about them, if their inner self is abundant, and that poverty therefore is only relative to a person's cultural riches. Much of the second part of the book dealt with how to enrich people inwardly, and how an awareness of the magicality of ordinary things, makes them extraordinary. Most of all, that wealth redistribution was pointless, because the Rich were too terrified to allow it and that inner wealth creation was simple and did the same thing better.

It is probably a simplification to write that there are two kinds of wealth: inner and material. But I shall write it anyway.

It is a cheering thought that the living conditions of a Medieval Monarch would be abject poverty to that of a modern citizen today. If only poverty were not relative we would all be rich as kings.

Artists have long been famed for working in penury. They are obviously being paid with an inner coin.

It is often said that the Rich are getting richer. The great delusion is that the Rich are rich at all. It is increasingly apparent that the Rich are getting poorer. Inside.

A person with an awareness of the magicality of very ordinary things all around us – a leaf, insect, pebble, or raindrop, will find an out-sized cheque killing the spell.

Giving riches to the inwardly destitute is like handing candy floss to the starving.

Let us abolish those things that impoverish our inner lives.

On and on it went, a manual for life, but not, unfortunately, *my* life, for I had no inner or outer riches beyond the book itself. Every week it was returned to the mobile library bus and renewed. I read the words so many times they would unconsciously recite themselves in my ear.

Eventually, seeing *Let Them Have It* borrowed week on week, the mobile librarian, a woman who looked like she had been born bibliographic, swaddled in a cardigan and tweed dress with tiny horn-rimmed spectacles, said softly, "It's by your grandfather?" She looked about her, then smiled," You just keep it, love. Here. But shhh. Just between you and me." She winked, "Don't bring it back. I'll mark the book lost and take it off the stock list."

That woman had inner riches for sure.

I hid the book under a floorboard knowing my parents would flinch at every word. Had my father even read what his had written? And if he found such incendiary literature in the house, what then? A tiny bonfire probably. The treatise became my most cherished possession: a literary lifeline to my Granddad.

Throughout all this, I had one other minor occupation. On days when I'd finished four books or was dulled by a tale, I would venture over nearby fields to a disused mill beyond the village, some half mile from my home. The mill had long fallen into disrepair and a large sign on its decrepit gate said: **Private Property**
Keep Out
Trespassers Will Be Prosecuted

This must have deterred the village youths for I mostly had the mill and unkempt grounds to myself. There was a large pond encircled by willows, and having read Izaac Walton's book *The Compleat Angler*, I cut a long hazel rod and fished for perch and roach returning them afterwards, I hoped a little wiser. It was a soothing pastime.

From the roof of the mill, a weathervane had fallen long ago and it lay in a weed-strewn courtyard, still revolving, but not according to the winds. It revolved, even spun violently, when there was no wind. It had spun ever since we had first met. Its spinning might have been the result of falling off the roof, but I felt only a *very* resounding tumble would make a weathervane spin for five whole years, though I'm not saying it couldn't happen. The reason it spun is perhaps not important. However, one morning, sat in the courtyard, I considered the vigorously rotating compass.

"I like your spinning. It's weird. You know, I think my aunt and grandfather would like your spinning too".

Then it stopped—on a blustery day—the very moment I'd appreciated its whirling round and round.

Which was a bit much, for I'd never previously admitted out loud that being peculiar was a likable trait.

"Oh, for goodness' sake."

But was not its stopping at that moment also peculiar? A communication of sorts. I didn't know whether to be downcast or cheered, but noted the weathervane's North was pointing South and its South, North and had a suspicion (understandable given my experiences with smashed plates and moving chairs) this would lead to trouble. The question was, *what* trouble? Suddenly, I was gripped by an intuition or paranoid vision, call it what you will, that within minutes a penguin would waddle breathlessly into the courtyard from a southerly direction heading towards Iceland. And that this would trigger a stampede of disoriented creatures such as snow-white bears and elephant seals, swapping polar regions—with me caught in the middle of the scrimmage. Even at this remove, I can't say for certain it wouldn't have happened. Losing my head, I immediately snapped both North and South arrows from the weathervane—they were fortunately weakened by rust—and lay them pointing in the correct directions in the grass.

It then occurred to me that if East became West and vice-versa the fauna exchange might be even worse, so I snapped off both those pointers too. And this *is* important, for in not wanting any subsequent environmental catastrophes to be traced back to myself (should creatures start switching hemispheres) I made a bow to fire the arrows as far away as possible. And if I hadn't done this and dispatched them to the correct points of the compass, I'd never have ended up in court and been tried for not killing four people, nor ordered to leave home and the little I held dear. Most of all, I would never have fallen in love with the Two-Headed Girl and she would never have betrayed me.

I made a bow from the fishing rod's line and pole and fired arrows East to the East and West to the West. Then North to the North and South to the South. There was something about these actions that reminded me of Aunt Essie's kite being nailed to the sky. It was unfortunately witnessed by several local youths, peering through the Mill gate.

I won't dwell on the shooting incidents. Nobody was hit or hurt, but as was pointed out to me by the judge, at least four people *could* have been killed had they not stumbled out of the arrow's flight path after being chased considerable distances—in the case of one man, three miles. It seemed draconian to arrest me afterwards, merely because the arrows returned and thudded into the front door of our house. In court I confessed to my part in the events and was sentenced for 'Crimes That Might Have Happened', to a train journey of indefinite duration to an undefined destination with only myself for company.

Two   *Suitcase*

At least it was a steam train, which I have always admired for their clanking jolliness and sooty oldfangled airs.

My parents waved me off from the station platform, undoubtedly relieved I was going. My mum pretended to sniffle into a handkerchief which I thought touching. Dad shook my hand.

"Goodbye Alphonso," he said. "Leave the communication cord alone."

Sage advice.

In the carriage compartment three men sat well apart paying no attention to each other, nor myself when I boarded with a suitcase. Expecting to have the entire train to myself, their presence felt odd. I heaved the suitcase up onto a rack, hoping this normative action would commend me to my fellow passengers, for the length of my journey being unspecified, this trio might be companions for many miles. I didn't want them burning with resentment from the outset: *put your ******* suitcase on the rack.*

The train lurched and began chugging from the station. I waved goodbye to my parents from the carriage window, though they had already gone. The platform and a series of goods sheds receded in backwards motion before a succession of seedy backyards came into view. I risked a glance at the three passengers. One was an old man with an Einsteinian thatch and eyebrows, but also a Marxian grey beard. He looked engaging but sat staring at the floor as if concerned that it might *do* something. The second man was younger and bore a resemblance to the elder passenger but had less rampant hair—they might have been father and son sat far apart, as if estranged. The second man was knitting a long scarf of many different colours—it looked like a fallen rainbow slumped over his knees. The knitting was passionately done—as if it really mattered. Opposite me the youngest of the three men was reading a book: *Long Train Journeys. A guide.* He also appeared to be related to the other two. It was like sitting in a compartment with a grandfather, father and son who had all recently argued about a matter that had not been resolved. It dawned after a while, that each of the men shared physical characteristics with myself and therefore I might be sharing a carriage with me in several different stages of my future existence. It was only at this point that the thought of an endless train ride with only myself for company, became disturbing—especially as one might at any moment pull the communication cord. Though if that meant I could disembark and escape, it might be worth the scream of brakes. Feeling both claustrophobic and hungry I broke the silence, "Is there a restaurant car?"

An open question to all three men.

"Yes," said the one knitting after a pause, without looking up.

I stood and was about to vacate the compartment for the corridor, when the older man took out a pair of scissors and snipped off the end of his beard.

"Here," he said, as I stood at the door, "Have this."

"Why would I want these ... hairs?" I asked with some asperity.

"You wouldn't."

"I don't."

"But they won't go back on and I'll grow more. Give them to someone else. Give them to the Girl With Two Heads."

I accepted the whiskers with a grimace and thanked him, restraining a desire to shout: *What a stupid and bizarre thing to do!* But knew we could not help it. There was some comfort to be had in thoughts of reaching a ripe old age, but obviously I would never be anything other than deeply weird.

I left the carriage and walked past another incarnation of myself in the corridor. To keep meeting older versions of myself—and this one was maybe in his 30s—was spoiling life's tantalising uncertainty. In the restaurant car, half-a-dozen me's were sat at tables, not in conversation and another self was serving behind a counter. When asked what was on the menu he replied, "Leftovers."

"Of what?"

He shrugged and pushed a half-eaten sandwich across the counter towards me with a mug of tea inches down from the brim.

"Why is everyone on the train like an older version of myself?" I whispered.

He shrugged again.

I sat at the only empty table and considered the tea and sandwich. They were probably only my own leftovers, but the temptation was slight. There was a book on the table: *Even Longer Train Journeys. A guide*. I was about to open it when the train began to slow, brakes scraping like knives being sharpened. With the side of my head pressed against a window to look ahead, I watched a station arriving, the carriage gliding by posts, signs, a porter and ticket office, before we jolted to a standstill. Hastily I rose and made for the door to egress the carriage. Nobody moved to stop me jumping down onto the platform, which was empty but for a man in a railway company uniform wheeling a trolley into a goods shed. Not a single person appeared to get onto the train. Strange. Then doors were banged open along the train's many carriages. About thirty passengers stepped down after me onto the platform. *Thirty or so older me's*. I glared at them as they stood in huddles beside the train. They stared back.

"No!" I boomed in a deep voice, as if to a dog following me home. *"No!"*

Their faces formed a group expression of crushed disappointment. I said again with finality,

"No. Definitely *not*."

They turned slowly and climbed back into their respective carriages. A stationmaster appeared and slammed all the doors, then blew his whistle. Borne off by the puffing locomotive, my own selves stared balefully at me through the windows as they left.

I felt a pang of guilt, but to have a gang of elder Alphonsos hounding my footsteps into the future, knowing what was going to happen before I did would have been unspeakably trying. Meanwhile, no authorities had appeared on the platform to rearrest me for breaking my sentence so soon after it had begun. It felt odd to be allowed off the train, though the duration of the journey never had been stated. Reluctant to draw attention to myself, for I still felt an outlaw despite having done nothing amiss, I chose not to ask a Porter of my whereabouts and approached a large station sign that read:

Not Waterloo.
Not Piccadilly.
Not Liverpool Street.
Not Euston.
Not Victoria.
Not Little Upton.
Not Crewe.
Not Lime Street.

I liked how much trouble they'd gone to be unhelpful. The train having chugged off very completely, I sauntered out of the arched Victoriana of the station entrance, trying not to look fugitive. A thought arrived that it would have been helpful to have the suitcase I'd forgetfully left on the train luggage rack. This was a blow, for there might have been any number of useful things in that baggage: money, food, a change of clothes, a comprehensive list of stations. Not to be dragging it into a gloomy townscape that looked to be settling down for the night was a dispiriting start to adulthood. I was without the means of buying so much as a cup of tea. Being nothing if not resourceful, I decided to knock at a house for help.

The first door I thumped on was opened by a kindly old couple who listened politely to my pleas.

"Hello. Sorry to bother you. I was on a train journey and stepped off at the station nearby, without my suitcase which I left on the luggage rack. I was wondering if you could lend or give me a suitcase with which to continue my journey and perhaps some of the filling to go inside it such as clothes, foodstuffs, toiletries and money."

The old man pursed his lips. "Suitcases don't grow on trees you know."

I agreed with this observation but added that it would not be altogether a bad thing if they did. The old man offered left-overs of their dinner.

'But we both ate everything, Sidney," the woman informed him.

"He could lick the plates."

I thanked them and left. The town, now alive with house lights in the gloaming, had nevertheless lost its lustre. Doubtless, it had been premature to step off the train so early in my punishment. I decided to walk until something better happened to me. A lane with no streetlamps and a serpentine disposition led, as I had hoped, towards open countryside. Before long, the moon's pellucid glow became so intense, that a roadside cottage, its garden, a farmhouse, then another cottage, could all be seen with clarity. After a mile or so, I began to wonder if it had been altogether wise not to have licked the two plates freely offered. There might even have been dessert bowls. Worse still, after leaving civilisation behind, a landscape of gloomy fields had unfolded in which beggable roadside dwellings played no part. Instead, moonlight fell spectrally on rows of leafy vegetation. I stopped to consider this. Might those rows not be carrots or courgettes? Or King Edwards that could be baked in a fire? I crept down a bank to look.

Sinking to my knees beside the nearest plant, I found it had sprouted a large oblong vegetable, troublesome to identify in the gloom. My hands went over a rectangle two feet long and half as wide. Firm and flat. With clasps and a handle. *It was a suitcase.* The farmer was growing luggage! Other plants in the row nearby, were the same, though varying in size. Suitcases? Who would grow such a peculiar crop? Had it somehow mutated because of ... *because of me?* It was enough to fill anyone with disquiet. For like cubist cabbages, cases had seemingly sprouted in ploughed lines across the field. The farmer would be apoplectic about such vandalism. How could he take harvested luggage to market? Who would eat them? How would a chef serve one up? Unless the plants grew with belongings inside. In which case, so to speak, had each grown differently packed?

Here, I was reminded of my luggage on the train, in a way that I hadn't when disembarking at the station. A replacement suitcase would not go amiss. I could not, of course open all the plants to inspect their innards. That would possibly decimate the crop and infuriate the farmer further. Whereas the loss of a single fruit might not be noticed at all. So, feeling conspicuous in the spotlight of the moon's disapproving stare, I sneaked on all fours up a row and reached for the biggest and healthiest looking specimen that sprouted close to hand. The suitcase, attached to the plant by a fibrous juicy stalk, came away easily when pulled, suggesting it was ripe. A strange leathery smell arose. I crept back to the road, freshly harvested valise in hand.

Feeling more of a fugitive than ever, I hurried from the scene of the crime. Fortunately, clouds moved in and the road darkened, though at the cost of a more blundering progress. Agonising about my criminal act, I wondered if the farmer would come after me with a shotgun. Not only had their field of cauliflowers been transformed into travel accessories, but I'd stolen one of them. Unless. Unless he actually *was* a luggage farmer and then would the loss of a single fruit even matter? I lumbered onward, desperately keen to snoop inside the case, but wanting to be some miles clear of the farm before laying it flat to lift the lid.

The road was long and dark and with the moon behind clouds I stumbled in my flight and wondered if there were a torch in the suitcase. Would I need a torch to investigate the contents for a torch? My ruminations were disrupted by the sound of a distant engine in the hills. Headlights sliced through the night like a knife through black butter. A car was speeding along the deserted lane. Was it the farmer? Surely not. It was to be hoped that they would pursue in a tractor. I watched twin shafts spear a grove of trees, sweep hedgerows, rake fields and vanish into dips. It occurred to me to ditch the suitcase or, even better, throw myself into a bush. I don't know why I didn't. Either action would have been sane. That I merely kept on walking was to not think on my feet in a manner that would have been dismaying to watch in another person similarly beset. To my horror, a car approached and slowed, spotlighting me in its headlamps as if I were onstage. Momentarily blinded, I groaned inaudibly when the vehicle pulled alongside me and stopped. It was the police. Were they onto me for the suitcase or escape from the train? I'd only just done both. A chubby man in a uniform leaned slightly from an open window and looked at me critically from beneath bushy policeman's brows.

"Going far?"

"Not really. I had insomnia. I decided to go for a walk to clear my head."

"With a suitcase?"

"I didn't want to leave it in the hotel. Because I couldn't sleep there, it was half in my mind that I might not go back."

"Noisy was it? Which hotel?"

"The one on the main street."

"The Dog and Bucket?"

"Is there another one?" I asked, trying not to sound slippery.

"Not on the main street."

"Then it must have been the Dog and Bucket." I concluded.

"That's not on the main street either."

"Then perhaps ascertaining the main-ness or otherwise of thoroughfares is not my forte. It's not a criminal offence is it, walking along a road at night with a suitcase?"

"Depends what's in the suitcase."

"Just clothes and other personal belongings."

"And if it's your case."

"It's got my name embossed on the handle," I blustered.

"It does seem strange to find a man walking down a country lane in the middle of the night with a suitcase and not knowing the name of the hotel he's checked into."

"But strangeness isn't illegal is it?

"Not yet. At this stage only suspicious."

"Are you going to arrest me for walking down a country lane at night with a suitcase of my own belongings?"

"Depends ..."

"Then are you going to take me into custody for questioning?"

"I can question you here. What's your name?

"Portable Designs."

It was a name I had seen embossed on the handle of the suitcase by the light of the police car's lamps.

"What?

The policeman looked as if he had hearing difficulties.

"Portable ... Designs ... P ...O ...R ...T ...A ...B ...L ...E ... D ...E ...S ...I ... G ... N ... S."

"Strange name. Almost as strange as walking along this road at midnight with a case."

"Well it's embossed on the handle of my case. Look, my name, imprinted in the leather. Portable Designs."

"You must have had strange parents."

"Can we leave Mr and Mrs Designs out of this please? I came nocturnal walking to clear my head of worries that were causing insomnia. I think after this conversation I won't sleep for a month."

"What were you worrying about?"

"I can't believe you are asking me these questions on a deserted road in the middle of the night. My life is in ruins. My wife ran off with another man, I hate my job as a travelling salesman and I'm having a midlife crisis years before midlife has arrived because my future has no future. I don't know where I'm going in life and walking along this road with my few belongings seemed to be somehow fitting and helpful until you pulled over to interrogate me."

"Ah."

"Ah what?"

"Now I understand. Sorry to have stopped you. I often feel like that myself. Being a policeman doesn't really agree with me. I just don't go so far as to wander aimlessly at night as a result. Enjoy the rest of your evening. I hope things sort themselves out soon."

He drove off and no sooner had the noise of this been swallowed by starless silence than distant sounds of another car's approach took over. This had me clambering hastily into a hedge, thorns notwithstanding. Minutes later, a second police vehicle went by. Slowly. Eerily. As if searching for some lone, late traveller with a stolen suitcase. After which the road held no further attractions for me. I hurried instead, albeit as if blindfolded, over farmland finding refuge eventually in a barn on top of a hill. Keeling over onto a stack of straw bales, I fell almost instantly asleep.

I woke famished to daylight filtering through a hole in the roof. I still hadn't opened the suitcase and did so now in the hope of finding it crammed with food. It was a 1930's affair with two silver clasps that sprang up when keyhole buttons beneath were side-pressed. Throwing the lid back eagerly, I was aghast to find tightly-packed wads of banknotes in rows. This was depressing. I tasted a fifty-pound note, for having been grown in a farmer's field there was an off-chance it might be edible – some money is, chocolate gold coins for instance. The fifty was however revolting and tasted of people labouring in unpleasant jobs.

Finding a suitcase crammed with used fifty-pound bills might bring a sunbeam into the lives of some, but even before reading my grandfather's book, money had never enthralled me. Undifferentiated, humdrum rectangles, paper bills reminded me of the housing estate I'd been brought up on. It stands to reason that mass-produced artifacts are of less value than those that are handmade, therefore hand-crafted artisan banknotes might have been of greater interest. Coins were worse. Round, flat and annoyingly jingly with the heads of historically unpleasant people franked on the smelly metal. Though it has to be said, there weren't any coins. I was disappointed in the case and slammed the lid. I had carried it MILES in the hope of more eclectic contents. First and foremost, some food: sandwiches, carrot cake, milk, tea bags and a flask of hot water. A false nose, moustache and glasses would have been welcomed, also a wig and clothes – stylish and unlike my own. Yes, some pin money but nothing to roll about in. I had obviously picked the wrong variety of case and so abandoned it in the straw, feeling famished but attuned to my grandfather's spirit. Besides, a man scampering over fields with a suitcase looks sufficiently odd for a certain prying type to want to report them to the police.

So, having taken just as many banknotes as seemed insufficient to corrupt my soul, I emerged from the barn to find myself surrounded by a Constable landscape on the sort of cloudy day he liked to depict. From my lofty position, I spotted in the not-too-far-off distance, a woodland where the desperate might forage for nuts, berries, and apples, despite it being too early in the year. I set off ravenously downhill, having had only half a fifty-pound note for breakfast. Taking the path of least lanes and farmhouses, I eventually came to an overgrown orchard, unhelpfully bare of apples, plums or mulberries. The trees in some kind of sinister reiteration of a theme, hung heavily with suitcases – a dark and forbidding fruit. Walking beneath this canopy of branches and leaves which bore a formidable crop of luggage, I feared to be brained by a windfall. Not for one moment was I tempted to pluck a valise from a low hanging bough, (though it could not be denied there might have been apples inside them), such was my dread of that second police car the previous evening. It felt too risky to scrump suitcases.

It so happened however that in a glade at the end of the orchard, there *was* a windfall: a case, lying battered and bruised in the grass, where a buffeting wind had doubtless knocked it down with a thud. I paused thoughtfully over this large brown object. A hungry soul cannot be reprimanded for gathering windfalls, or be tried in a courtroom surely, for partaking of one. The catches of this valise opened easily to reveal four half-eaten sandwiches. After only a momentary hesitation I lifted one of the cheese and pickle delicacies from the case and nibbled away. I wondered if somebody had already discovered the windfall and sampled its contents, but would a person hungry enough to take four large bites from a sandwich do so from more than one sandwich at a time? It seemed less implausible that the innards of the valise naturally grew half-eaten sandwiches. Whilst tucking into this simple and perhaps already sampled fare, I surveyed the rest of the case's contents. There were garments of some description and closer rifling revealed these to be a simple white dress with a laced bodice and puffed sleeves, accompanied by a blonde, pigtailed wig, beribboned bonnet and a collapsible crook. A shepherdess's costume no less. Still possessed of a fugitive mentality, I disrobed and donned the disguise which fitted perfectly. There was even some strap-on padding provided to give the wearer an appearance of being buxom. Of flasks, tea, milk and liquid refreshment generally, there was none, but I let this go. A shepherdess such as I had become would undoubtedly find a mountain spring with which to refresh herself. Suddenly, the world and my own prospects looked more cheerful.

Three   *Shepherdess*

It was unlikely in my winsome pastoral disguise that I would be recognised, rearrested and sentenced to another harrowing train journey—therefore I was free. Free to do *what* was moot necessarily. I might not wish to be a shepherdess all my life, particularly one without a flock, which would inevitably lead to existential crisis. It mattered only that for a while at least, I could pass myself off in the world as a normal person, until fresh opportunities presented themselves with regards to a more fulfilling occupation. Extending the crook to its maximum length, I skipped out of the glade and along a woodland track, noticing how easily I fitted in with the banks of flowers and trilling of birds. Emerging onto rolling meadows, I wondered how did shepherdesses find work? Present themselves at farmhouse after farmhouse? Though to play the part of a modern Bo Peep who had lost her sheep might lead to awkward questions. Whose sheep had I lost and where? With regard to future employment, I would certainly need a backstory and stopped to practice on a tree.

"Hello," my voice squeaked, "I am a shepherdess looking for employment. Unfortunately, if you desire a reference, the farmer I worked for previously and for many years died suddenly in a sheep-dip accident. Yes. Most upsetting. But if you would like to see me shepherdessing and have some sheep, I could give you a demonstration of my skipping and other skills."

Hopefully the farmer, enamored of my pitch and authenticity of apparel, would nod sagely and bid me go into the kitchen for a cup of tea and some home-baked bread. Perhaps this nursery rhyme existence – peaceful, Arcadian, and normal might turn out to be my calling. I would have put this plan into action immediately had it not been for a timely and momentous meeting with an actual sheep. I rounded a hilly outcrop, and from behind an arrangement of gigantic stones a woolly creature emerged, took a look at me and uttered that single word in the sheep lexicon the world over.

"Baaaaa."

I was taken aback and stopped in mid skip. It was a nanosecond of *substance*—a snapshot that would be stuck forever in the photograph album of the mind. Here was the very creature I was destined to spend much of my near future tending. With this magnificent shaggy individual, I could practice and hone my abilities. Show Bo Peep where she had gone so disastrously wrong.

The beast stared at me and though I had never been on close acquaintance with a horned, woolly ungulate before, it occurred to me that eye contact might be crucial to the pair of us getting along. I had read that in zoos, creatures continually stared at often become depressed, as prolonged eye-contact is a common way for one animal to establish dominance over another. A gorilla in a zoo might become demoralised by the thousands of stares. Try it in the wild and the beast will rip your head off. And of course nobody fears or is intimidated by a sheep, so *everyone* stares at them. In an effort to be friendly then, I looked away from the sheep and then fleetingly back, as if unable to hold eye contact, and again away. I sat on a boulder and repeated this several times. The sheep looked shocked. It is rare to see astonishment in a creature so lacking in facial expression but there could be no doubting that something momentous shifted in the history of sheep/human relations. I could almost hear the curly-horned head thinking*: what is this? A human—a sovereign of the pastures and wool-snatching despot—is treating me as an equal! More than an equal—giving me respect!* There was a sense that, for the sheep at least, the world had turned upside down: for the exploited and downtrodden a new day! She tottered a couple of steps towards me, transfixed.

The sheep had the name 'Horton' dyed into its woolly haunch—an unusual name, not that I am anyone to cavil at an outlandish appellation. My experiment with eye contact having arrested Horton's attention, she came nearer, head tilted ever so slightly to one side. I considered grabbing her with my crook, purely a practice swipe for the experience of having done it at least once, should a repetition be required at a future interview, but that would have been a breach of trust. I also considered offering some grass but felt this could be interpreted as facetious when the field was overflowing with it. Using verbal communication as an overture of friendship seemed futile for Horton's vocabulary came from the world's tiniest dictionary. What is a translation of baaaa? Do sheep fundamentally, have only one thought? Surely using the B word over and over when I didn't really know what it meant, could only undermine my fraternal advances. Especially if there were nuances in the word which I was unable to detect and which altered the meaning. There seemed to be nothing for it but to continue with the fleeting non-eye contact.

In fact, this was easily enough to win the sheep over. Clearly Horton had seldom met so fascinating a shepherdess as I, and who knows how beautiful our friendship might have become had not three further sheep appeared round the rock. They went stiff at the sight of me, but I met their ovine stares of suspicion with a couple of fleeting sidelong glances which left them stupefied—or at least, more stupefied. As my submissive overtures continued, they, like Horton, stumbled closer, and I saw that each also had the name Horton dyed on their rumps in red. Really, how are sheep to develop any individuality if they are all called by the same name? True, they looked pretty much identical and if a shepherdess were to name them all differently it might afterwards be tricky to remember which was who. Safer I suppose to choose one name and baptise them in the dip as a job lot. Still, given these circumstances it's no wonder that sheep are such sheep. A shame, because taken singly, unflocked so to speak, they are extraordinary creatures to look at and it is only there being millions of them dotted all over the world like little fluffy clouds on burned matchstick legs, that leads us not to notice them. The more of a thing there is, the greater its invisibility becomes. If there were only two sheep in existence, almost as rare as the dodo, we might wonder more at their extraordinary magical appearance: the whorled horns and gaunt Roman-nosed faces so wildly at variance with the abundant frizziness of their coats; they might then be viewed as a beast worthy of reverence and awe instead of a succulent accompaniment to mint sauce or provider of an unwanted Christmas jumper.

There I was then, with a flock of four—an excellent opportunity to gain experience in my new shepherdessing career. (Being a *shepherd* did not appeal to me incidentally, there being no glamour in it, nor poetry.) At this point I had to confess that I had not a notion of what a shepherdess might actually do. Round up a flock, look pretty as a ceramic figurine on a mantlepiece and then what? I was saved from immediately confronting my own ignorance by the timely arrival of the rest of the flock. Many sheep. All called Horton. Twenty or thirty baaing ungulates poured around the rock and met my inconstant gaze. It was not long before the entire flock was gathered around me, spellbound. Surely whatever modest duties a shepherdess might perform would be easily accomplished with this sort of mastery over the creatures in my care? If this was not success then it was failure of some magnificence. Who owned these Hortons and did they have or require a shepherdess of my evident gifts?

"To whom do you belong, my dearest four-legged sisters?" I inquired of the assembly in a high-pitched voice.

They looked up at me dumbly. Not even a Baaaa.

It appeared to be a question of finding the nearest farmhouse and presenting myself with a polite curtsey. But which way to go?

"I suppose it is quite hopeless to expect any of you to lead me to your owner's abode?" I squeaked. There was a silence. "Well, it has been a great pleasure to make the acquaintance of you all and I hope we will meet again soon in circumstances to our mutual advantage."

There was a pathway up and around the rocks suggestive of a not-too-distant 17th Century farmhouse with whitewashed walls and cobbled courtyard, so humming to myself in a girlish falsetto, I picked my way through the flock to seek out a new life of humble agrarian employ. It came as a surprise to find the Hortons at my heels after only a few yards skipping. I pulled up and spoke to them in my cute shepherdess's voice.

"You don't need to follow me *yet*. I must first be engaged by your owner to tend you, *then* ..."

I broke off because their blank looks suggested my words were just so much human baaaing. Still, there was no harm in having an obedient flock as accompaniment when I met Mr Giles or whoever dwelt in the picturesque farmhouse of my imaginings and I resumed a springing of steps to the fore of my adopted herd before a sudden doubt brought my limbs once more to a standstill. Might not the Giles' be displeased by the sudden appearance of thirty ewes in their front garden?

"Dearest Hortons, one girl to another, I have decided to go alone on this quest to find to whom you belong. So whilst I am searching, employment-wise, for pastures new, you might loll here on pastures old until I return. We shall not be parted long."

This was not an admonishment, but I was firm and wagged my finger. There were a few isolated *baaas,* which I took to be consent. However, on continuing along the grassy knoll there came the unmistakable patter of cloven feet. Once again I stopped and turned.

"Now look," I became stern and dropped my voice several octaves, "You *cannot* come with me, understand?"

I stared at them, holding eye-contact to an extent that would have horribly depressed a gorilla in a zoo. But it was too late for that. My earlier antics had established me as a sheep messiah and these—my disciples—were expecting to be led to promised pastures in a revolutionary overthrow of the established order. The eyes of my flock were filled with a fanatical fervour. They had become my followers in a way that short of turning them into mutton chops, I could not undo. As a shepherdess I'd been altogether too successful. There was nothing for it but to hike up my skirts and make a dash for it across the meadow towards a stone wall.

Don't get the idea that sheep are waddling loafers whose days slowly nibbling hill and dale leave them wheezing and unfit; this lot were athletes. A pack of worsted thoroughbreds, they kept up with me effortlessly with enough breath spare to baa all the way. They could have run the Derby! On reaching the wall I vaulted over it in relief only to see the flock hurdle after me as if from the fevered imagination of an insomniac counting to a million at three o'clock in the morning. I stood on the other side of the enclosure aghast as they tumbled over the stonework in a woollen waterfall.

"No! Back! Back you fleecy morons! I'm not even a shepherdess. I lied. You've been taken in. I'm a just a bloke in a dress and a wig."

Again, surrounding me, there was nothing in their eyes but a fixed determination that wherever I went, they would be sure to go. Their devotion and levels of fitness necessitated the immediate birth of a plan to pull wool over the eyes of what was only a flock of sheep, for God's sake. There was a small gathering of trees and thicket nearby and I sauntered towards this as if any notion of escaping the Hortons had been left on the other side of the stone wall. It was monumental ill-fortune therefore to round the bushy perimeter of the copse and meet, coming the other way, *another herd of sheep*. There was almost a head on collision. Both parties performed an emergency stop with a jostling pile-up at the back and bleating protests. I attempted no funny business with eye contact and gave them a stare that hardened into a menacing glare before turning back through a parting sea of Hortons to retrace my steps. Sheep being sheep they *all* followed me. A nightmare would be a pleasant dream in comparison. I knew if I hopped back over the wall the entire lot, two whole flocks, would jump after me.

"Now listen you lot," I blustered, "Get it into your bony heads, *I do not want to be followed*. I want to be alone.

You are not gazing up at the cult figurehead of some sort of Sheep Liberation Front."

It was like they were hanging onto and yet ignoring every word. The new flock were at least not all called Horton, but they did have 'Tim' dyed into their woolly sides. I mean, *really!* No wonder they couldn't think for themselves—mind you, this lot couldn't take orders either.

"Might I suggest that the Horton's hop back over the wall and the Tim's stay here. I am, meanwhile, going to a sheepless place."

With this, I marched back to the copse, albeit with an unheeding cohort of woolly companions and selecting a lofty oak with obligingly climbable boughs, ascended until the ground looked giddyingly far down through the leaves. The sheep gathered round the trunk in silence, gazing up at my dangling legs and I dare say, frilly bloomers, with imploring bleakness. I resolved to ignore them completely, certain that in their own good time boredom would set in and when one drifted off, the rest, unable to help themselves, would inevitably follow suit. This did not happen. Hours passed and my ambitions with regard to future shepherdessing, shrank with the heat of the day, the hardness of an oak's pew, and rampant hunger. Even for half-eaten sandwiches. To climb down was a climb down, there was nothing for it however, but to seek out the farmer of one set of sheep or the other and explain that the flocks had inexplicably followed me probably because I was a shepherdess—though on holiday and so not looking for employment. I was welcomed at the base of the tree by hearty bleatings—flattering in a way but in the circumstances, enough to make a drover want to lead swiftly on to the nearest abattoir.

It ought not to be difficult to find a farmhouse in the heart of the English countryside, but it is an unwritten law of finding things that they never turn up until you have long finished searching and are looking for something else entirely. Any Mr. or Mrs. Giles would have done and it was all the more galling that in the course of my unsuccessful explorations, I somehow managed to acquire five more collections of sheep, each additional flock stamped with a different appellation. Coke. Lud, Rog, Mimm and Ard. After only a few hours of roaming butterfly-strewn farmland devoid of farms, I amassed an army of sheep. A legion. Caesar probably crossed the Rubicon with fewer followers. I tried any number of ruses to escape: climbing gates, jumping ditches, finding a very high stone wall, nothing worked. I even took off the shepherdess dress and twirled it round my head as an example of someone too lunatic to follow. At one point, I turned to see a moving carpet of woolly grey, funnel down a hillside after me, like dirty suds down the plughole of a sink, then got on my hands and knees and barking, impersonated a collie.

A couple of Horton's attended me closely for the entire journey, the most devoted I fancifully imagined to be the one I had first met—an apostle of sorts—but I couldn't be sure. Whatever, as my hunger increased (for I'd had no sustenance since opening the windfall suitcase) so did guilty thoughts as to whether it was immoral to eat lamb in the present company, with roast potatoes and peas. Would I be able to eat a Horton, barbecued over a spit? Or a sandwich with slices from a Tim's tender rump? What would the rest of the immense flock think? Did they think?

That evening, disconsolate, I settled to camp on a hillside in the lee of a hawthorn brake, surrounded by my companions. There were none of the little comforts one imagines make shepherdessing such an agreeable pastime. No rustic abode where a maid might luxuriate in a tin bath of warm spring water to remove the whiff of sheep and cares of the day. Nor sweet cot smelling of aired linen and lavender. No nightdress or mirror in which to unbraid one's hair. Not a single dainty sandwich with the crusts cut off, nor glass of cooling lemonade. Instead, there was damp grass, hard earth, the heady odour of matted wool, and a stomach that felt empty even when I was asleep. Not that I did sleep as my dreams were disturbed by grasshoppers that went up my dress and pinged about.

I woke after dawn with a dozen or so ovine faces pushed enquiringly into my own, like owners of a guest house anxious to know what I wanted for breakfast. Only there *was* no breakfast.

"What?" I started and groaned. "Yes, I know its morning. I suppose you've all had a sumptuous feast of grass and are raring to go?"

Thus far in my life, farmhouses had failed to play much of a significant role, being a scenic adornment at best. Now I needed one more than air. I needed breakfast and somebody, anybody, but preferably a farmer, to take a few hundred sheep off my hands.

A thought occurred that perhaps, overnight, the multitudes might have forgotten that they were following me, or got fed up with it, and that I might be able to saunter off whilst they remained grazing on the hill. True, it would only take one of them to bleat and follow me, but it was worth a try. With what I hoped was inconspicuous nonchalance, I stood and began slowly to amble across the field. The flock rose as if choreographed and as one jogged after me – I felt like a cat with hundreds of cans tied to its tail.

It was enough to make a shepherdess break a crook over her knees. *Shepherdess!* As I looked hopelessly into the far horizon, across the backs of many ewes, for faint glimpses of a distant farmhouse, an extraordinary vision met my eyes. Over the brow of a nearby hill, not more than a couple of hundred yards away, came a group of seven shepherdesses, skipping furiously over rolling pastures, crooks bristling. A great operatic chorus of baas filled the air as they approached and I almost fell to my knees in relief. Up, up the knoll on which we stood came the maidens, bounding towards the herd and myself with angry skips. Picking my way through the flock, I went to meet them. They skidded to a halt, breathing heavily, some glaring at me, whilst the others investigated the sheep.

"They're ours alright!"

"Mimmstead!"

"Cokenstop!"

"Hortondale!"

Amongst the seven there was a great variation in height—from the extremely tall to not very—and width also, if I might be so unchivalrous. All were dressed in full shepherdess regalia, including pigtails, and all I daresay, were charmingly pretty, though it was hard to be completely sure, so fearsome were the expressions on each face. Still anxious that Alphonso might be a train-jumping wanted man, I decided to preserve my feminine identity and thus, high pitched voice.

"Ladies, I am extremely pleased to ...."

"THIEF!" They shrieked in an ensemble.

"Well, if these sheep are yours ..."

"THIEF!" They repeated, as if I might have missed the earlier point.

I think there is nothing more infuriating for angry people than attempts to calmly reason, however, I did so in a hoarse soprano. "If you were aware of the circumstances surrounding the surrounding sheep ..."

"Who are you?" The tallest one snarled, pointing her crook directly at my throat.

"Where were you taking our flocks?" demanded another, her shaking stick also aimed at my collar.

They were nothing like the illustrations I'd seen in books of nursery rhyme.

"THIEF!"

"Please, I have not stolen them, they followed me because ..."

"Hey!" the smallest one looked at me keenly. "You're not a shepherdess at all. You're *a man!* A man *pretending* to be a shepherdess!"

There were scandalised gasps from the company. They gave me as one, a penetrating stare then closed in and surrounded me, picking at my dress.

"Those are false breasts!"

"His chin has three hairs!"

"A cross-dressing shepherd!"

To have seven affronted women picking holes in my disguise with such hostility was unsettling.

"Alright!" I ditched the falsetto. "Alright, I'm not a shepherdess. Or a shepherd. The truth is that I found the shepherdess costume in a windfall suitcase that had fallen off a tree …"

"Fallen off a tree?"

There were skeptical jeers.

"And thought I could try being a shepherdess as a new vocation, so I went in search of a farmer to ask if they needed some sheep rounding up and on the way …"

"Ha!" They screeched at my naivety.

"It's not just *anybody* that can choose to be a shepherdess these days," said the foremost Amaryllis with a haughty toss of the pigtails.

"Though it helps to be a woman for one thing," came a snide addendum.

"You have to have a degree in shepherdessing at least," a third Phoebe opined.

"A BA."

One of the sheep spelled it out further.

"*At least*. I have an MA," said the smallest shepherdess, somewhat smugly I thought, "Priscilla has a doctorate."

The one with a crook still at my throat inclined her head modestly.

"You need a four-year course in all the techniques: counting, crook handling, going to market, flock management, health and safety, pasture, dips, skipping ...There's so many different philosophies and schools of thought about the best way to herd and nurture sheep. You need to know which branch you belong to and wish to follow. So I don't think you should go on masquerading unqualified as you are."

"Yes. Don't think you can trespass on our pastures again and steal our flocks Mr Unqualified Shepherdess."

The other six murmured their galled agreement. I restrained a yell.

"I didn't steal them! They just *followed* me. I was trying to escape the bloody morons all of yesterday. I don't want your sheep. I never *did* want your sheep. I'd be delighted if you drove them away and I never saw a single sheep again for the rest of my life because they're driving me nuts!"

"Well, if that's the case," said Priscilla primly, "you can hand over the shepherdess costume and we can know for certain that your words are sincere."

"I don't have any other clothes," I explained as if to an idiot. "I left them in the case and haven't a clue how to get back there."

The smallest snorted. "Hand over the crook, pigtails and dress and we'll take what you've done no further. Otherwise, we go to the police and report you as a sheep rustler."

I was flabbergasted. "For goodness' sake, I don't have *any other clothes.*"

"That's your problem," said one of the wider shepherdesses sternly. "We want no recurrence of your crimes. It will take us all day to sort out the mess you've made as it is."

The wig was snatched from my head, the crook from my fist and then two of them began lifting the dress.

"*Ladies!*"

The rest joined in and dragged the garment over my head. My ineffectual struggles were not so much because I was outnumbered, more the threat of the police. I was left standing in bloomers, breast pads and grimy white plimsolls.

"Let him keep the rest," granted Priscilla.

"That's kind of you."

"We could be less kind if you like?"

"I don't doubt it."

So there I was in light drizzle on a hillside, wearing little more than bloomers, having been defrocked by seven shepherdesses in a manner that was extremely humiliating, but worth it to get rid of a pacifist army of sheep that surrounded me. I was glad to have been left with the chest padding for I'd stuffed three fifty-pound notes down the cleavage.

"I don't suppose any one of you would have a spare sandwich?" I asked meekly—penitently even, "I'm famished. Haven't eaten since dawn yesterday."

One of them took pity on me. Just for a moment she might have been a mawkish piece of porcelain come to life.

"Here," she thrust a paper packet into my hand. "It's half-eaten, but I didn't feel like lunch yesterday and couldn't finish it."

I thanked her profusely and picked a path through grazing sheep towards a gate at the bottom of the meadow. A couple of Hortons started hesitantly after me but found crooks immediately collaring their necks.

Four *Scarecrow*

In life, when one set of problems packs their bags and leaves, it is only to make room for another set of visiting predicaments—equally bad or even worse. There were blessings to count:

    firstly, I had food,

    secondly, no sheep.

Yet having clambered over a barred gate into a country lane, I found myself in danger of arrest for wearing only breast pads, bloomers and shoes on a public highway. Eating sandwiches was the priority—they were Wensleydale cheese and pickle, with the crusts cut off and only mouse-like nibbles taken out. Still, whilst savaging this ladylike repast, I was in full view of any passing motorist, cyclist or pedestrian who cared to report me to those who seize citizens inappropriately clad. Throwing my cloth breasts up into a tree improved matters only slightly, I still needed an entirely new wardrobe, and that meant a visit to town and shopping for a suit in nothing but frilly pantaloons. It would hardly go unnoticed. Better perhaps to let the banknotes now stashed in my left shoe be and approach a hamlet by night to steal from a clothesline. My problem with this was, in the main, getting caught.

    Needing some place to lie low and think, I struck off over farmland once more (in the opposite direction to the shepherdesses and their sheep), thereby making the discovery that a person cannot be inconspicuous when crossing open fields dressed only in bloomers. Moreover, to crouch and run beside a hedge in frilly undergarments looks even worse. Endeavouring to appear as much a part of the landscape as a robin or stone wall, I eventually reached a woodland where the chances of a meeting someone who would scream and run to the authorities appeared small.

It was still morning and I followed vague paths, drank from a refreshing stream, ate some dandelion leaves, and explored the limits of my arboreal refuge. After much thought, it seemed the most sensible plan would be to wait until nightfall, then set out in search of another crop of suitcases. It was late afternoon when I heard a wuff and a female voice calling. "Blue! No! Come back! Blue!"

A dog walker? Or had they got the bloodhounds after me? Was the owner of Blue a policewoman? *Blue* ... police uniforms were *blue*! I looked about in panic for a tree to climb and found myself overwhelmed by choice. Pulled ditheringly to and fro by the merits of several candidates, a second, closer wuff sent me scrambling up the girth of the nearest, an enormous horse chestnut. No sooner was I perched breathlessly, legs astride a lofty bough, than an Alsatian trotted below and sniffed about at the base of the tree.

"Blue." A young woman in uniform appeared beside the dog. "I wonder where we are? I'm lost. They do say, you're never lost if you have a dog's nose. But I think I'd look stupid with a dog's nose, don't you? Let's sit here a while and have a bit of lunch. Perhaps the others will find us."

Others???

The policewoman sat against the trunk of the tree, opened a Tupperware box and began eating a sandwich, speaking to the Alsatian with her mouth full, which made the following one-sided conversation hard to follow.

"I must say, that shepherdess got my back up. Fair enough, she'd recovered her sheep without help from us, but to call me crap to my face—well I nearly punched her in hers. They'd reported rustled sheep, we had three officers and three dogs—you, Bob and Sooty—on the case, then she says we aren't needed anyhow and that a shepherdess impersonator, still on the loose, had been punished enough. It didn't help that you chased the sheep, but you *had* been given a fleece to smell to help find the flock's trail. At least we have a description of the man. He won't get far wearing only bloomers. And if looks could kill when I asked if you could sniff *her* bloomers to help track the fugitive down. Blimey. Here you are, have the rest of this sandwich, I'm not that keen on beef."

I was worried that she'd look up, even though under normal circumstances, people never do. It would only be when it was imperative that a person shouldn't look up, that they *might*, it's some sort of unwritten law of the universe. In this case, the Cosmos adjudicated in my favour and not even the dog looked up, which is something that dogs do do having irritatingly alert senses that pick up on things that are none of their canine business, (though strictly speaking

I dare say Blue was being paid in pedigree chum and beef sandwiches, to look up and find me. He didn't however. There's only so much Pedigree Chum and beef sandwiches can buy.)

After a while, the forces of the Law wandered off in search of me. I listened in relief to fading sounds of their departure. Something about the policewoman and her quest, the impossibility of finding an object that she was moving further and further away from, brought a poignant smile to my lips. Still, two further police-persons might drop by at any moment with dogs that *did* look up. And how long before these representatives of the Law put two and two together to make a train-hopping, frilly-bloomer-wearing, sheep rustler Alphonso Blink?

Hastening to earth, I returned to the stream I'd drunk from earlier and paddled up it to leave no spoor for the sniffer dogs to snuffle. Soon enough I came to open farmland—a cornfield that would be hard to cross without leaving an obvious trail of bent stalks. At least the corn was higher than my bloomers, for I could see only the jacket and shirt of a scarecrow in the middle of the ...

On closer acquaintance, the scarecrow was found not to be a fashionista. His jacket was nylon. Stained, torn and weatherbeaten nylon. However, needs definitely did must. I had an anthropomorphic pang of guilt at depriving the poor guy of his clothes, for what would he be without them? A crucifix of wood standing aimlessly in a field, less purposeful than a fence post. His face, a stuffed hessian bag with daubed-tar eyes and a mouth, looked both expressionless and aghast as I undressed him. The shirt was almost serviceable—white but ochred with age, with frayed cuffs and only two buttons. His trousers, which only on an Armani scarecrow would match the jacket, looked like a family of ferrets had lived down the legs and then manically bitten their way out. At least all the garments were freshly laundered by rain and well aired. Whilst no undergarments were found of any description, I still felt it was time to bid the bloomers a fond farewell, though offering them to the scarecrow as hand-me-downs was a possibility I discarded. It would only provide evidence of my whereabouts and latest disguise and hopefully a jackdaw or rook of any imagination would find a naked scarecrow far more terrifying. I stuffed the lacy underwear in my new jacket pocket and continued on through the corn.

By now it was mid-afternoon, and it was a relief to be able to travel openly and be thought, if seen, only a tramp – albeit a particularly down-at-heel tramp – but not a degenerate in need of handcuffing. Though I hoped very much not to be mistaken for a scarecrow. Call me paranoid, but the thought of being accosted by a militant band of field mannequins and scolded for not being qualified to frighten Ravens, Jays and the rest of the extended Corvid family did not bear thinking about. Nor did standing in a field for an hour with aching arms outstretched as policepersons with sniffer dogs ate sandwiches beside me.

The cornfields eventually gave way to a steep gully where a waterfall tumbled six feet into a pool. Crossing a small river, boulder by boulder, I considered the possibilities for a night's sleep. Not a shepherd's hut. Nor open pastures where a flock might surround my recumbent form and pounce on me with loud *baaaas* when I woke. A bed and breakfast reverie had to be quashed, for a vagrant would probably not be admitted in the garden gate, never mind the house. Perched on a large stone in midstream and considering my non-options, my thoughts were interrupted by sounds of riotous progress approaching from the ridge above me.

A crowd of men careered over the gully's edge and gambolled down the slope shouting *wheeeeeeee*. There was nowhere to hide, but it soon became apparent that there was no occasion to. They were *me*—or at least a gang of me, whooping it up, having presumably escaped from the train.

With a yell of recognition, they frolicked towards their own self, coming to a halt on the riverbank opposite where I stood stricken, midstream, on a stone. As one they gave a mock salute.

"What are you doing here?" I groaned.

"Same as you," one me answered.

"Meaning what?"

"Escaping the train."

"Did you get off at the next station?"

They guffawed at this. The eldest, who had once cut off the end of his beard as a gift, replied. "It could be said that a communication cord was tugged."

I acknowledged the inevitability of it.

"By you?"

"No," the greybeard reassured. "It was a group effort."

The me of the rainbow scarf said, "We *all* did it. And if you're looking for a place to sleep, there's a nice castle just down from the river and then up the hill."

"I'd rather not know," I stated with frigidity.

"Don't worry, *we* won't be there. *We'll* be somewhere else. And you'll be sleeping in a marsh if you don't go and knock on the portcullis. There or the police station because there's a lady in uniform with an Alsatian not far behind us."

"Can you tell me if I'm wanted for leaving the train early?"

"I thought you'd rather not know?"

My breath felt suddenly heavy. "Please, could you carry on to wherever it is you're going?"

"We don't know!" They laughed. "We haven't a clue what's going to happen next."

They galloped off, following the river, whilst I remained on the boulder and watched them go, almost toppling into the water with irritation. Though in desperate need of clothes and accommodation I had absolutely no intention of finding the castle because knowing what came next in my life would be like skipping to the end of a book. Cheating existence. I *did* regret not asking them for sartorial donations. A shirt from one me, a jacket from another. It was pathetic that my own selves didn't care enough to offer so much as a sock! To spite them, I stomped up the steep slopes of the river valley in what felt like the opposite direction of the castle, thinking it improbable anyway that I'd meet the policewoman and dog if I kept my wits about me. And her being at the top of the slope with Blue, standing amongst some trees beside a cornfield was taking an unfair advantage, as my wits had not really had time to be collected and were caught off guard by her frown.

"Hello," she murmured suspiciously. I must have looked guilty for her voice went stern. "What are you doing?"

"When nobody's looking," I replied, "I'm training to be a scarecrow."

As proof my arms outstretched themselves. She looked skeptical, even Blue, sat beside her, seemed to narrow his eyes. Though they were narrow already.

"Why?"

"When I get good enough, perhaps one of the local farmers will employ me."

"Not, surely, when they can make one for free?"

"Stuffed dummies," I huffed as if affronted, "can't wave their arms about, yell loudly and throw stones. They're inanimate oafs. Crows aren't fooled for more than a day and next morning are roosting on a scarecrow's head cackling in contempt. Before you know it, half your crops have been burgled. Whereas with *me* ..."

Still the policewoman frowned. "But can *you* hold your arms out all day?

"No," I admitted, "that's what I'm practicing now – building the muscles."

She weighed things up. "I don't expect a farmer would pay much."

"I'm not ambitious. A beef sandwich twice a day."

She gave a grim shake of the head. "That wouldn't do for me." There was a pause before she changed tack. "You haven't by any chance seen a man in bloomers?"

"No," The moment was undeniably sticky. "But funny you should ask, for I *did* find these, caught on a fence earlier this morning, a few fields away." I handed her the crumpled underwear. "If your dog sniffed them, he could probably track the man down."

The policewoman looked a little apprehensive. "A naked man ..."

Blue sniffed the bloomers then pointedly sniffed me.

"They've been in my pocket, which must interfere with the scent. But why on earth would a man cavort around in bloomers?"

"Who can fathom the criminal mind? Some shepherdesses ..."

"Look!" I interrupted. "A crow!" I ran at a tree waving my arms and yelling. "Whaaaaaahhhhh!"

The bird flapped off with a couple of laconic caws.

"Very impressive," my companion observed. "Worth a beef sandwich I'd say."

"You wouldn't have one spare?"

"No. Sorry. Only crab. Went back to the station to get a couple."

"Oh well. If you *like* crab."

"I do."

"Yes. Crab *is* nice."

She gave a sigh and hooked a brown lock behind her ear. "I'd better be on my way. Thanks for your help with the bloomers." A thought seemed to suddenly occur. "Why did you put them into your pocket by the way?"

"Er ...Believe it or not, I thought they must belong to a damsel in distress that I might meet and save from embarrassment by restoring them to where they belong. I'm glad I didn't meet a naked man."

"It's troubling for sure." She gave me another curious stare and then said slowly, "You're not ... Alphonso Blink are you?"

At which point, I conceded that the castle might have been a more sensible option, and that there was much to be said for knowing what might happen in advance and avoiding it.

"Who?"

"Alphonso Blink."

"My name's John. John Smith."

Again she appraised me.

"A very ordinary name for somebody embarking on such an extraordinary career."

She was testing my impromptu powers to the full.

"If you must know ... I'm trying to make myself more interesting. I ... I can't get a girlfriend for being so dull. That's why, with the bloomers, I was hoping to meet a damsel in distress, scare some crows in front of her, and maybe she'd find me more interesting than my name suggests."

She looked amused, as if at my simplicity. "You're certainly not dull."

"Well ... "and I only intended this as a jokey parting shot "... if you ever need a boyfriend ..."

She met my goofy smile with a baleful one of her own. "I do."

Which was awkward. One ought to expect the unexpected, but how?

"Right. But I didn't mean ..."

"... And you need a girlfriend. So ..."

I croaked, "Yes .. but ..."

"*But* I'm a policewoman," she sighed. "Is that it?"

Trouble is, it was.

She grimaced. "It's as difficult for me to get a boyfriend in this uniform as it is for you to get a girlfriend being called John Smith."

I realised a man needing a girlfriend so badly that he'd become a scarecrow and run around with bloomers in his pocket, would never turn her down and my story would be undermined if I didn't say what I eventually did, dry mouthed. "We could make a date then?"

She blushed and tried to repress a shy smile, which made her look much less like an officer of the law.

"I wouldn't turn up in these clothes," I continued. "I have better ones at home."

For a moment she stopped being my nemesis and I wondered if her policewoman's legs would seem quite so straight and narrow and upstanding if they were not encased in regulation black tights.

"I wouldn't turn up in these ones either," she observed, as if reading my mind. "We shouldn't be defined by our clothes,"

"Or names."

"No. So ... *where?*"

Not having a clue about the area we were in I said, "Um .."

"What about Merton Cross tomorrow night at The Sheep's Head?"

I flinched inwardly, but nodded with an enthusiasm that a little part of me felt and a big part of me didn't. She came closer and touched my nylon jacket with a sort of disbelief.

"But only if you promise to change the jacket. And trousers and shirt."

"A promise, I promise."

There was a moment between us. A short longing. Blue moved closer, head tilted as if trying to understand.

"I can't kiss you on duty."

"That's okay," I reassured. "It will be something to look forward to tomorrow night." I was going to stand her up anyway.

"7.30." she suggested.

Wasn't I? For when she turned to go, I held her arm. What was I doing? *This was a policewoman.* But my hand tingled. "Hang on. You didn't say *your* name."

She looked surprised at this omission. "Oh. Oh yes." She giggled. "How could I not? It's Betty."

"*Betty?*"

My entire world deflated.

"Short for Elizabeth. But everyone calls me Betty. See you tomorrow."

"Yes. Goodbye."

Blue gave me a canine nod and trotted after his mistress along the cornfield and out of sight. Watching her go, I felt it a shame we could never meet again, for although dating a policewoman was like stepping aboard a love cruise on the Titanic, she ... she was ...she ... oh for goodness' sake! *She was called Betty.* Having miraculously escaped capture, and in desperate need of a bed, food and new clothes, I felt it would be best to forget her *and* my philosophical convictions and give the nice castle down the river a try.

Five   *Soup*

The ruin stood in wild and unruly grounds. Seen from across a narrow moat, silhouetted by dusk, it was not the grim and intimidating fortress I'd expected. I doubt any *real* castle has an irreproachable history, but the bijou crenellated battlements of this one had surely never seen a fight and looked like they could be stormed by primary school children. Small and postcard pretty—swarmed over by dog rose and ivy that wound up turrets and over crumbled parapet walls—the castle possessed a sense of idyllic dereliction. As if, having Quixotically appeared on a cloud, it had drifted to earth and landed with a little too much of a bump.

The drawbridge, prostrated, was squidgily rotten underfoot, and the rusty portcullis up, which was not unwelcoming; and there were lights on in several window embrasures. But still I hesitated at a formidable arched door before giving the iron knocker three hefty blows. Expecting a suspicious 'who's there', I had an explanation for my garments already composed:

"Sorry to bother you at this time of night. My clothes were stolen by young lads when I went for a swim in the river. I think they did it for a lark. I was forced to borrow some raiment from a scarecrow. Fortunately, I'd *put my money in my shoes, so I could pay for some food and a night's accommodation if you ...."*

A light flickered behind the door, bolts shot back and hinges creaked. An elfin, white-haired lady in a pale dressing-gown appeared on the gatehouse step with a lantern.

"Hello?"

She peered from round glasses into the gloom. Her hair was waist-long and face beautiful, though old. But for the spectacles, I might have thought her a faery queen.

"Sorry to bother you at this late hour ..." I began.

"Alphonso." She held the lantern outstretched for a closer scrutiny. A small smile appeared, "Alphonso Blink. I knew you were coming. It was in the air."

I was flabbergasted—more than anything because she *smiled* to say *Alphonso Blink*. Nobody did that. And how did she know me?

"Come inside, you are *most* welcome."

She saw me over the threshold, bolted the door and led us by lantern through a passageway.

"How do you know who I am?"

She stopped, turned and smiled again. "You're the image of my husband and your grandfather, Alphonso Blink. You couldn't be anyone else but my son's son. I was at your christening but we haven't met since."

She continued past a fallen suit of armour. The first chamber we entered was cluttered with numerous bird cages and what looked like half a biplane. There was a grandfather clock facing the wall as if it had done something wrong.

"Excuse the mess. I've tried to employ cleaners but they never last. There's no electricity in this part of the castle, so it's hazardous after nightfall."

A second stone corridor was almost entirely blocked by a tractor tyre. "Nuisance." She bent to step through it.

The place was a rag and bone yard. At least I felt appropriately dressed. That is, until she came to another room and switched on an electric light.

"Come in. Sit down and tell me all. Not least, how you came to be so atrociously attired."

With grace she seated herself, but I stood stunned.

"Forgive me, it's such a shock to suddenly have a grandmother. Especially one who doesn't look in the least like one."

She looked amused. "With more forewarning I might have put my hair in a bun and knitted half a jumper."

Had she been living in this castle, surrounded by frayed tapestries, threadbare furniture and baffling junk all my childhood? Why had nobody said anything?

When I eventually did sit down to recount my adventures, it was hard to concentrate for the wonder of being with a long-lost grannie. To meet this porcelain-white relation who looked like she'd lived and aged in a pre-Raphaelite painting and then stepped out to meet me, was at that point, the most incredible experience of my life.

Whilst listening, my grandmother thoughtfully brushed her long white hair, but at the first mention of food, tutted in self-admonition and went to make me some.

"Not leftovers." She put a pyramid of sandwiches on a silver platter in front of me and also a bowl of soup. "Not turtle. Pea."

She sat beside me then, an intimacy that was so affecting, I could barely finish the sandwiches, not to mention my tale.

"And then I knocked and my grannie opened the door."

"You can call me Imogen."

"Yes. Oh. Of course."

"You had a lucky escape with Betty," she reflected and began again grooming her white waterfall of hair. "The police searched for you here already this morning."

I was aghast. "But why? I haven't done anything. Honest."

"*I* know that. But it's not what you've done that bothers them, it's what you are."

"*What* am I?"

She stopped mid-brush as if meeting a snag. "*Different.*"

"Aren't *you*?"

"To them I'm a little old lady. Your grandfather was always on and off trains for things that never happened but might have. It embarrassed John to death."

"Is that why I wasn't allowed to know you or granddad?"

"Your father hated his father's eccentricities. The two of them were as different as a chalk sandwich and a cheese sandwich. Irreconcilable."

"So why did he call me Alphonso?"

"Esmeralda demanded it."

"He didn't have to agree, surely?"

"Esmeralda is *Esmeralda*."

I remembered the kite.

"So why did you call *him*, John?"

"We all make mistakes," she sighed and laid down her hairbrush. "You must be exhausted. Let me take you to your room. You'll like it. It's full of Alphonso's inventions."

"He was an inventor?"

"Of sorts." She led me up a spiral stone staircase to a landing with an arched door.

"There's a bed in here somewhere," Grandma Imogen switched on a light.

It's hard to say which thrilled me more – that the room was round or that it was crammed with peculiar contrivances made of junk: buckets, pulleys, coach-horns, dials, teapots, bedframes, boilers, giant bellows.

"There's a berth over there," said my grandmother encouragingly. "Behind the remains of a machine to make people happy."

"And did it?" I picked my way through a small heap of scrap.

"Well one man felt it didn't and smashed the mechanisms with a hammer. Though as your grandfather pointed out afterwards, the fellow laughed a great deal as he delivered the blows. Alphonso concluded after the experiment that there was something about cheerfulness which made other people want to kill you. So he dismantled The Happiness Generator and used the components for a machine which made already existing things that we take for granted. Such as a blade of grass or a frog. He thought that if people saw how stupendous the apparatus needed to be to make something ordinary like a leaf, they would appreciate the staggering singularity and genius of the world around us much more."

"Like he said in his book," I recalled.

My Grandmother looked astonished. "*Let Them Have It?*"

"Yes, I found it in a mobile library, but he never mentioned a machine for making things we take for granted."

She frowned and smiled simultaneously. "Well fancy that being still available. There's a copy in the library here of course. And did you like it?"

"I must know the words by heart," I confessed.

"Then you'll recall that bit: *Cup an oak leaf, still on the tree, in your palm for only a minute and the miracle of it will become apparent. But only if you are as alive as the leaf itself.* I think he invented the contraption as a joke. In a fit of irony. The apparatus took up a whole acre of land. He made these ..." She lifted a small wooden box from a shelf and opened it for inspection. "They look dead now. But once they were green."

I picked two leaves from the box. Dry and crumbly, they were as real as anything my father used to rake off his lawn. The fine detail in the veins and stalks was extraordinary. "Are these really made by machine?"

The box went back on the shelf.

"That photograph on the wall is Alphonso setting it in motion to manufacture the first leaf."

My grandfather, skinny and bearded with a mass of frizzy hair, stood dwarfed by a colossal contraption which reached higher than surrounding trees that made the same 'product' so effortlessly.

"I'm off to bed Alphonso. I'll find some of your grandfather's clothes and put them outside the door for the morning. You'll want to look nice for Betty."

"Betty?"

"One of these inventions is a shower. I'm sure it still works."

"But ... I can't actually *go* on the date with her Grannie. She's a policewoman."

Imogen looked stern. "I think it would be most ungentlemanly not to if you've made an arrangement. So long as you don't tell her about this place or who you really are, you should be alright. She sounded like a nice young woman to me."

"But ..."

"Slumber on it. When you find the bed. Goodnight."

How soothing to sleep in a round room, where dreams can spread their wings without getting stuck in the corners.

How had I ever managed repose in a house on an estate that boxed everything up? I woke encircled in an embrace. As if I'd arrived at my *home*, home, though I had never visited or dwelt in the castle before. For several minutes I lay and ruminated on roundness. The natural world didn't do square. No square planets, square middles of a daisy, nor square pupils to an eye. The pupils of Betty's eyes were beautiful because … Why did she have to be called *Betty*? A woman by any other name … Eliza, possibly. Beth at least had an atom of poetry. Zab went pleasingly with Alphonso. But *Betty*? It was a barwoman's, charwoman's, policewoman's name. I mean, could somebody called Betty *appreciate a leaf?*

I went around the round room touching inventions reverently. There *was* a shower of sorts, once I figured out how the clanking mechanisms were set in motion to fill and refill a bucket that spilled water repeatedly over my head. My Aunt had left a pile of garments outside the bedroom door. A shirt and tie, grey knitted sleeveless jumper, beige trousers and matching jacket. Not what I imagined Grandpa Blink would wear at all.

"Sometimes he had to go out disguised." My grandmother confided over breakfast. "Especially in later days when he began uninventing things."

"Uninventing? Can a person do that?"

"Alphonso invented a machine to uninvent. He felt strongly that there were things in the world which others had invented which should never have existed, so he set about uninventing them."

"So, they ... *vanished?*"

"Alphonso's greatest ambition was to uninvent the atomic bomb, but he never managed that. Which *is* a shame. But some of the things ... yes ... he was such a difficult man – so impulsive, volcanic and headstrong. We argued at least once a day. Three or four times a day on a good day. For arguing that is. I shouted at him over this very table that it was a foolish idea to uninvent things however desirable. Even smashed some plates."

"You don't look the sort to break china grannie."

"It wasn't the *best* china. And we mustn't be defined by our appearances. When I was younger, my tantrums were legendary. The trouble was, that people missed the things Alphonso uninvented and felt lost without them, without knowing why, feeling only a distant ache. I'm sure it was for uninventing things he was killed."

I dropped my toast. "Somebody killed him?"

"I *did* warn him. But it's a sombre subject for a fine day and I'll blub if I go into it now. Let's roll out that tractor tyre.

The rest of the day grannie showed me round the castle and grounds as if we were tourist and guide. In an outbuilding filled with contraptions, there was a square-wheeled bicycle leaning against a stone wall.

"It used to get me to the shops and back. Alphonso was going to enter the Tour De France on it but was arrested by gendarmes a few days before the race for things that could possibly have happened if he'd won."

Well, man-made things *were* square.

In one room of the castle there was an invention which featured potato peelers, sieves, whisks but also a headscarf and even a bra.

"This is another of the workshops. He would always be taking things of mine unasked, infernal man, I'd wonder where they'd gone and then see them going round and round and round in some preposterous mechanism. He'd doodle away at mealtimes, completely incommunicado, then disappear into this room and draw up some fantastical blueprint onto squared paper to bring yet another useless machine into being. Such as *this*: the external combustion engine."

The walls were papered with sketches including a vast and intricate design for the machine to help people appreciate a leaf.

"One day, the day before we were due to go on a tour around Europe, he disappeared and never came back. He'd gone to a nuclear processing plant in an attempt to uninvent the splitting of the atom and was caught. In trying to escape … Well, that was that."

We were in the grounds, beside a small lake, when I tentatively asked about Aunt Esmeralda.

"Does she ever visit?"

"Oh yes. But only when I'm really not expecting it. Out of the blue in a way that makes me gasp. *Like now.*" There was a pause, as if to give Esmeralda an opportunity to rise out of the waters and wade to the shore. "Only she hasn't. A shame. Her company is so lively."

"It would be nice to meet her without …"

"… your parents being around?"

"Yes. And when she wasn't rushing to a meeting."

"She's *always* rushing."

"What does she do?"

"She's a chartered accountant. Fancy your not knowing that."

It was one of the most unbelievable things I'd ever had to believe.

"Aunt Esmeralda an …?"

"Yes, she has a gift, like her father's, of making things not add up."

The tour ended with our reflections looking back at us from the castle moat, and I saw myself in the watery mirror ask, "Grannie, could I stay a little while? I need somewhere to hide and this place … it feels like where I belong."

"It's your ancestral home. In the Blink family since … well, ever since your grandfather built it."

I saw the surprise in my face. "*He* built it?"

"With a little help. Yes."

"So why is it a ruin?"

"We thought that more romantic than a shiny new castle," she recollected.

I gazed up at the building anew. "It must have cost a fortune."

My Grandmother demurred. "Not really. At the time he had developed a splendid money machine."

"*Counterfeiting?*" A ripple went through me.

"Oh no," she looked shocked. "What was produced was just very similar to legal tender."

My grandmother was re-inventing my grandfather!

"But I thought money disinterested him."

"That's true. But it wasn't actual money, was it? Just worthless paper. Fortunately, it paid for the land, the castle and a coat of arms. Anyhow, I'd be much offended if you went rushing off like Esmeralda. We may get searched by the police a few more times, but Alphonso made a priest hole behind a panel in the library. Which reminds me, you *do* have to rush off to a meeting quite soon. Let's go and make you look presentable."

We went over the drawbridge. Carved in stone above the portcullis, were two turtles staring at each other over a shield-like shell with a motto underneath:

Deorsum Cum Suppa!

"Down With Soup." My Grandmother translated.

Six   *Leaf*

Grandma Blink directed me to Merton Cross and The Sheep's Head, a village pub pleasingly devoid of pastoral herders and their flocks. Betty was sat with a beer in a murky corner. I approached with an orange juice.

"I thought you might stand me up," were her first words.

"That would have been ungentlemanly."

I sat opposite her and removed my jacket, hanging it over a chair.

"John."

"Yes?"

"Whilst your clothes are a great improvement on the last time we met, I can't believe you're wearing a sleeveless woollen pullover. How do you expect to get a girlfriend wearing a tank top? Did your mum or your grannie knit it and give it to you for Christmas?"

"I thought it was stylish. A bit suave and dashing."

"For a trainspotter maybe. Let's just say that if I was in trouble, my life in danger, I couldn't imagine you rescuing me in that particular garment."

"Well, if your life is imperilled tonight, I'll take it off."

"Can't you do that *before* somebody rushes in with a chainsaw?"

"Fine." I did. She really *wasn't* a Betty. "Here, I've brought you a leaf."

She watched me push an oak leaf across the table in perplexity. "How nice."

"You see, I realised today, leaves are *amazing*. So detailed. Intricately veined and designed. Nice to rub. Aromatic. Smell it."

With a pained look Betty refrained from even touching it. "John, you don't have to try to be interesting with me. *You're fine as you are.* At least now you've taken off the sleeveless pullover."

"Don't you want to marvel at it though?"

"Not in the slightest."

"I think it's incredible. So unique."

"Along with all the billions of others."

"And they just grow out of a tree. Amazing!"

She gave the table a small slap. Froth rocked in her beer glass. "*Stop.* Can't you see? Leaves are *not interesting*. Talking about them is *not interesting*. So the more you go on about them, the more you become John Smith."

"Oh."

"Yes, 'oh'. A box of chocolates might have been interesting. A bunch of flowers maybe."

"*They* have leaves"

She held her head and groaned. "Help. Shut up about leaves or I will leave. They are boring. Very, very boring. So boring I might get up and go."

"Alright. Sorry. Did you have a nice day at work?"

"No."

"Alas."

"Though at least I wasn't looking for sheep that had already been found and a man not wearing bloomers."

"Well then?"

"I was put on the case, along with the rest of the team, of finding Alphonso Blink."

With some insouciance, even a sense of enjoyment, I replied. "The man you thought *I* was."

"Only you are *way* too uninteresting to be him."

"Maybe *he* likes leaves."

"I doubt it."

"When you catch him you should ask him. I bet he does."

Betty glared. "What did *you* do?" She said between ever-so-slightly gritted teeth.

"Me? I er ... tidied up the house. I gave up on the scarecrow thing after we met, so I went back to my old job."

"Which is?"

"Chartered accountant. Working from home."

"Do you like it?"

"Not really. It can get way too exciting."

"Exciting?"

"When the figures don't add up. Tally. That's always happening to me. I'm not good with numbers."

"So why are you a chartered accountant?"

"*I* don't know. Are you any good at *your* job – arresting people?"

"It isn't *only* arresting people."

"How many people do you arrest a week? A day? Arresting Alphonso Blink will probably be extremely exciting."

"To be honest," Betty lowered her voice confessionally, "this may sound strange, but I've never arrested anyone."

"What?"

"I was in the traffic police for two years. I gave out some parking tickets."

"So, Alphonso's safe."

"It's not funny. The higher ups thought he might be in the area. His grannie lives in a castle not that far from here. But we've searched it and not found him. I'd be scared making the arrest. He's supposed to be very dangerous."

"But I'd protect you. Now I've taken off the tank top."

She giggled. "You could bore him to death,"

"Hey! I'm actually not that boring. I'd punch him on the nose. That would be interesting."

"I'd pay to see that."

"Huh. Maybe we should start this date again," I protested as if injured.

"Sorry," she smiled ruefully.

"The trouble is, I don't really know what to do or say because ... because you may not have arrested anyone, but I've never been on a date before."

She looked incredulous. *"Never?"*

"Well you know—being called John Smith."

Betty picked up the leaf and twirled it in her fingers as if it explained much.

"Oh, I see. Well, I've been on a few, but they always go wrong."

"Why?"

Her eyes met mine in a way I hoped was not her wanting to lock me in a cell. "They've all been with policemen."

Her constable-dating disaster stories were extremely funny. I made up some chartered accountancy tales merely by talking about my father as if he was me. Before we knew it, the bell had rung for last orders.

"Come on." Betty stood up. "It's dark. You can walk me home unless you've had too many orange juices."

"I think I can still walk in a straight line."

"We shall see."

Ten minutes later we were outside a small house on an estate like all the other estates. When she reached the doorstep, there was another one of those moments between us. In fact there had been several in the pub and I hadn't really known what to do about them.

"Goodnight," I said simply and almost turned to go.

"Aren't you going to kiss me at the door?"

"If ... if you want me to."

"Sometimes, at the end of a date," she teased softly, "people do."

Her eyes and mine went molten and mixed up, which ended in my confessing, "Only I've never kissed a woman before so you'll have to show me."

She did. Several times. Until, she said, I'd sort of got the hang of it.

"Do you want to come in for a coffee?" she whispered.

"I don't drink coffee. Do you have orange juice, or just water."

"Oh, just say 'yes'. I'm not going to make you coffee anyway."

"Right. Yes."

She pulled me inside the front door and shut it behind us. A person wouldn't need to peer through the letter box to know what happened next.

Fortunately, Grandma Blink left the drawbridge down in case I was late. Which I was. *Very.*

After which, Betty and I met every evening, each assignation concluding as the first. By the fourth date I bypassed The Sheep's Head and went straight to her front door. She opened it. I tumbled inside.

"How was the chartered accountancy today?"

"Terrifying. Not a single number added up. How about you? Did you arrest anyone yet?"

"No. I don't think I ever will."

"I hope you never do."

However, no relationship can be entirely satisfactory that divides a person from themselves and creates a feeling of being two people instead of one. Dating Betty, I caught myself wanting to spend the rest of my life as an alter ego. John Smith would fantasise in her arms about becoming a policeman, for then, not only would he be above suspicion and arrest—but also he and Betty could live in personal and professional serenity. Kissing me would not compromise her. My being a bobby would make our love life simple. Until, I would later remind myself, cells spontaneously burst open releasing criminals back into the wild and emergency sirens began to play nursery tunes like an ice-cream van. All of which pointed to Law Enforcement being inimical to me and I to it. A slap in the face to my now beloved Grandmother and namesake and round bedroom. So should I stop seeing Betty? *Could I?* How sensible was it to fall deeply in love with a woman who might put me behind bars on discovering my identity?

In the end, sitting with my grandmother in a drawing room after lunch, I asked for advice. To Betty or not to Betty. That was the question.

"You seem to be enjoying yourselves."

"But only when I don't stop to think of the possible consequences."

"There would be ever so many of those. Almost as many as the impossible ones."

She smiled, only to frown at a clattering noise from somewhere in the castle. My Grandmother gave me a sharp look. "We have a visitor."

"Police?" I panicked.

"No, they are always perfectly polite and knock. Hide behind the curtain."

Only moments after I'd stepped behind a drape, there was a creak outside the drawing room door.

"Come in, John."

I heard the door open and shut.

"How did you know it was me?"

"Oh, burglars make less noise."

A pause.

"Is Alphonso here?"

"Your father passed away some years ago. You surely can't have forgotten."

"My *son* Alphonso."

"Why on earth would he be here of all places? You never brought him to the castle in childhood. Does he even know I exist?"

"I've come to tell you, mother, that if he *is* here, you must hand him over to the Law. He's a wanted criminal. He jumped from the train before his sentence was completed. A communication cord was pulled. Who knows what he might do. Things happen because of him. Disturbing things like with …"

"Esmeralda?"

"Not just her."

"Your father too."

"And look what happened to *him*. I don't want Alphonso to turn out that way."

"Because?"

"For his own safety. Moreover, it's a disgrace to the family. People in the village won't even speak to us. Patricia is terribly distraught by what the neighbours might be saying."

"Well I don't know where he is. If he was here, things would be happening I presume and they're not."

"You know very well it doesn't work that way. Never here. Look, you always knew how to be discreet. But the others …"

"Do you want to search the place?"

"You wouldn't lie to me mother?"

"Never. Unless it was absolutely necessary for your own wellbeing."

"I might have known you'd be on his side."

"I might have hoped *you* would be. Should Alphonso arrive over my drawbridge I shall write you a letter immediately. Now, I presume you're going to stay for dinner and perhaps the night?"

"I can't stay. Patricia is in the car."

"Won't she come in?"

"No."

"Well at least I can go out and say hello. Perhaps she will accept an invitation to dinner if it's personally delivered."

"It's most unlikely."

"I will at least then say hello. It's only polite."

The door opened and closed again. The room fell silent. I emerged from behind the curtain and puffed out my cheeks. Half an hour later I heard footsteps returning and hid behind the curtain once more.

"They've gone."

We sat together on the sofa.

"Will he tell the police do you think?"

"He suspects. So yes. No doubt he will tell them of the priest hole, but I dare say we can invent something of our own to conceal you."

"If it's going to bring trouble down on you, I'll go. But I don't want to, because of ... *Betty*".

She sighed, "I do wish she was called by any other name. However, for me, it's no trouble. And if she's on a team of constables deputed to track you down and arrest you, she should be privy to their plans and so can forewarn you of their dastardly intentions."

"Only if she knows I'm Alphonso Blink."

"I'm sure John Smith could wangle that information out of her, with a little guile".

Unfortunately, he couldn't.

That evening in her bedroom, putting our clothes back on, I seized the nettle, in fact an entire clump.

"Betty," I casually ahemed, buttoning my shirt right to the top by mistake, "There's something I have tell you."

She hitched tights up under her skirt. "By the tone of your voice, it's not going to be something I want to hear." The waggle of her hips and snap of elastic felt moody.

In retrospect, there might have been multitudinous ways to gently break the news, but a feeble smile, hand wafts and breezy confession was not one of them.

"Yes. Betty ... The thing is ... um, I'm not John Smith. I'm Alphonso Blink."

There was an uncomfortable silence. Betty looked agitated. "I know *that*. I guessed ages ago. In the field, when you were a scarecrow."

I was stunned. "So why didn't you arrest me?"

"It just seemed ... impossible. I'd been told you were a monster. So at the beginning, when we met above the river, my nerves failed. Anything might have happened if I'd tried to arrest you. It might have been different if there'd been some colleagues around. But I was too terrified to try on my own. Then after a few minutes, you seemed so inoffensively sweet and funny that I decided in a cowardly way, to put it off, saying to myself it could be done on that first date. And that I should do it all on my own because I'd never made an arrest before and that was professionally embarrassing. A sergeant had taken me to one side a week earlier and said 'Betty, you are the worst copper the police constabulary has ever employed. I thought how amazed everybody would be if it was *me* brought you in. But then you pretending to be John Smith and giving me the leaf – it was all too lovely and fun. You were the first man I'd kissed who I wanted to kiss again. So it was impossible to arrest you. I brushed the whole thing under the carpet and joined in pretending you were John Smith and not Alphonso Blink. It was *so hard*! Each time you paid a visit, the contents of every cupboard and drawer would be switched round afterwards. There would be toiletries in my knicker drawer. Knickers in the fridge. Salad in my jewellry box. Scarves in the bread bin. Still, somehow I managed to block the whole Alphonso thing from my conscious mind. But now you've gone and brought your identity into the open, it's like I have no choice but to arrest you. It's my job. You *complete idiot*. Why did you have to tell me!"

"But you just said, *you knew!* Anyhow, I'm an honest man. I haven't actually done anything wrong."

"You skipped your sentence prematurely. Jumped off the train. That's unlawful. Like breaking out of prison before your time is served.

"The length of the journey was never specified."

"You had to wait for it to end."

"It doesn't matter – the punishment was for a crime I didn't commit."

"You could have killed somebody."

"So could you."

"But I wasn't caught *not* doing it."

"I cannot believe that you would arrest me."

"I'm an officer of the law. It's my duty."

"You can't lock up your own boyfriend. Me. You have to *stop* being a policewoman. Your sergeant has already told you you're hopeless."

"I am a copper through and through," was her hot-faced rejoinder. "I was wearing a blue uniform as a toddler."

"Betty, you're not a Betty. You're not a policewoman *inside*. You can't be if you like me."

Her face wrestled with her professional self. "Alphonso. I'm sorry. This is it. Now. You're under arrest."

It was impossible to take seriously.

"I'm not. You're not in uniform."

Her uniform, still on a hanger, was folded over a chair. I snatched it up. There was an outraged howl.

"Give those to me!"

I held the distasteful garb behind my back. "We shouldn't be defined by our clothes."

"I can make a citizen's arrest."

"Leave the police force and come with me."

"Where?"

"*I* don't know."

"Exactly. You're so completely impractical and unpredictable. Strange things happen when you're around. I'd never feel safe. My present and future would be all out of control."

"They are anyway."

"They're not. I'm fully insured and I have a pension scheme."

"You could come and live in my granny's castle."

"So that *is* where you've been staying."

Her standing there, too distraught to be on the beat, or anywhere but in my arms, undid me. I said miserably, "Can we stop this and go back to being in love?"

She scoffed unconvincingly. "You can't fall in love with someone in only a week."

I hugged her uniform to my chest. "We can. I have. I love you even though you're called Betty. You love me though I'm called Alphonso."

"We mustn't be defined by our names."

There was one of those moments when our eyes met and intermingled darkly. Then she turned around and sobbed. "You're. Under. Arrest."

"You can't apprehend me with your back turned."

"I can."

"It's no wonder you've never made an arrest."

"I'm giving you a chance to get out before I run you in."

"Betty."

"I'll count to ten. If you're still here ... One ...

"You're *not* a policewoman ....

"Two ..."

She turned. "If you don't go, I'll hit you with this truncheon." And there was indeed a cudgel in her hand.

"I don't believe you will, because deep inside you, you're not ..."

She hit me. Hard. Ow. *Darkness.*

Seven   *Foxy*

My head throbbed as consciousness returned and a front door slammed. Betty had gone for reinforcements. Staggering up groggily, I found her uniform was still in my hand and cast it from me in disgust. Then with equal distaste, retrieved the garments – *for revenge*. She couldn't be a policewoman without being dressed for the part. I'd burn the lot. True, she'd hit me in plain clothes. *But I was still going to burn them!*

I staggered in fury almost all the way back to Blink Castle only to hear, on reaching the tumbledown gatehouse, a wailing of sirens break out behind me, shattering the night with renditions of *Oranges and Lemons* and *Teddy Bear's Picnic*. Ducking behind a rubbled gatehouse that had never been a dwelling, I watched three vans, lamps frantically blue and dazzling, screech into the castle grounds. Was Betty with them? I touched my sore brow. If so, she still hadn't made an arrest. Would she arrest my Grannie? Surely not.

In a moment of weakness undoubtedly brought on by a doughty blow to the brains, I half-wished for the 'me's to run past and offer their advice. They didn't. But I figured they would only have suggested something utterly ridiculous anyway like pulling on Betty's uniform which was still in my arms and passing myself off as a policewoman.

Even more exasperatingly, I felt my grandmother would have agreed and advised me to pedal off on Alphonso's square-wheeled bicycle. Betty's truncheon wallop probably accounted for the fact that I actually did what both might have counselled.

Fumbling blindly, I found the bicycle propped where I'd last seen it inside an inventing shed. Here, I pulled on Betty's skirt, blouse, tights and tunic, then stuffed my real clothes and little cash into panniers before tiptoeing into some bushes with the machine. Meanwhile further vehicles tore down the drive as if a national emergency had arisen. Which was ridiculous. Their crisis of state was a policewoman trying not to ladder her tights in getting on a square-wheeled bicycle.

Now I do not want to give the impression in this narrative that I wear feminine garb by inclination, delightful though much of it is aesthetically and next to the skin, underwear in particular. The costumes, I think it can be clearly seen, were forced onto my body by desperate circumstance which is not to say there is anything inherently wrong with wearing garments normally worn by the opposite gender. Though, outside of a suit of armour, just about *anything* might be considered normal attire for a woman. A female may wear a shirt and tie, tiepin, cuff links, trousers, Stetson, waistcoat and pretty much what she likes and still be counted feminine and face no serious social condemnation. Only underpants and sock suspenders would raise an eyebrow and these would be hard to see unless worn on top of the other garments. In the pursuit of transvestism therefore, as with so many other things seemingly, a man is at a great advantage. For the slightest daintiness, such as blowing the nose with a lace handkerchief, would be considered down the pub as dangerously effeminate, whilst standing at the bar sipping a gin and tonic in a floral dress, stockings and high heels, would undermine a fellow's masculinity to the point of ridicule and even violence. As would a man's attendance at a football match garbed in a ballgown, even if a matching silk scarf draped around the neck *were* in the colours of the home team. So despite the undeniable attraction of transvestism for many men, I doubt I would have worn Betty's uniform under any other circumstances than myself being a national emergency, for it was not nearly so becoming as the shepherdess rig. However, the garments *did fit*, as Betty and I were of similar height and build, and they smelt of her, which had to be an advantage should sniffer dogs ever be loosed on my trail. Blue apart.

  I set off in any direction as fast as the wheels would turn. There was something of a rodeo about the bicycle, and the front light tended to rise and fall with each rotation of the bumping quadrangular tyres, making navigation in the dark a sort of guesswork. My plan, such as could be devised on the borrowed bone-shaker, was to ride till dawn and by nocturnal pedaling, get far enough away from Betty and her colleagues, to breathe a sigh of relief. If a secretive lair could be found, I might masquerade as a policewoman for a few weeks – merely to buy food and other such stuff – before attempting a stealthy return to Blink Castle.

Riding a square-wheeled bicycle was not so slow and uncomfortable a means of transportation as might be imagined. My grandfather was obviously a gifted engineer, for the machine and I soon settled into a perky rhythm that ate the miles. Only an hour after my escape a signpost was passed that said: *Blink Castle. Quite far.* In fact the peculiar motion of two right-angled wheels kept me alert and awake. Once or twice cars passed and only once one didn't. Not long after seeing the signpost, an automobile of the Law drew up beside my panting form causing me to pull over onto the verge. The car was populated by a single officer. Rather young with big ears.

"Hello there," he smiled. "Late to be out."

"They do say better late than never," I puffed as if my voice had never broken. His must have about a week earlier.

"I thought you had flat tyres. But I see the wheels are square."

"It's French. Designed for people training for the *Tour de France*. Builds up the muscles. I'm just getting fit on it myself."

He leaned out of the window to squint more closely at this gallic curiosity. "Strange bicycle. I don't see an insurance disc."

"Insurance. For a pushbike?"

"You're not very on the ball are you? The new law came in weeks ago. Insurance for pedestrians and cycle riders. If you haven't insurance it should be impounded."

"Actually, I *do* know about the law, I was briefed by my sergeant. But it being a French bike, I couldn't get insurance."

"Really?"

"French bikes are impossible to insure because they drive on the other side of the road."

He gave a low whistle. "Of course …"

"Their view was that it was too risky, because if the rider wasn't concentrating, the bike might suddenly think it was back in the Loire or Dordogne and then a pile up would occur with large payouts."

"You can see their point." The policeman grimaced.

"Though for myself I'm not sure this bike is a sufficiently sentient creature to behave that way."

"But if it's foreign and did start to drive you on the wrong side of the road thinking it was in France or one of those other places you mentioned, a serious accident could occur. I do sometimes think, from a health and safety point of view, it would be better if everyone just stayed in their houses. It would lower insurance premiums. Parliament was discussing bringing that in as a new law. Makes sense when you think about it."

"Yes, well I wouldn't normally do anything as dangerous as ride a bicycle, or even leave the house except to work or shop, but my mum bought this for me as a 21st birthday present when she was on holiday in Paris. I thought it would be most ungrateful to send it back unridden. So I decided to just bend the law a tiny bit and cycle at night when the roads are empty. Anyhow, I can get off and walk with it. What about my legs if I'm ambling? Those can't be impounded can they?"

The young man frowned. "That legislation hasn't been rubber-stamped. But bending the Law? A police officer?"

"Not a sufficient bend to break it. More flexing it a tiny bit after midnight. My mum's a magistrate and she said the Law is like a tree. If it doesn't bend a little, it will be uprooted in a strong wind. And some of these new laws *are* a puzzle. Should I really need insurance to walk along a pavement?"

"Anything could happen. Like say you trip up and accidentally headbutt another person and they make a claim for a new nose and you don't have any money. It's a prison sentence."

"You're right. I see it now. Let's hope the legislation comes in soon. I should walk home immediately before disaster strikes."

"It might be best. And that bike would surely be happier for a refund in Paris."

"I might leave it in the garage for now and *pretend* to ride it at night so my mum doesn't get upset. Then sell it to the next Tour de France rider I meet."

"Do you live locally?"

"Not far."

"I could give you a lift home of you like. Put the bike in the boot. My name's Tim by the way."

"Tim. Nice name. Suits you. Well…"

"I'm from Little Mumbridge. Quite close by."

"That must be handy."

"What's your name?"

"Er ... Donna."

"Funny. You don't look like a Donna."

"I didn't choose my name," I lied.

"You look like more of an Alison or Alice."

"Maybe I should change the way I look."

"Don't do that." He looked suddenly shy. "We could go on a date one night, Donna, if you liked."

"Er ... that would be wonderful, yeah. I don't actually have a boyfriend at the moment. So, why not. Um, not tomorrow night though. I've got a hen party. Not the night after either. Babysitting my nephew. But the next night is free."

"Great. Do you know Little Mumbridge?"

"A bit."

"Where would you like to meet?"

"Oh anywhere."

"What about The Royal Oak?"

"Okay. I played darts there once. Police girl's night out."

"Darts? Phew, you want to be careful with those. Seven o'clock?"

"Say seven-thirty. Give me time to get ready after work."

"Okay. If you hop in, I'll take you home."

"You know, I'd sooner walk. There's not many people to fall onto and head-butt at this time of night. But thanks for the offer. Why are *you* out so late?"

"I'm looking for Alphonso Blink."

"*The* Alphonso Blink?

"There can't be more than one surely."

"Let's hope not."

"See you at seven thirty. Wednesday."

"I'll be there."

Tim drove off, and on reflection I decided that any man with big ears named Tim, deserved to be stood up. Apologies to other big-eared Tims everywhere but take it up with your parents, not me.

This harrowing brush with jurisprudence persuaded me that the road I was following was too much travelled. Thinking a lesser path might make all the difference to my avoiding uniformed officers, or even those in plain clothes, I attempted to take a turning down the first inconsequential country lane that branched off into the gloom. A left. The bicycle apparently demurred, for it just stopped dead and I was almost thrown over the handlebars. Thinking the brakes had seized, and having dismounted by necessity, I checked the machine for obvious malfunctions but could see little in the pitch black. I attempted to wheel the machine down the lane but it wouldn't budge an inch. It would however go backwards and also, I discovered by trial and error, continue down the main road. An attempt to about turn and head for the country lane once more, brought another bout of stubborn rebellion. I dismounted and ticked it off,

"So you'll go along the main road but not a minor one? Is this some kind of petty obstinacy for my saying you were not sentient? If so, I'm sorry. Honest. All my previous encounters with transport have been of the non-sapient variety. It would greatly help us both, I think, to find a less conspicuous highway, as you are certain to be impounded at any scene of my future arrest. Hence, let us ..." I made a third attempt to navigate towards the little left turn. The bicycle was mule stubborn.

"Fine. Have it your way."

We proceeded at great pace down the main road once more, this time however, the square-wheeled conveyance began driving on the right-hand side of the road. No matter what I did with the handlebars, wrestling them strenuously to the left, we careered along as if in a benighted Avignon or Bordeaux.

"This is madness!" I shouted at the contraption. "We're not in France you moron! If something comes the other way we'll crash!"

By great good fortune, nothing *did* come the other way and after we'd careered continentally for several miles – or kilometres – the bicycle lurched right down a country lane as inconsequential as the one I had earlier tried to steer us into.

"Why is this better?" I yelled, for it was worse. Grass grew down the middle and the tarmac was cratered with potholes. At least it felt safer. I thought the only oncoming traffic we might meet on such an obscure road would be a 17th century pack-horse and drover.

In the end, not really having much choice, I left navigation entirely to the contraption. Did it matter which way I went so long as the destination wasn't populated by police officers, shepherdesses or my parents? Once, the eyes of a fox flashed in the bike's headlamp and it scarpered, which left me reflecting that we had an affinity, for here was I being hunted, presumably by dogs. And my thoughts streamed into a monologue thus:

'This foxy flight overland is different only because my antagonists wear blue and not red, though my scent might be less pungent to follow being of rubber bicycle-tyre. Still, are we in fact, either of us, deserving of a huntsman's horn? I carry no horrible diseases like a rat, for which the term vermin has a certain justification. A fox carries none either and might even be considered a farmer's friend, for they eat creatures detested by most agriculturists: rats and mice, slugs and rabbits, and I do not. To which one might say: advantage fox. Except that I don't steal chickens, ducks or geese, an undoubted vulpine character flaw. Then again I *did* steal a police-uniform. True, I have not killed or eaten it but *have* chosen to wear it as a disguise to escape the Law, whilst a fox never pretends to be anything other than they are. A person does not see them gallivanting about the countryside in a helmet and buttoned blue ensemble. To which I say, alas. For a fox impersonating a constable would be a most arresting sight, if the pun might be forgiven. Actually, no pun should ever be forgiven. A pun, not sarcasm is the lowest form of wit ...'

And so my inner monologue, truncheon-induced no doubt, went on.

"Wherever you're taking me," I shouted down to the bike after a while, "presuming you're sentient enough to have a purpose, and not just steering randomly, I would like to find a place to hide before dawn."

On and on, along a mind-boggling imbroglio of minor, minor roads and grassy tracks we sped until dawn opened its bleary eyes. At last, I could almost see where we were going, which appeared to be headlong into the very middle of nowhere.

"*Whoah! Whoah! Whoah!*"

The blur of a signpost had me hauling at the brakes. I dismounted and rested the bicycle against a hedge before retreating twenty yards to see what intelligence the wooden arrow had to impart.

Dover: Still A Very Long Way.

My brain, addled by a night of sleepless jolting in the saddle and a still throbbing truncheon blow, could barely take in the word. Dover. *DOVER*. DOVER? Why? *WHY?* I returned to my steed and stared at it.

"Dover?"

The bicycle looked immobile and expressionless.

"Dover? A busy port. Why would *that* be a safe place to hide?"

It remained leaning against the hedge like a load of metal bars and rubber tyres.

"Unless you're thinking that in France we'd be less likely to be caught. Which is probably true. But getting there? *How?* Dressed like this. There's bound to be police at the ports watching out. It's not worth the risk."

The handlebars seemed to sulk. I could have sworn they gave a shrug. The whole attitude of the contraption, almost the way it was leaning, suggested it felt the risk was negligible.

"What does it matter to you?"

And then I saw very clearly why it mattered.

"*Ohhhh* ... You want to be in the Tour de France, don't you?"

The front wheel turned and the headlight stared at me beseechingly.

"But how will I get over to France? Stowaway on a fishing boat? Looking like a policewoman?"

It remained staring at me, like a faithful hound expecting to be fed.

"Though I suppose I could dress up as a fisherman. Hopefully not a fisher-woman. No. There's no such thing as that. Not that I've heard of anyhow." It did make a sort of sense. Going to France that is. Nobody would really know of me there. But ... "I don't know much about the Tour, still I doubt if just *anybody* – a nobody like me especially – could enter. It's not the same place as when Granddad created and rode you. A rider would probably have to be in a team, we couldn't just wander into France and elbow our way into the race. Well could we?"

The front wheel straightened in a woebegone movement, the front light turned away. It was hard not to feel compassion, even in my own dire circumstances. After all, the Tour de France was what the machine had been built for.

I went over to the bicycle. "If we *could* get across the channel, I daresay a genuine competitor might be persuaded to ride you instead of their normal bike. But I won't be able to stow away on a fishing boat in this outfit. I'll need a big woolly jumper or Breton shirt and beret from somewhere. And right now, apart from a place to rest my dizzy head during the day, I need food. *And* a razor for my legs so people don't see through my disguise, which they will if they see through my tights." I looked down at the sheer hosiery and obvious furriness beneath. "Only a man or a spider would have legs this hairy. Okay?"

The bicycle remained stock still—assent or as good as—and we soon continued our peregrinations over a landscape so empty and uncultivated it could only be a *very* long way from Dover. My head ached, and though for some while we met no other traveller, nor habitation, it felt imprudent to pedal on in the early morning light, I desperately needed to stop. So on approaching a lone house on the crest of a hill, I gave another, "Whoaaah!"

At which my mount inexplicably sped up a steep stretch of tarmac towards the dwelling and jerked to a standstill. Although there were no other habitations as far as the eye could see, I found myself outside a shop frontage of well-coiffured head-shots where a red and white candy stick was revolving over a door.

"I need a razor, not a barber's shop," I fumed at the bike. "A supermarket or something. This is no good."

But too late. A blind went up inside the front door and a hand flipped a closed sign to open. A man's face peered out at me. A lock clicked and the door was thrown wide.

Eight *Fish*

"Good morning."

A barber, I presumed: small, middle-aged and impeccable, with a whiff of the Mediterranean about his accent. The hair on his head was black and parted with precision in the middle, emphasizing the symmetry of a face adorned by a neat twirly moustache. Costumed in a black waistcoat, white shirt and red bow tie with matching sleeve garters, he appeared in the early dawn light, like a second tenor from a continental barber's shop quartet. A castaway on some island of bouffant sophistication amidst a sea of empty moors.

"Would you care for a trim?" he asked politely.

"Thank you, no." I piped.

"A pity. You have the most beautiful hair. Though, that would be a reason, perhaps, not to shorten the locks. But I could wash and perfume them for you? It does not cost much. You are early, well before the rest of my appointments."

I was surprised. "Do you get many er ... customers out here? It does seem to be in the middle of nowhere. An odd place to find a barber's shop."

"My appointment book is pretty full for the next few months."

"With farmers? Shepherds? Policemen?"

"Oh no. Sophisticates from various metropolises. They drive out to see me, for my work has a modest reputation. Some people arrive from distant countries for a trim."

It all sounded rather unlikely to me. But then everything does that actually happens. After a moment's hesitation I said, "I know this may sound odd ..."

"Not as odd as a square-wheeled bicycle surely," he smiled, looking past me to where the conveyance was leaning against a wall.

"No, perhaps not. It's a training cycle. A sort of keep-fit machine that we use sometimes in the force."

"Strange."

"I was wondering if you had a spare razor I could buy off you?"

The barber looked a little taken aback. "Why no. I use only strop razors. They are specialist and imported into this country from Venezuela. I need the few I have. Besides they are quite a challenging instrument and not entirely safe for personal use by a layman. Or laywoman. Why do you need one?"

"I'd rather not say. It's an embarrassing problem. I couldn't tell a man."

He looked down. "Ah. Your legs."

"Yes."

"They are unusually hirsute."

"All the women in my family have legs that are hairy as a man's. My mother. My sisters too. And the girls at the station tease me about it quite cruelly. Recently I've been allowing the hairs to grow back as a sort of protest. Taking pride in my own body, my own family heritage so to speak. But this morning, after setting out from home, I kept seeing my knees covered in ... in ...well it's almost like fur, and realised I couldn't face my female colleagues without shaving my legs. So if you had a little portable razor ...?"

The Barber shrugged sadly. "I don't. But let me shave them for you here? It won't take long, and it is an hour before my first client will arrive."

"I'm not sure that would be very easy for me. I'm too inhibited. Couldn't I use the razor myself?"

"It will be no easier to arrive at work with cut and bloodied legs. But if you stand in my shop now, remove your tights, I will have them smooth as glass in ten minutes. Less. It will cost nothing. I do it because I can see you are troubled. Please bring your bicycle inside."

I've no wish to gloss over this episode as it was a powerfully unique and strange experience, though almost nothing happened, *at first.* His use of a shaving brush to lather my bared legs with foam might sound lurid but didn't seem so at the time. My only concern was preserving a female identity. Standing in the centre of his salon, I demurely removed my shoes and tights whilst he, humming softly, approached with bowl and brush and began to apply lather from my ankles up.

"No higher than the bottom of my skirt please." I squeaked nervously.

"Of course," he answered as if going higher would be an affront to his professional integrity.

I hitched the hem a little so as not to get froth on it.

"My name is Maxime," he declared, crouched on his knees and daubing mine.

"Mine is Donna," I answered in kind.

Soon my legs were entirely white, as if I'd been wading in snow, and I stared at them in a wall mirror whilst he went to strop a razor.

I have to say, Maxime was a consummate artist. I barely felt the pass of each stroke over my thighs or back of my legs. He had a tendency to make slightly extravagant gestures on removing foam and hair, before cleansing the razor in a silver basin. His humming would intensify at the end of each sweep with a satisfied *tra-la,* as if each cut were a master craftsman's ultimate achievement. He was a perfect gentleman, only commenting once on my legs to say that they were strong, shapely and feminine. Though he did add at the end, "Ah, a man would be proud of those hairs."

"Please, they're embarrassing."

"No longer. I have removed them all."

So there I was, in a policewoman's uniform, having my legs sheared by a strange man in a barber's shop in the middle of nowhere when, as my legs were being towelled dry, we were interrupted by the entrance of a young woman from another room in the house. For a moment, the world stopped. *She had two heads.*

She had two heads.
She had two heads.
She had two heads.

It happened so quickly. My mind's-eye blinked an astonished snapshot of a blonde *and* brunette—both sets of hair tumbling over the shoulders of a single body clad in a short flowery dress. There was a flash of recall that my elder train-bound self had spoken of a girl with two heads. Then she began speaking herself.

"Father …?" said the blonde.

Seeing me naked from the thighs down, the long-haired brunette, said only. "Oh."

Maxime turned from me in dismay.

"Girls!"

"*So*-rry," they chorused.

I dropped the hem of my skirt and gaped. The two faces, not identical, were both charming and each possessed an upturned cupid's bow for a top lip.

"Beatrice, Celeste, how many times do I have to tell you? Don't come in when I have clients."

"You don't normally have clients this early," the blonde head reasoned.

"Even so …."

The dark-haired head spoke to the blonde.

'A single-headed person Celeste. How dull!'

"I've always wanted to be dull," came her reply.

"Can't be hard with only one head. And yet…."

"And yet what?"

"Nothing." Beatrice replied. "Just *and yet*…."

By this time Maxime had marched over to his daughter throwing the towel testily behind him onto the floor. "Girls please. How can you be so rude?" he hissed, agonised. *"To an officer of the Law.* She has come in here for assistance!" He turned to apologise to me. "You mustn't mind my daughter. They're sometimes inappropriately outspoken."

"That's fine." I falsettoed. "Thank you, I must be going. Don't want to be late for work at the station."

"Yes," fretted Maxime, "Forgive their seeming lack of respect."

"But Father," Celeste interrupted, "this *isn't* a policewoman."

Maxime, appalled, clutched his brow.

Beatrice having appraised me in amusement added, "I believe she is a man."

"Agreed," Celeste nodded. "On the run and in disguise. But fearful of asking for assistance because he doesn't know us."

"Girls ..." Maxime intervened, looking from me to his daughter and back again in panic.

The raven-haired Beatrice ignored him, "How to reassure the poor fraud?"

"We could ask sooner than try things that might disturb him all the more."

"Could anything disturb him more than a two-headed woman in a barber's shop discussing his concealed gender being ridiculously obvious? Still, will you ask or I?"

"You. Because it was my idea. I've done all the work so far of thinking up a plan."

"Very well." Beatrice eyed me with interest. "Excuse us sir?"

"Yes." I replied, absurdly as a soprano.

"You admit then to being a man?"

My voice tumbled in pitch. "I overheard your conversation. It was hard not to, in an intimate room such as this."

"An excellent reply." Celeste remarked to Beatrice.

"He is obviously a replier of some substance and skill."

Celeste turned back to me. "Then you know we would like to offer you assistance?"

I gave a wan smile. "A sandwich would be extraordinarily helpful."

Maxime approached to examine me.

"Sorry to have misled you." I squirmed.

He stroked the smooth side of his face as if for a renegade bristle.

Beatrice tutted. "Father. We know you're myopic. But really. He didn't even have a good high voice."

Maxime gazed at my legs and shook his head. "It's none of my business. My business is mowing the lawn of the head, the face and sometimes, not very often it's true, the legs."

"Though not a woman, or a police officer," I confessed, "I'd be grateful if you would not speak of this to anyone."

Maxime half-smiling, brought his utensils to a sink. "O' clever daughter, you must at least concede he has a very pretty face."

"He does." Celeste agreed.

"Passable." Beatrice allowed.

Maxime looked back at me, chuckled and shook his head once more. "And many a woman looks more like a man,"

"Though few," Beatrice replied as I pulled on my tights, "look less like a police officer."

"Make him a sandwich," he shushed. "We will say nothing er … Donna of your visit."

"*Donna?*" the daughter's heads winced in unison.

"Well, you couldn't call a policewoman *Celeste*." I explained defensively.

`Beatrice sniggered. "She actually *did* want to be a policewoman once."

"*When we were five.*"

"But as we share the same body …"

"There has to be unanimity about things."

"So we fell out didn't we, Celeste dear?"

"Yes. But with hindsight, you were quite an astute little five-year-old to see the constabulary would be no career for a two-headed girl like us. Even if it was only because you thought the uniform unflattering."

"Well look at it."

"Quite right. Though it's unfair to judge this one when he hasn't the figure for it. Anyhow, it was a long, long time ago and I'm quite over it. Let us cut sandwiches."

"We had better take the bicycle with us or Father's clients will get nosy."

Bidding Maxime farewell, I trundled it from the salon. My tandem-headed hostess led me through the house to a kitchen where, after leaning my mount against a cupboard, I sat at a table.

"Your bicycle having square wheels, both like and unlike ourselves, is singular," remarked Celeste.

Groggily, I only then recalled what had happened on the train. "One of my own selves, the eldest, once told me I would meet a two-headed girl. He cut off some of his beard to give to you when we met."

They looked understandably nonplussed.

"I've never met anyone who has met an elder self before." Beatrice remarked.

"Neither have I."

"Obviously, if I haven't either. Curious. We may have two heads, but at least there's only one of us."

"Let us not pry."

"No. We should demand our bristles however. Well?"

The hand on Beatrice's side outstretched demandingly which led to a guilty confession,

"Unfortunately I left them in my trousers when I changed into a dress."

The two heads stared at each other.

"How inconsiderate."

"To dash our hopes so." Celeste tutted.

"I'm not sure if we *should* help him now."

"Though I have to say ..."

"Spit it out ..."

"Revolting phrase, please don't use it again."

"What were you going to say?"

"I can't remember." Celeste banged her brow, then continued. "Anyway, would either of us actually *want* the clippings of an old man's beard? In all likelihood, quite disgusting bristles with remnants of soup sticking them together."

"True. Our squeamishly not being able to even touch them might have lost the trust of our new friend."

My head pounded in recall. "As he gave no word of warning along with the bristles, I'm inclined to trust you anyway."

"Ha!" Celeste brightened. "I've remembered what I was going to say."

"Excellent. Proceed."

"I was going to ask Donna, if he left the whiskers in his trousers to change into his current garment, which is a skirt or as he originally said, a dress, which is different."

It looked bad, but I was in no condition to dissemble.

"A dress."

Beatrice laughed, "A police-impersonating transvestite aboard a square-wheeled bicycle in our very own kitchen. Delicious."

I was too befuddled to respond.

"Do take off your cap, dearest Donna," Celeste teased placing a kettle on the stove.

At which, the truncheon blow told.

"Perhaps I might lie down."

With a groan I slumped over the kitchen table.

I woke on a sofa, beneath a blanket, head aching and bandaged. On a chair beside me, the girl with two heads was playing chess with herself, the board balanced on bare knees.

"Oh hello." Celeste turned to Beatrice, "Your pawn defrocking my bishop has woken Donna."

"You conked out."

"For long?" I croaked.

"Six hours."

"Oh. Thank you for looking after me."

Beatrice spoke to her other self. "He is greatly in our debt."

"Especially for dragging his unconscious body all the way to this sofa."

"But we couldn't leave it sprawled on the kitchen table."

Celeste agreed. "It was in the way for lunch. However, we will keep all of this to ourselves so as not to discomfort him."

Gingerly, I sat up.

"How is your head?" Celeste continued.

The question seemed funny from a girl with two.

"Aching."

"At least we have a spare if one gets hit."

"That must be a great comfort." I replied dryly.

"Yes." She looked thoughtful. "But the downside is that we spend twice as much on hats."

"And then argue about their stylistic incongruity when we go to a party," frowned Beatrice.

"Our tastes are different," the blonde head lamented.

"And when we argue, we can't stamp off to another room and slam the door to get away from each other."

"I slam the door and she's still there."

"And so are you."

They stared at each other so fiercely, I laughed. Celeste changed the subject.

"Let us find a pill for Donna's head. And ask if he still wants a sandwich and cup of tea."

"I wonder if I might have a sandwich and cup of tea." I murmured.

"Very forward of him to ask," tutted Beatrice.

"He's obviously not himself, brained on his only head."

Over the aforementioned sandwich, I explained my bruised brow and disguise.

"My girlfriend, well now ex-girlfriend, was—no, still *is*—a policewoman and she finished with me by truncheon blow."

Beatrice grimaced. "That sort of thing would be implicit in the relationship, I suppose."

"She was called Betty."

"It gets worse and worse." Celeste fretted. "I can't see the attraction from here but go on."

"She felt it was her duty to arrest me, even though I hadn't done anything wrong."

"Because …?"

I confessed. "Because I'm different from everybody else.

"We have much in common," said Beatrice sardonically.

"For instance," Celeste chimed in, "we also wear women's clothes."

"Look, I only wore Betty's uniform to disguise myself and escape on my grandfather's bike from the long, truncheon-wielding arm of the law."

"Thus fetching up here."

"Yes."

"Which is all very well," Celeste went on, "but why does your grandfather have a bike with square wheels?"

"He doesn't really. He's no longer alive. I borrowed it from my grandmother, without permission."

Beatrice turned to Celeste. "He obviously *does* have to be watched."

"My grandfather designed the bicycle to win the Tour De France, fifty years ago. But his entry was thwarted and the machine he built … well, it still yearns for the race."

"Yearns?"

"It's sentient and I've promised to pedal it to Dover, smuggle us onto a fisherman's boat and once in France, find a Tour de France competitor to ride it. The wheels go incredibly fast when the machine feels like it."

The two heads looked at each other, raised their eyebrows and then turned to me. Celeste spoke first. "Your story is about as plausible as a two-headed girl. And as we *are* a two-headed-girl, I absolutely believe it."

"It's too good *not* to be true." Beatrice laughed.

"I also thought it might be wise to put the channel between Betty and myself."

But they weren't listening.

"Ooh la la, let us be properly introduced to this sapient velocipede." Celeste enthused and the girl with two heads, ran into the kitchen.

"Roi des velos," I heard Beatrice sing, "welcome to our humble abode. Should you require anything of us, a little oil, or pumping of the tyres, please ring your bell and we will be glad to be of service."

Soon after, the bicycle was wheeled in and leaned against the sofa beside me.

"We think the velocipede," said Celeste, "would like us to find you some appropriate clothing for the journey to Dover and beyond. Though not another dress."

"Something a mariner might wear," I agreed.

"Fishnets?" suggested Beatrice.

Celeste ignored this, "Father might help. But we will have to wait for him to down the scissors and comb."

We were eating dinner when Maxime finished work and entered the room in a long, green quilted-coat over black trousers. He gave me a stern smile.

"So, Donna. You are really Alphonso Blink's grandson, also Alphonso Blink?"

Rumbled, I could only nod, ignominiously.

"One of my clients, a foreign Minister in fact, told me that the grandson of the Great Alphonso had escaped a train, and that anything might happen as a result."

The two-headed girl, who had been eating from a single plate, stopped in mid-chew to stare at me. Beatrice swallowed and spoke. "Who is Alphonso Blink?"

"I'm named after my grandfather, whom I never met." I explained. An inventor, who apparently often fell foul of the law. But I myself haven't done anything wrong."

Maxime looked grave. "Of course not. It is what you *might* do that worries them."

"Might do?" Beatrice looked perplexed.

"I seem to inadvertently cause strange things to happen."

"So *that's* how you're different," breathed Celeste.

"And nobody knows that better than ourselves," said Maxime, "that it is not a time to be different. For which reason, Alphonso, I cannot shelter you long in this house. So long as I am on the right side of the state, or at least those that run it, our position is just about tenable. But they would not be forgiving if it was discovered that *you* were under my roof. Especially with the current regime."

I pushed my plate away apologetically. "I can leave after dark. Only, these clothes ... My own in the bike pannier would be known to the authorities."

"He wants to look like a fisherman, Father." Celeste said. "To escape on a boat to France."

They summarised my circumstances. Then ...

"He could have that woollen beanie of Celeste's," Beatrice mused. "Technically women's clothing, but it looks terrible on her."

"*It does not,*" the owner protested.

Beatrice went on. "A thick woolly jumper and overalls would complete the transformation to a trawlerman."

"So can we ransack your wardrobe Father?"

"Yes, but don't ..."

His daughter was already out of the room.

"Your dinner is in the oven," Celeste called back.

When Maxime brought his meal to the table, I spoke.

"You called my grandfather 'The Great Alphonso'. Did you know him?"

He hesitated. "Not well. I took my wife, Georgetta and Bryony, to see him once," and here he took a photograph from the windowsill and put it in front of me. Two heads on one set of shoulders. "To disinvent her heads."

"Their mother?"

He nodded. Neither of them looked very like Beatrice and Celeste, except one head had a fetching upturned lip. Maxime continued.

"The endless close proximity meant they grew to hate each other. Though I loved them both. I thought your grandfather, such was his genius, might be able to make her whole. Even though that was not what I myself wanted."

"But my grandfather couldn't help?"

"Couldn't or wouldn't. I never found out. He thought she was the most wonderful creature he had ever met. So did I. But ..."

"Is she still alive?"

"I doubt it. Many years back she was sent away on a train journey of indefinite duration. She has not been heard of since. I am constantly fearful that they will do the same to my daughter."

"But do they even know Beatrice and Celeste exist?"

"Unfortunately, yes. My daughter has a high profile."

"Oh?"

"She is a singer-songwriter and performs twice a week in a nearby town. My own work, on the heads of the heads of state, is all, I fear, that keeps her from danger. But for how long?"

"Singers?" I wondered aloud.

"They are exquisite in harmony together. The current minister of foreign affairs, against his better judgement, is a huge fan."

Then Maxime quizzed me about the bicycle, its single-mindedness and whistling velocity. He was mopping a plate with bread when his daughter returned bearing disguises. Both faces were glowering.

"Celeste wants Alphonso to see us play tonight." Beatrice told her father.

The blonde head tossed. "Well, *I do*."

"Is it wise?"

Maxime didn't answer the question but only looked at Celeste, as if for her reasoning.

She answered, "Nobody will know it's Alphonso Blink, once he's incognito. And we won't be giving him a lift. He can cycle into town once it's dark in time to see the gig. Why not? So long as he doesn't approach or talk to us. I want him to hear us play. It won't take long, then he can continue on to Dover."

Beatrice stared at me. "She is attracted to you."

"Beatrice!"

"Well, you are."

"You are so horrible sometimes." Celeste looked at me, blushing deeply. "I *am* attracted to you. And unfortunately, she is not. In such things, we must have unanimity. *Though there never is.* But if I can't kiss you because of her, you could at least come and listen to me sing at The Umbrella Club tonight."

I returned her blush. This mindbogglingly frank exchange between Celeste and Beatrice left me bereft of words. We had only just met and the thought of kissing anybody but Betty, had not wandered into my mind. Maxime intervened calmly,

"Avoid each other in the venue and I cannot see the harm."

Beatrice looked so thunderous I feared for plates stacked on the table.

"I'd love to hear you sing." I said recovering somewhat. "And thank you both for rummaging out a better disguise. Perhaps I should try it on?"

I retired to an adjoining room.

The fisherman costume was a little *haute couture* – the beanie, roll-top pullover and culottes had obviously never participated in hauling a net. Tears and tufts were needed and the perfume of mackerel, haddock and cod, though the garments could be rubbed with something raw from a fishmonger on arrival in port. A stubby pipe and sandpapered complexion would not have gone amiss, but the biggest omission, really essential in a fisherman of any legitimacy was a beard, and my chin, being callow, did not have the wherewithal to grow more than a few wisps.

It was whilst lamenting the baldness of my chin that I began to feel attracted to Celeste. Once the idea had been planted in my head, kissing her seemed so beguiling I could scarcely believe I hadn't thought of it myself. She *did* have the most tempting upturned lip. And I felt for her being brutally exposed by Beatrice and wished I had not looked so nonplussed at her finding me attractive. Not least, Celeste would never bash me over the head with a truncheon, though of course, Beatrice might. For a moment, the thought of not seeing either of them again for the sake of a square-wheeled bicycle's feelings seemed a stretch. But then they were kicking me out anyway, and perhaps once I had delivered the machine to a future yellow jersey, I could nip back across the channel, by which time Blue, Sooty and Bob might have been called off.

Returning to the kitchen, I found Maxime had gone but that the atmosphere could at least now be cut by a wooden spoon. The two heads giggled when they saw me.

"The young salt." Celeste teased affectionately.

"Or not-terribly-able-seaman, Swabber Blink."

"It feels easier than being a policewoman," I confessed.

"Ah now," Beatrice sighed, "if we only had a fish for him to chase, to test him out in his new career."

"We could pretend to be fish and see if he could catch us."

"He's already caught you."

"Perhaps I'd like to be caught again."

"Do fish flirt?"

"Yes. When they want to catch a fisherman. And I think it's been made quite plain that I do by the rest of the shoal." Celeste spoke a little hotly.

"You *have* caught one," I told her.

"Huh, well we had better get ourselves ready," Beatrice decided, and the tension between the two heads returned. "Here is father to keep you company."

Maxime entered the kitchen as his daughter briskly left it. He sat at the table clearly ruffled beneath his immaculate exterior.

"Alphonso, Beatrice is right. For you to go and see my daughter perform this evening is not a good idea. But for you *not* to go might be worse. They cannot afford a war. Besides, their performances are amazing. Just don't be seen together. I briefed your bicycle here with directions to The Umbrella Club whilst you were changing. Also, once you are across the channel, you might want to find the address on this piece of paper. It's in Normandy."

I took the scrap of paper and read: *Le Château Sans Passé.*

"The machine was shown the route on a map. Friends of mine live at the address. Keen cyclists. They will help you for sure. Just say Maxime cut your hair."

The girl with two heads reappeared with a guitar case. Dressed in a denim jacket and jeans with a white T shirt, they might have stepped from inside the cover of a gate-fold record sleeve.

"We're going early," Beatrice announced.

Celeste looked tearful. The guitar case banged a door as they left. Maxime smiled ruefully at me. "Better go outside and say farewell."

They'd backed a Citroen 2CV out of the garage and left it fuming blue puffs whilst loading the guitar case onto a back seat. I approached tentatively.

"Excuse me, girl with two heads." They slammed the back door of the car and looked at me pointedly. "I just wanted to say goodbye and thank you for helping with my transformation. And Celeste, although we may not meet again, I want you to know that the attraction is definitely mutual and I *would* ask you to kiss me but ..."

"No buts," she rejoined darkly. "Beatrice kissed somebody once that I didn't like. *He was called Reg.*"

The other head hung a little in shame. "True. But in my defense, we didn't find out until after the deed was done."

"It was obvious from the beginning. His hair was lank and guitar playing out of time and he said *Hey, cool chick.*"

Beatrice winced. "He kissed me and then said: *I'm Reg by the way.*"

"Despicable. So Alphonso let us proceed."

"Yes, but ..."

Beatrice laughed. "He doesn't want an audience of me."

"Only because I'm imagining you might find it disagreeable. Though I do find you incredibly attractive as well."

She looked dumbfounded.

"Why?"

"I don't know. I seem to have no control over the part of me that deals with finding people attractive or not."

"We have that in common at least. Alas, much though I like you Alphonso, you do not make my lips tingle or jumble my mind with delicious romantic absurdities."

"But you do mine." Celeste laughed, taking my hand and pulling me close.

At which we kissed, a slightly tricky operation as Beatrice spoke in my ear after about ten seconds of osculation. "Strange to be turned on by somebody kissing Celeste who doesn't turn me on. You see the problem?"

Celeste made an appreciative noise. "He kisses nicely."

"Yes, I can tell. I feel as turned on as you do, without a shred of reason."

Celeste murmured. "I have only one word to say to that. *Reg.*"

"So you understand well the voyeuristic situation I am in, where I am feeling erogenous sensations that belong to somebody else."

"Beatrice, for once in your life, SHUT UP!"

There was an explosive silence. I stepped back to witness a fierce mutual glare between the heads, then a pleading look aimed at me from Celeste. The singers turned and slid into the CV2 then, with a slam of the driver's door and angry revving of the engine, went weaving off along the lane. All I could manage in response, was a limply apologetic wave. After a few minutes waiting for my confusion to settle, like snow in a paperweight globe, I went inside to incinerate Betty's uniform and my own clothes from the bicycle panniers in a stove. Afterwards, Maxime replaced my head bandage with a much less obtrusive plaster and talked about his early life as a barber and meeting the mother of Beatrice and Celeste. Dusk eventually arrived and I bade him farewell before heading off in the gloaming to the Umbrella Club.

Nine   *Cocktail*

The ride was ridiculously uneventful and while it is tempting to fabricate something to enliven this part of the narrative—best stick to the facts. My lips were not tingling as I pedalled off, for though Celeste's kiss had been eager, Betty's were better. In mitigation, having Beatrice as a seething chaperone was no aphrodisiac. All the same, our awkward parting had not left my mind jumbled with delicious romantic absurdities, suggesting that, after I'd heard them sing, we might be better strangers.

In less than an hour, the bicycle conveyed me to a benighted town park which, according to Maxime, the Umbrella Club overlooked. I hid the contraption in some rhododendron bushes, covering it with branches and leaves, reasoning that only a lunatic would steal a square-wheeled bicycle. Though it was pointed out to me, by myself, that *I* had. Then, emerging faux-nonchalantly from a park gate, I made my way towards a large, half-umbrella awning protruding from a wall across the street. Beneath this canopy, at the top of a small flight of steps, stood a bouncer, or so I surmised having never met one before. Certainly his features had been rearranged by some sort of pugilism and spoke more of breaking noses than kindly explanations. I advanced warily up the steps, whereupon he opened the door and smiled.

"Enjoy your evening sir."

The club was crowded, which made buying an orange juice at the bar a feat of considerable self-promotion. The drink eventually appeared, of course, with a mini-parasol.

Following sounds of a live jazz band, I squeezed through a press of drinkers and entered an intimate auditorium where the umbrella theme was also unconstrained—the band on a podium playing beneath a giant sparkly gamp. I groped my way to a dimly-lit and secluded table at the back. For a while nothing much happened, a few couples smooched on the dance floor, and the level of my orange sank slowly by straw. Then a woman carrying a cocktail approached, an attractive brunette in a long red gown that was slashed daringly high up the leg.

"Would you mind if I joined you?"

"Not at all," I stammered. "Please do."

She sat beside me placing her cocktail alongside my orange juice. I thought her at least five years older than myself.

"Are you on your own?" She asked.

"Er ... not really." I didn't want any further entanglements. "I'm waiting for my wife. We're meeting here."

The arrival smiled at me from behind a curtain of black hair. "You don't look like a married man."

"It's only just happened," I explained. "It might take a few years for being a bachelor to wear off."

"And you look young to be hitched up."

"It wasn't really my idea, she proposed and I sort of went along with it."

"Interesting. I'm married myself."

"So why aren't you sitting with your husband?" I quelled an impulse to look around for some large rugby player approaching with a pint.

"He's abroad. Being a cyclist."

I nearly blew bubbles down my straw. *"A cyclist?"*

"Yes. Quite a strange job, I admit. He's a professional and is in France now working with a team for the Tour De France."

"Oh. Does he have a bicycle?"

I saw her mind boggle. "Of course he does. You can't *walk* the race."

"Yes. Silly of me. What I meant was … well, I don't know what I meant."

Nor did I know what to think. Here was a possible entrée into the world of the Tour de France, I didn't want to mess it up. "My name's Jack" I lied, recklessly adopting yet another non-de-plume.

"That's funny. My name is Jacqueline." She laughed. "But somehow, you don't look like a Jack either."

"Being married must have made me a bit less like myself," I reasoned feebly.

"And what do *you* do?"

"Me? I'm a fisherman. Working from Dover. Supplying cod and herrings to outlets across the country. You might have eaten fish with your chips that I have caught personally."

She looked sceptical.

"You're going to say that I don't look like a fisherman aren't you?"

"You don't."

"My wife will be here soon and she will be able to verify all my biographical details." I said a little desperately, "Though quite what she'll say when she finds me deep in conversation with a beautiful woman, I can't think."

Jacqueline shrugged carelessly. "My husband might equally ask what I am doing deep in conversation with a beautiful man. But he's abroad, and besides, there weren't too many other places to sit. So what is a fisherman doing in the Umbrella Club? Shouldn't you be down the tavern in Dover? I don't think I've ever met a seaman who drinks orange juice through a straw."

"My wife is a fan of some woman who sings here."

"Oh. The Two Headed Girl."

"Yes. That's the name of the band. Are they good? I'm not much interested in music myself."

"Very good and most unusual. Your wife will miss them if she doesn't hurry up."

"She's always late for everything."

"And what's *her* name?"

I haplessly blurted the first name that came to mind. "Betty."

"*Betty.*" My companion turned this over thoughtfully. "Betty and Jack. They do go together. How did you meet?"

"It's a bit of a fisherman's tale."

"But of course."

"She's a police constable and was one of several who arrested me for smuggling brandy into the country on my boat."

"How exciting. And *were* you doing?"

"No. It was a wrongful arrest. It was actually the Captain from a neighbouring boat they were supposed to nab. But being handcuffed to Betty for an hour, well, we sort of got to know each other a bit and after my release and their apology, I asked her on a date."

Jacqueline sighed, "If only my life were half as improbable as yours seems to be."

"About your husband's cycling ..."

My words were drowned by an introductory razzmatazz from the band.

"Now look. Your wife will be vexed. They're coming on."

Beatrice and Celeste walked from the wings to cheers, wolf whistles and applause, seating themselves in a circle of light beside the band.

"Hey," I whispered as if amazed to Jacqueline so as not to blow my cover. "She actually has two heads!"

"It's one person."

"Is it a trick? She can't really be like that."

"Shh. They're about to start."

In fact they were only tuning up. Or Beatrice was whilst Celeste spoke to the audience.

"Hello everyone. We're the Two Headed Girl."

"Unfortunately," Beatrice added whilst finely adjusting a machine head.

"We're in a bit of a grumpy mood with each other tonight. Well, most nights really. But if you bought our last record, you know all about that in some detail. We'd like to start with *Something Cheerful*. This is a Beatrice song."

"Credit where it's due. When I was making it up, she had our fingers in her ears."

My expectations are nearly always wrong. Whether this is bankruptcy of the imagination or having so little working knowledge of what life is really like, I can't say, but predicting accurately what might happen next has never been a strength. In this case, my expectation of some tasteful folksy blues with an underlying spirit of soulful innocence lasted about one line.

"*There's nothing worse than cheerful folk declaring all is well*

They make me want to scream"

"*and me*"

"*and shake them with a yell:*

Shut up and cry, please sob and weep, for everything is shit

I can't believe you're smiling when we're up to here in it

In fact we could be cheerful if you'd only go away

And be all bright and breezy on a ten-lane motorway

Or under water, one more happy remark and I'll see red

and slap you or quietly raise a vase and break it on your head

I'll pack my troubles up and stuff them in your mouth and that

Is all that just might cheer me up you fucking annoying twat."

I was particularly shocked by the last three words being so exquisitely harmonised. Whilst singing, they pogoed in a boisterous way and kicked the stool over, without the guitar accompaniment losing time.

Jacqueline was watching my expression and laughed, "They're fun aren't they?"

Fun! It went way beyond *fun*. A two-headed woman boinging up and down with a guitar whilst singing a venomous song with faultless harmony, was everything that Betty was not! Never before had I met a poltergeist spirit and as the gig progressed and they threw more pots and pans, I fell in love with Celeste and Beatrice all over again. The kissing would surely improve if Beatrice would only come round to an understanding of my romantic possibilities.

They started with songs that the clientele seemed to know and delivered them dancing, screaming, shouting, pouting, and above all with pristine musicality and harmonies that I longed to rewind and hear again. Between songs they jumped down into the audience and stole drinks or knocked them over by kneeling on tables to strum, flirting outrageously with the men.

"Which of us do you prefer?" Beatrice asked one merry gentleman at a table. "Be careful, there's no right answer, but there's definitely a wrong one."

"In other words, preferring me," Celeste warned.

He helplessly spoke the truth, "You're both divine."

Which brought only snorts of derision from Beatrice, "Ha! He's sitting on the fence!"

"Uncomfortable perhaps," Celeste observed.

"Especially an electric one."

"Though this is an acoustic set.

"Barbed wire then," Beatrice decided. "In which case he'd be better admitting which one of us he prefers and have the other one pour a drink over his head." The guitar twanged. "We shall make up a song for him. Let it be called, *Sitting On A Barbed Wire Fence*.

It helps to make up your mind
when stuck in your big fat behind
there's a spike of barbed wire
stabbing like fire
a dozen of them rustily tined."

And that was the astonishing thing about the performance. They made up songs on the spot. Improvised words, melody and harmony for compositions that sounded too perfect to have been off-the-cuff, although several ended abruptly in a fit of giggles and once with Beatrice confessing,

"I can't think of a rhyme for *pint*."

Midway through this chaos, they stopped to lean on the edge of the stage whilst Celeste introduced a song. "This one's from our first record and I'd like to dedicate it to our good friend Donna if she's in the audience tonight."

"She is." Beatrice grumbled whilst appearing to tune the guitar. "I caught a glimpse."

"It's called *I Can't Make Up My Minds.*"

There was a cheer from the crowd, many of whom obviously already knew the song.

Celeste: *It's hard for me to make up my minds*
Beatrice: *Cos it seems they can never*
Both: *agree.* (discord)
Celeste: *In two minds about this and two minds about that*
Beatrice: *There's no seeing eye to eye with me.*

The two heads turned to stare at each other.

Celeste: *I want to go sliding down the banisters of love.*
Beatrice: *Only to find myself stuck halfway.*
Celeste: *It's no good saying please*
Beatrice: *Will I open my knees*
Celeste: *And let go because they*
Won't always be there
At the foot of a stair
whilst my stupid minds
don't even try to agree.

This unbelievably moving composition, sweetly sung and delivered with a wry detachment, had me almost slithering under the table, which did not escape Jacqueline's attention.

"We appear to have broken a string," Beatrice remarked at the end of the song.

"There's a spare in there." Celeste motioned to an open guitar case on the stage beside them.

"I'm glad we thought of that."

"They do say that two heads are better than one."

"Who does?"

"The people who say things, stoopid," Celeste answered as if to an idiot.

"They're wrong," said Beatrice whilst also attending to the guitar.

Celeste thought for a moment.

"But I've never heard *anybody* say one head is better than two. Except us."

"Well if as they say," Beatrice argued still winding a string, "two heads *are* better than one, having two heads, we must be right and one head is therefore better than two."

Celeste stage-whispered, "I'm glad you've cleared that up for us."

"It's tuned by the way."

"I have ears by the way."

And so it went on, a catalogue of songs, outrageous improvisations, witticisms and audience engagement. There was an absurd interlude in which they impersonated Bach and Handel, each vying to sing their own composition and thus creating a fusion called *The Messiah's G String*. When this slipped into discordancy, there was a vociferous argument in German which ended with Celeste explaining, "Ve don't see ear to ear."

When Celeste took a trumpet from a case Beatrice remarked, "Oh no, the coach horn is coming out."

"Do we have time?"

"The night is yet riding on a tricycle in short trousers. But we do need a title for the song you're going to play along to."

"*My Kind of Guy,*" someone called.

The music immediately began. It was an arresting highlight to see Celeste playing the trumpet and Beatrice singing whilst their body danced along.

"My kind of guy
lives in a pie
And how I just lust
to kiss
beneath his pastry crust
With the filling just us."

Celeste paused breathlessly to laugh at Beatrice, "You're weird."

"Pastry is under-rated," came the indignant reply. The song went on,

"What a recipe I'd be
So sweet and so, so, savoury ..."

It thereafter became lewd, and they advised us not to listen. But the audience couldn't help themselves. There was such a fizz in the air. Such excitement at witnessing a performance so mind-blowingly one-off. An exhilarating feeling of: *I was there!*

The set ended with a song about screaming, in which they got the entire audience to scream along and screamed into each other's faces whilst jumping up and down on a sofa. It oughtn't to have been musical but it was, for they screamed in harmony. I could have watched all night and cursed that in their company earlier, I'd had no notion of quite how extraordinary they were. Two heads were the least of it.

"That was incredible," I applauded after they'd bowed and run from the stage, leaving an aftermath of dynamite having banged.

"A shame your wife missed it," Jacqueline wryly observed.

Caught off-guard, I groped for words, "Betty will be er ... disappointed. She must have had ... a lot of ... um, arrests at work."

"You know," her eyes looked into mine and slowly undid my innermost thoughts, "I don't believe a single word you've told me."

"Really?"

I felt very exposed by her scrutiny.

She smiled and with deliberation added, "But I am very attracted to you nonetheless." At which she drank the rest of my orange juice through the straw, noisily hoovering the bottom of the glass. "Would you like to come back to my place for a coffee?"

"A coffee?" My mind whirled. There was now red lipstick on the top of the straw. "But your husband?

"He's in France for a couple of weeks at least." She leaned, elbows on the table, close to my face, hers soft, all dark eyes and darker hair. "So he'll never know you've drunk a cappuccino with me."

Whilst my interest in the girl with two heads had been totally reignited by their performance, I also remembered coffee with Betty and how it was served. As a way of taking any beverage it would be my first choice. Moreover, here was an undeniable opening into cycling circles that I desperately needed. It would be harder on the other side of the channel for a person of such retrograde French. Not least, Jacqueline, though a little older than me, looked like she made great coffee.

"Alright. Give me your address. I'll drive over."

"What will you tell your wife?"

"I suppose I'll have to make something up."

And with this she slowly took my hand and very deliberately placed it on her bare thigh, revealed by the slash in her dress. Her skin was hot and my hand sizzled as she moved it slowly up and down along her leg beneath the table.

"Incidentally," she purred smokily, "What *are* you doing here?"

"It's all a bit complicated," I breathed.

Jacqueline left my hand to move itself and reached for a small silver purse on the table. Taking out a pen she wrote something on the back of a card. "My address."

"Thankyou."

I removed my hand from her thigh with some regret to accept the offering and stood up.

"Hopefully, we'll meet again soon."

"If you don't live too far away." I agreed.

"I don't."

I looked at the card: *Jacqueline Dupont, The Umbrella Club.*

"You work here?"

"Sort of. I own it. My flat is only three doors down. Number 17, Umbrella Street. I'll meet you there in an hour."

She stood up, smiled and wended her way between tables of animated clientele. I turned the card over and over. Number 17. To leave the bicycle in the park till morning felt risky, for come daylight it could hardly escape notice. I'd have to wheel the machine to her flat – and tell her what? Had she worked out that I knew Beatrice and Celeste? She must be sympathetic to them if they sang in her club. Then again, surely Maxime and the Two-Headed Girl would have known Jacqueline was married to a tour de France cyclist? Why had they not said so? Then it occurred to me that her husband was probably a guest at *Le Château Sans Passé*.

Not wishing to compromise Celeste and Beatrice by hanging about to congratulate them on their performance, I left the club, thanking the bouncer at the door.

"Enjoy the rest of your evening sir."

"Thankyou," I rejoined, "What's your name by the way?"

"Basher sir. Basher Harrison."

"And what was your line of work before this?"

"Worked in a flower shop sir. On Grundy Street. Selling tulips mostly."

Ten *Passwords*

After an uneasy glance up and down Umbrella Street I bade Basher farewell and crossed the road. There's something not entirely savoury about town parks at night. One imagines they are a sanctuary for deviants and malefactors of every kind, waiting to spring with a sudden rustle from behind bushy silhouettes. This was my first encounter with municipal gardens circa midnight and playing Blind Man's Buff in the rhododendrons, groping for the handlebars of a square-wheeled bicycle, lifted hairs on the neck. I had a paranoid sense of Umbrella Park being a densely populated underworld. That if I were to stumble upon the playground there would be burglars on the swings, drug dealers on the roundabout and murderers whizzing down the slides. Distracted by such thoughts, I realised my fumbling progression had gone way past the point where the Tour aspirant had been hidden. My camouflaging skills were so good I had concealed the machine even from myself. Or was it hiding? I retraced many elongated, slow-motion steps, outstretched hands grasping countless twigs and leaves and even a park railing in my quest for the Great Alphonso's steed.

    I felt up and down one side of the park three times until concluding the bike had been stolen by thieves from the see-saw. Or maybe it was just too dark and I should go drink some coffee with Jacqueline until dawn. At least I would not have to explain why such a bicycle was on my hands ... *my hands* ... my hands met a dog's head. There was a happy snuffling sound. I couldn't really see anything much in the shadows except more shadows. However, this one felt extraordinarily like an Alsatian.

"Blue?" I whispered in dread. "Please not." To my relief there wasn't much response. "Sooty?" This brought some panting and my hand was lapped at. But it still did not feel like recognition. "Bobby?"

The animal jumped up and licked my face at our being on first name terms.

"Down!" I hissed. "Down you daft bloody animal. Bobby, sit. *Sit!*"

Bobby's obedience levels were tested no further because the surrounding bushes erupted in a way that only many giant hedgehogs or a posse of policemen could accomplish. A number of arms grabbed my own.

"Alphonso Blink ..." a voice intoned in the dark.

"No!" I babbled, "My name is Frederick Nunns."

"You are under arrest."

There seemed to be dozens of apprehending constables. As many as all the criminals I had imagined earlier.

"I'm innocent. I'm a fisherman looking for my boat."

"I'm sorry Alphonso," came Betty's voice from behind me, moments before my head felt a crack of violent pain. "There's no other way."

I fell unconscious backwards into her arms. Or so they told me later.

I awoke in a police cell, head throbbing and bound like a turban. The room was dazzlingly white with no windows. A table and two chairs were the only furniture but for a bed on which I lay, wincing at the fluorescents and stink of disinfectant. At least the mattress had a bit of give.

For a long time I just stared at the walls. Wishing there were posters. Even Wanted posters. Even Wanted posters of me. At last a grille on the door slid back.

An adenoidal voice said, "You awake?"

"Yes."

"Good, because we need to set up your account."

My thoughts swam at this. "I'm not sure I quite understand. Maybe because my head hurts."

"Think of a password."

"Why?"

"To open your account. You can't have an account without a password. It should be at least eight letters long with a mixture of capitals and lower case and throw in a number and special character for good measure."

"Could I get a drink of water and an aspirin."

"Well, this is the thing. I'm not authorised to do that until you open an account."

I eventually came up with Help(meescape)999.

"Don't tell anyone what it is."

"Who can I tell? I'm alone. Can I have a glass of water now?"

"Not yet. I have to authenticate your account."

The throb in my temples worsened considerably. "I've been arrested. What is all this?"

"All prisoners have to have an account. And we need to authenticate it so we know who you are."

"But you must know who I am? Or you wouldn't have bashed me over the head. Where's Betty. She'll tell you who I am."

"According to GDPR she can't legally reveal any of your personal information. Now first of all we have to prove you're you. When you ring the buzzer to ask for something like a glass of water, a constable will come down and give you a special number you write down, using a pen and paper found in the table drawer. The constable will then go, and a second constable will visit. They will ask for the number. If it is the same as the one that the first constable took away, you will be authenticated and can make a request."

"Do I do this just once?"

"Oh no. Every time you want something. Here's your number, which only you must know."

"Well, and you."

"I'm not allowed to look at it."

"Where did you get it from?"

"It is immaterial. 439008. Now ring the buzzer for your water."

And with that the grille slid back and the voice was gone. I somehow keeled out of bed and on wobbly legs approached the grille. There was indeed a buzzer beside it, which I pressed, but heard nothing. Not long after returning to the mattress, I heard the grille scrape open once more.

"Yes?" another disembodied voice called. Much more sonorous.

"I'd like a glass of water please."

"What's your authentication number?"

"I don't know. The other guy said it really fast and I didn't write it down."

There was an irritated sigh. "You'll have to buzz for a new authentication code."

"What? But can't I just have a glass of water. I'm new to the system? Couldn't you just bring it down to me this once?"

"No. How do I know you're you? Could be a case of identity fraud. I'd be giving a glass of water to a person who shouldn't be drinking it."

"A glass of water?"

"It's for your own protection."

The grille shut again and again I heaved myself up and staggered to the buzzer. After this monumental effort, I went to the table and took a pen and scrap of paper from a draw. The pen barely worked.

Eventually the grille opened. The first constable's nasal voice returned. "224776"

I wrote the number down without the aid of ink, merely pressing hard enough to leave deep imprints of the numbers on the paper. Then another buzz and another wait for the second constable's deep sonority.

"Yes. Number?"

"224776"

"Correct. What is it you want?"

"*Water!* I've already told you. So you *know*. In fact, I want food as well. Sandwiches with all different kinds of fillings and a variety of little cakes and pastries."

"Very good. Just press the buzzer and a constable will come down with a menu of things to choose from. There will probably be four or five options. Which might lead to pressing the buzzer for a further menu of options. If you don't want any of these, press the buzzer once more which will lead to a constable arriving to ask you in person what it is you want, if it's not on the menu."

"But I've just told *you*."

"It's not my department or sphere of responsibility."

"Well, why couldn't I just ask the first constable to get me what I want without the menu."

"They wouldn't be allowed to proceed in that way. The constable will listen to what you want and tell you if you can have it. The only thing is, whatever you want will take a long time arriving."

"Because you're understaffed?"

"No, the staffing is excellent here. It's because many constables who respond to the menu options live in Asia and have to travel from there. One arrived last week from Bombay with a chicken sandwich for a prisoner who had been released three months earlier. The funny thing about that was, because of the language difficulties, the constable had brought the wrong sandwich, the prisoner had actually ordered egg."

"It's insanity."

"On the contrary, it is all part of making the organization more efficient and responsive to the general public."

When I had calmed down sufficiently to press the buzzer for a menu, the grille slid back and I heard a Constable playing guitar beside the door. Every twenty seconds he stopped playing and said, "Thankyou for waiting. One of our constables will speak to you shortly."

After this communication, his playing, which was the same twenty seconds of Faure's Pavane with different mistakes and mutterings of annoyance when he fluffed a note, would recommence. Still I thought it nice work if you could get it. Eventually, after much buzzing, and many voices, I received a glass of water and placed an order for some dry bread to arrive at some unspecified point in the future.

There was no clock and thus, having no watch, no sense of time. I didn't even consider pressing the buzzer to get authenticated and receive a menu requesting the hour of the day. So I couldn't be sure quite when it was that Betty showed up in my cell, only that she caught me asleep. It was a shock, opening my eyes to find her staring down at me, in glasses, with tears in her eyes.

"Hello," I croaked. "Don't say you're coming to brain me again, please."

"Sorry. Can you ever forgive me?"

I sat up with a groan. "Yes. I think so. Not sure about the glasses."

She sat beside me on the bed. "Only you can't be above the law. Nobody can. I need them at work for reading."

"I keep telling you I'm innocent of any misdeeds."

"The facts speak differently."

There was nobody else in the room and the door was shut.

"How did you get in here. And why are you here?"

"We're locked-in together for my visit. As *I* arrested you, I got special dispensation for a private interview."

"With nobody else in the room?"

"Rules were bent a little." She reddened. "I had to agree to a date with the Desk Sergeant. But don't think you can try anything funny. There's armed guards outside the door and all round the building. Everywhere in case the locks are picked. You couldn't escape if you were Houdini. You have to have special passwords and a pin to get out."

I pointed to the pin on her tunic lapel. "Like that one?"

"Never you mind."

"Perhaps, just at this moment I don't want to escape. Though we might try a bit of funny business if you would bend the rules just a little bit further."

Her abashed face said 'kiss me' so I did. Because for some reason, I still loved her.

"Better stop," she said breathlessly, before we got carried away. "I'm on duty. Are you hungry? I've smuggled in a sandwich."

She took a brown paper bag from the jacket pocket of her uniform. Inside the packet were large triangles of white-sliced-bread filled with cheese and pickle. However ...

"Betty, there's a bite taken out of it."

She shrugged apologetically. "It was the Staff Sergeant's. I borrowed it after agreeing to the date."

"Stole it you mean." Why was she continuing with such an unsuitable career? "What kind of a constable are you?"

She sensed where the conversation was going and said defiantly, "I'm a detective constable now. I was promoted for tracking you down and hitting you over the head. I think *especially* for hitting you over the head. And that was just the first time. I shall probably be made Sergeant for hitting you on the second occasion. Don't think I wouldn't do it a third time if I had to."

"I see you've brought the offending implement with you." It was attached to her belt. "And if it's going to help you get promotion. ..."

She unclipped the bludgeon angrily and threw it on the bed. "I brought it just in case."

"Just in case what? I kissed you too many times?"

And then I kissed her again. In the end she had to push me away by the chest.

"Please, Alphonso." She looked suddenly hot and bothered.

Her speaking my name had me wondering. "So. Betty. How *did* you track me down?"

She looked immensely pleased with herself. "After searching your grandmother's castle ..."

"You were kind to her I hope?"

" ... She's a dear old lady. Gave us tea and little fairy cakes. Anyhow we got nothing out of her and completely lost track of where you'd gone. We were thrown even more off the scent when Blue tracked you down to a fisherman's boat in Dover. But you weren't there and obviously never had been."

"Crazy dog," I observed feebly, "Better get rid of him."

"It was obviously the incident with the Foreign Minister's hair that put us back on track."

"What incident?"

"What do you mean, 'what incident?' You know it was you?"

"Know *what* was me?"

"You making his hair go haywire in a public meeting with the President of France."

"I didn't do anything."

"Only you *could* do it. Besides, there were witnesses. His hairdresser said you did it."

"Maxime?"

I stood up.

"Ha. So you see, you admit you know him?"

"Well yes."

"And you were in his house which adjoins the salon when the Foreign Minister was having his hair coiffured."

"That's true but ..."

"Who else could have done it?"

"What exactly happened?

"You must know?"

"I never knew that your knicker drawers had been rearranged with food from the fridge. It just did it. What happened? Tell me please."

"As the French President and Foreign Minister shook hands, in a public meeting before all the international press, the Minister's hair began behaving as if it had a mind of its own. First it stood on end as if electrified, and went all the colours of the rainbow. Then danced about, grew really long and grabbed the President, binding the two men closely together in knots before shrivelling up, to leave the Minister completely bald. He was apoplectic. Though his hair has since grown back."

Had I really done all that? It did seem, taking my past into account, quite likely. "So Maxime got into trouble?"

"The Minister in a fit of rage ordered him and his daughter to be arrested."

"Maxime was arrested?"

"He *was* the hairdresser."

"Did Maxime tell you about me?"

"He didn't have to. His daughter did first. Thinking she must have something to do with it as she is as weirdly outrageous as you are apparently, the Minister ordered their arrest as well. So we went to the Umbrella Club, arrived just as the gig finished, and arrested them. When they discovered that they and their father had been implicated in the surreal event, the dark-haired one blamed you, and said you'd only just left and had been advised to hide your bicycle in the park. That's where we found you."

"So Beatrice ..."

"A nasty piece of work, I must say. She was furious with you."

"Betrayed me." I went silent, trying to assimilate it all. "And *you* took the bicycle. You must have been quick."

Betty looked nonplussed. "No. There was no bicycle found."

It was enough to unwind my turban. "Maybe it was impounded for not having an insurance disc? It was my looking for it so long that gave you time to catch up with me."

Who had taken it and why? The Two Headed Girl? They didn't know about Maxime till after the show. Jacqueline? Basher? Nothing made sense. Had it gone off on its own? But then why hadn't it done so years before instead of languishing in a castle outbuilding?

"Talking of taking things. What did you do with my uniform?"

"I burned it."

Betty looked annoyed. "Might I ask why?"

"Because ... I didn't believe you were a police woman."

"But you do now?"

"Not when we kiss. Nor when you steal a Sergeant's sandwich and bribe him to come down here to see me."

She was as split in half as the two-headed girl.

"What's going to happen to me now?" I asked. "Will there be a trial?"

She looked astonished. "Trial? What for? You're guilty. I think you'll be put on a train of infinite duration, with only your own self for company."

"Sounds terrible." I despaired. "Anyway, it hasn't been definitively proved that I mussed the Minister's hair. Even I don't know if I did."

She looked disapproving. "There was a public scandal. The French President left the country immediately, insulted. I think the Minister for Foreign Affairs might even come and see you here personally to shout at you."

I took her hand, which felt oddly cold. "No chance you'd come with me on the train I suppose?"

She pulled her hand away and stood, embarrassed. "I wouldn't like the uncertainty of it. I like to know where I'm going. But anyhow, they'll only do that if they can find out how you got off the train in the first instance. Because otherwise you might do it as easily again."

"It was quite easy. I pulled the communication chord."

She took out a notebook and pencil and pushing out her tongue began to write, "Pulled ... communi-ca-tion ... cord." She folded the pad and put it away. "Of course. Who else would have dared? Though it was against the law and subject to a one-hundred pound fine. The driver of the train never mentioned your transgression."

"Fearing for his future employment I dare say. I hope I haven't got him into trouble."

"It was a she."

"Well, her then. Can't be that nice a job anyhow. Shovelling coal on a steam locomotive."

Betty looked fidgety. "I have to go."

We looked at each other in the way that we always ended up looking at each other until she burst into tears.

"Your glasses are steaming up," I observed moments before an embrace.

"I'm never going to see you again," she sobbed into my neck.

"Why would you want to? I'm a criminal you're a Police Sergeant to be. We are horrendously ill-matched."

She sobbed some more. I kissed her wet cheeks.

"Promise me one thing, if we do ever meet me again."

"What's that," she stammered.

"You won't bash me over the head with a truncheon."

I picked up the object with a rueful expression and whacked her over the head with it.

It sounds bad and it is not the moment in this chronicle of which I am most proud. As a rule, a person should refrain from knocking the person they love unconscious. But then sometimes, in the heat of a moment, lovers do and say things they later regret. I had invited her to board a train of infinite duration with me and she'd said no, which surely indicated a lack of commitment to the relationship. Moreover, my circumstances demanded urgent action. The Foreign Minister might turn up to shout at me and ship me aboard that infinite train at any moment.

Betty fell sideways onto the bed with a groan and I swiftly undressed her. I blush now to think of it, but I had seen it all before and she hadn't even officially stopped being my girlfriend. At least I didn't take her underwear, though fetching, except for the tights, and I did whisper an apology as I removed them—so there can be no call for the harsh judgement of others. It's not as if I wanted to do it and let me make this abundantly clear—*I did not bash her over the head to get her clothes*. My changing garments with her was purely for the purposes of escape. I dressed her in my fisherman's costume which, had she known it, was actually quite becoming. Then unwound the turban bandage from my head. With a pair of nail scissors from her shoulder bag, I cut strips of material to truss her hands and ankles. The remaining bandage I wrapped round her head to look like the turban. Except for the piece I used to gag her. I knew that would make her especially angry but didn't want any screams for help before I'd got clear of the police station. After all of that, I buttoned up Betty's blouse over my chest, pulled on her tights, zipped the skirt around my middle and shrugged on her tunic. At no point did I get any kind of pleasure out of it, for apart from anything else, it was all done in such a hurry. I grabbed her shoulder bag seeing a curious slip of paper had fallen out when I'd rummaged inside for the nail scissors. It said:

JohnsmithXXX1!

My pseudonym. She had put three kisses beside it. Clearly the numeral one and exclamation mark signified my importance. In private moments Betty was doubtless unbuttoning the blue serge of her tunic to press the scrap of paper to her bosom. It made me feel even more guilty about bashing her pate. Still what's sauce for the gander ought also to be sauce for the goose.

Placing her cap on my head and glasses on my nose, I went to the door and in as close an approximation to Betty's voice as I could get, spoke through the grille, "I've finished thanks."

"Password."

For a moment I panicked—*password???*—and almost said *Help(meescape)999*. Belatedly, I realised what Betty's paper slip was actually for and showed it at the grille. Keys rattled and the door opened. Passing quickly through, I informed the guard that the prisoner was asleep with a sore head and that I had to hurry off to authorise a menu for the Minister of Foreign Affairs who had booked an interrogation. He said only:

"Pin," and held out a much pricked piece of paper for me to pierce.

Keeping my head down, I took the pin from Betty's jacket lapel and stuck it into the offering, in the hope that I was getting the protocols right.

"Thanks."

Perhaps because he and Betty had never previously met, the Constable seemed not see through my flustered appearance, and in fact only looked past me into the cell where she was tucked under a blanket, turbaned head turned away on the pillow. I wondered if the password and pin were all that was important to him and if a bearded man wearing a suit of arrows might as easily have escaped if the password matched and paper was pricked. Anyhow, he locked the door as if it was a formality whilst I scampered up a flight of stairs, towards a pair of guards smacking truncheons into their palms.

"Password," the ugliest demanded.

"It's JohnsmithXXX1!"

"We're case sensitive" the other guard sniffed.

"Capital J and capital kisses, I mean ex's."

"Okay. Pin."

Again, a much perforated scrap of paper was held out for me to stab.

"On you go."

Clearly they either hadn't looked at Betty very hard on her way to the cells or their security system relied solely on matching up sequences of random characters and bizarre piercing practices. So far so simple, but what if I met her date? Hurrying along a corridor, I could only hope he wouldn't recognise me either and didn't flirt. But an open plan office had to be negotiated before exiting double doors into the outside world, and there at a desk full of paperwork, was a Sergeant.

I immediately appreciated the self-sacrificial nature of Betty's visit. The man was flab-faced and so generous of build that three chevrons straining on his sleeve looked ready to pop off and go flying across the room. Like an overpacked suitcase that has to be sat on to shut, he was crammed into his uniform. I don't want to dwell on this unnecessarily, but it looked as if he'd fallen in a river and on getting out, the uniform had shrunk on him. There was squeezed out flesh at the collar and cuffs. He had no business trying to date Betty. At. All. However, he couldn't fail to see I wasn't her.

"So, Betty. Visit over?"

I lowered my eyelashes modestly.

"How was the prisoner?"

"Oh guilty as anything." I falsettoed.

"Just need your password."

I gave it, this time wondering if the three kisses actually meant I was Betty's *ex, ex, ex*. There was no time to dwell on this however.

"And your pin?" He gave a leery smile, "Even though we know it's you, we have to be on our toes about identity theft."

Once more I skewered a dartboard sheet of paper.

"Goodbye then," I simpered and turned to go.

He frowned. "Hang on."

My heart sank.

"That didn't go through."

"Didn't it?"

"You have to push it all the way." He put his hand on mine to assist the piercing of the paper. "And tick the box: I am not a criminal."

"Oh yes, of course."

Taking a proffered pen, I lied.

He winked, "See you tomorrow night, treasure."

"Can't wait," I replied, saccharine pill sweet.

Providing all the boxes were ticked, I think he'd have let me through as Betty, were I stark naked or wearing a moustache.

Eleven   *Beige*

Through the double doors I went, expecting uproar behind me at any moment. Minutes later, I was a policewoman on the beat, walking briskly along a main thoroughfare of London Town. I was free, but for how long and whatever next? Most certainly, a change of clothes. I checked a purse in Betty's shoulder bag and found it plump.

Striking off down a secluded side street, I felt my ex-girlfriend's uniform had played its part and when no-one was looking (I hoped), thrust the hat deep into a bush. Moments later, the tunic followed. Her second uniform was going the way of the first. The remaining garments were no more than a dowdy civilian lady might actually wear, especially once the tie was stuffed in my shoulder bag and top three buttons of the blouse unfastened. I was slightly worried about my flat chest. But that is a common affliction. Whilst the easing of my identity was a relief, the head wound was now visible, a problem on reaching a road with busier pavements. I needed a hat or wig, in fact an entirely new costume – something incredibly unremarkable like … like the man in front of me was wearing: a pin-striped suit and bowler hat, with an accompanying umbrella. Perfect! But I doubted he'd consider a swap. Nor could I breeze into a gent's outfitters as a woman and wriggle into trousers, waistcoat and red braces.

Wrestling with this conundrum and all the while dreading a wail of sirens—especially to the tune of *Teddy Bear's Picnic*—I hurried down several more side streets and across a busy main road, and there noticed a charity shop. Pausing at a large window crammed with second-hand wares of doubtful provenance, I noticed the shop was manned (so to speak) by several elderly ladies who were distracted by customers or folding clothes into bin liners. There was a chance they would scarcely notice if I stepped inside and sauntered inconspicuously over to browse the Men's rails. So I did and swiftly discovered, whilst trying not to inhale a peculiar musty odour, a likely pinstriped three-piece and dodged into a changing cubicle when everybody was looking the other way. The trousers, jacket and waistcoat went well with Betty's blouse and retied tie, making the return of my masculine identity a breeze. After straightening the knot of my tie in a mirror, I slipped back into the shop and hung the skirt surreptitiously on a rail with barely a regret. As there was nothing in Betty's bag to identify it as hers, this was left carelessly on an appropriate shelf with many of its plastic and leather cousins. It only remained to buy a bowler. There wasn't one, but a black fedora, which covered my head wound and was not incongruous with the outfit, sufficed and there *was* a black umbrella. I thought the items dear at seven pounds conjoined, but as the suit had come free, said nothing to the white-haired lady who served me with a smile.

My misdemeanors were piling up: stealing garments, escaping from prison by coshing a police constable and making the foreign minister's hair assault a French President—I would soon be an extremely wanted man. At least my current disguise was more impenetrable than Betty's ensemble that had been easier to see through than a plastic mac. Even so, my situation was dire and I needed to escape London immediately. Returning to Blink Castle was impossible—it was the first place a vengeful Betty and co would look. Really, I needed my Aunt Esmeralda, but where did she live? What was her second name? Blink? If I knew where she worked I might visit. But only my Gran would be able to tell me and that meant ... unless ... unless I went in some other direction; one that nobody would expect.

In the circumstances, the last thing the authorities would dream of me doing was to rent a place close to the police station. All the better if a job of mundane ordinariness could also be found nearby—a window cleaner, road sweeper, traffic warden. Disguise myself as Mr. Average, take a bedsit next door to the constabulary and I might easily pass unnoticed in the Law's back yard. It needed thinking through, but surely becoming normal would be no bad thing? I'd had enough of two-headed women, sentient square-wheeled bicycles and policewoman girlfriends knocking me unconscious with a truncheon.

In need of a 'To Let' column, I went in search of a newsagent, trying to exude an air of conventionality. Being normal couldn't be hard; by definition, almost everybody could do it. It was merely a question of observation and copying what I saw. Select any average-looking male citizen, follow at a discreet distance, then adopt their mannerisms, body language and habits. I attempted this with a number of suited men walking before me on the pavement but my attempts to reproduce their walks led to questioning looks from passers-by. In fact, when three teenagers giggled at my contortions, I almost gave up, but then an extremely standardised-looking man stepped in front of me and stopped to tie his shoelace. I hid in a doorway to study him. Dressed in a beige suit, he had an air of the middlingly median—of being not much to write home about. Ever. The way he tied the lace of his shoe exemplified *average.* When at last he recommenced walking, with me only three yards behind, I felt, watching his gait, he would fit perfectly any situation in which *absolutely nothing happened.* When he stopped to buy a newspaper at a kiosk, I pretended to gaze into an adjacent shop window, even though it was boarded up, and saw him tuck an Evening News under his arm so sterotypically, that I knew he was the ideal candidate to stand in a bus queue or crowd and never catch the eye. He was so inconspicuous I would have missed him had not the inconspicuous been my especial concern. Eager to discover the secrets of his generality, I followed him into a cafeteria, to do as he did and so learn my trade.

Predictably, he went up to a long counter and viewed the fare on offer, cakes, pre-wrapped sandwiches and pastries. At the end of the line were tea and coffee machines and a young woman working a till. It is almost impossible to describe the banality of what then happened: *He took a cup, poured black tea into it from an urn, and then added milk from a jug, asked the serving girl for an egg sandwich and she got it for him.* Nothing else happened! Well, except that he paid. It was absorbing. The challenge was to replicate this. The man wandered off to an empty table whilst I did what he had done. It wasn't actually as difficult as it looked.

I sought out a vacant table just near enough to my archetype to see what he was doing which was naturally, nothing. He just sat and gazed from a window with a blank expression. What on earth was he thinking, I wondered. Anything? After a while he took a sip from his tea. I tried all of this. Window gazing. Tea sipping. Trying to look blank. It didn't come naturally. What was going on? He didn't look worried about what might happen next. Whereas I would be terrified that my unconscious self would make all the cars and buses I could see through the window, go backwards. Or cause traffic lights over the road to turn blue, purple and brown. Or have the zebra crossing rise like a magic carpet whilst people were walking across it.

Obviously, to be like the mentor I had chosen, it would be necessary to trust in the Universe that nothing much was going to happen next. So I tried this. Like him, I took a further sip from my teacup and no oddity occurred. Nor the next sip. Nor the next. Until the cup was half drained. For several minutes I was just like everybody else and lived a life of such wonderful emptiness that it seemed a posse of constables might enter the cafeteria and sit at my table without ever guessing my identity. Though I did wonder if a real John Smith would have so much going on inside them about the fact that inside them, there was nothing going on.

Meanwhile, the beige man's cafeteria experience progressed. After several more sips of tea, he reached for his sandwich, unwrapped it and placed it on a plate. This felt moderately eventful. Almost the highlight of his day. Especially when only moments later, he lifted the sandwich to his mouth and began to eat. Being quite hungry myself, I unwrapped *my* sandwich. And here, his life and my own diverged considerably. I saw immediately that there was a large denture-sized bite missing. There was no point thinking of what a normal person would have done in such circumstances. It was precisely the sort of thing *that would never happen to John Smith!* Not a REAL John Smith. How would it be possible to remain incognito in London if my inner self couldn't even be trusted to buy a sandwich? How was I to stop peculiarities giving me away? I surveyed the sandwich in despair, before adding my own bite to the first. And it was then that I had *my epiphany.* If it would not happen to a real John Smith, then there was nothing else for it—I had to become a REAL John Smith. I had to change my name.

CHANGE MY NAME!

It was a seminal moment. There was nowhere to hide in London, (especially not next-door to the police station), because my own weirdness would eventually hatch some preposterous sabotage. Drastic action was therefore required: go home to my parents, get the relevant paperwork, and change my name by deed poll so that the bizarre incidents stopped forever. Nothing else would do. For if I found a job miles from anyone, anywhere—a lighthouse keeper say, in the Outer Hebrides—even that would be fraught with peril as my uncontrollable psyche would be certain to send innocent ships and mariners not onto the rocks, but into a giant spillage of custard or porridge. So no, only legally altering my fore and surname to something profoundly dull would work. After which, I would find a commonplace occupation – packing boxes in a factory, working at a supermarket checkout, washing up in a restaurant, or fitting carpets! *Anything.* And then, only then, hopefully, would my sandwiches come to me whole.

After furiously thinking all of this through, I looked up to find Mr Beige staring at me in a most unconventional manner. His face was twisted with horror. For a millisecond his eyes met mine, then he stood abruptly, banging the table and upsetting his teacup. I watched him rush from the cafeteria and out onto the street, dodging other pedestrians. Bizarre.

Obviously, he was not the embodiment of beige I had believed him to be but a weirdo of psychedelic flamboyance. No matter, it was time to leave myself and return to the not-particularly-welcoming-arms of my parents. Passing the table of Mr Psychedelic-Flamboyance I saw the tell-tale sign of a sandwich triangle with a single bite taken from it. Poor man. However I was brought to an abrupt standstill by his Evening News, which lay abandoned and covered in tea on the tabletop. Because *I* was on the front.

It came as a shock to find such an unflattering photo-fit picture of myself beneath the headline: HAVE YOU SEEN THIS MAN? I'd only just escaped! The ink must be still wet, (tea notwithstanding) and the pages still warm from the press. Below the picture was a one-sided account of my offences and warnings I might look like a woman. This explained much: Mr Psychedelic Flamboyance was Mr Beige after all and had almost certainly scuttled off swiftly to inform a certain Sergeant where I was. Or wasn't, for taking the newspaper, I departed the cafeteria and hurried along the pavement looking distractedly not median. Finding a rank of cabs outside a cinema, I climbed into the one at the front.

"If I wanted to go north by train, what station would I have to go to?"

The large flabby cabbie didn't even look round. "Liverpool Street mate."

"Can you take me there?"

"Why not? It's me job."

And immediately we were off.

"Have you been a cabbie long?" I asked, after he had stopped a couple of times and scratched his head.

"All me life. Since I could hold a wheel. Me dad was a cabbie before me, and his dad started his days on a horse-drawn hansom."

"Did you ever think of anything else?"

He studied me in the rear-view mirror, and said, "I'm not that bad. But I do get the stations mixed up. Had the knowledge once. But stopped using it for some reason. It did cross my mind to be a copper."

"Police?"

"Yeah, you get to go faster and less traffic. Everyone has to get out of the way when you put the siren on. But in the end I went with tradition. You can't go wrong if you stick wiv the past. Wot about you? Just visiting?"

"Never been to London before. Thought I'd see the sights."

"Yeah. Feel the history. Wonderful innit? I mean, Shakespeare used to work here. That's a thought innit? The entire place full of blokes in codpieces wearing tights, and the greatest poet of all time swanning about, buying a sandwich or a cup of coffee in the middle of 'em. I sometimes fink of him buying a newspaper or whatever there was in them days, and reading a review on the very street corner where I've stopped at some lights. *'Romeo and Juliet. Not bad. Bit sad at the end.'* I mean, you think about it, I must drive sometimes over bits of London where all them years ago, he thought up a famous line. To be or not to be ... there, we just ran over it. To be ... brrmmmmmm ... or not to be."

"It's certainly a thought."

"I'd love to have given Shakespeare a lift somewhere. From the Mermaid to the Globe maybe. Ask him what he was writing. Oh, Hamlet. What's that about then? Really, you haven't a clue either. Did you have a plan before you sat down and picked up a quill? No. Right. Nah mate, don't pay me for the ride. An honour and a privilege. Wouldn't be legal tender anyway. Don't suppose *you* write do yer?"

"Me? Er...no. Never."

"Illiterate?"

"No. Not illiterate."

You can write your name then?"

"My name?"

"Easy one is it?"

"John Smith."

"Oh yeah. Easy. My names Harry. And my wife's name is Carrie. That's marriage for yer. Sometimes though, I've wondered as I'm driving along, if Shakespeare would have written anything decent if he'd been called Harry or John Smith. No offence."

"None taken."

"I mean you could hardly help being the World's greatest poet with the name he had."

"True. You seem very interested in Shakespeare. Have you read the complete works?"

"Nah. Print's too small. But I did go and see one of his play's once wiv Carrie. *Hamlet*. Fell asleep. But she raved about it. John Smith eh? So it's no wonder you're not a poet. Shame though, if you'd been a scribbler I might have let you ride half price – just in case you turned out to be the next Shakespeare."

"No way *I'll* ever be famous?"

"We can't all be bleedin' celebrities. Though tell the truth, you don't half look like that photo fit picture in the paper of whatsisname – Alphonso Blink."

Trying to look relaxed, I thought on my feet, though seated. "That guy they said made the foreign minister's hair attack the French president? Sounded a bit farfetched to me, that story. I mean how?"

"Who knows mate how these weirdo deviants do the things we hear about. The lot of them are terrorists, trying to undermine the state."

"The only thing I'm on the run from is my ex-girlfriend. Alphonso Blink's welcome to *her*."

He laughed. "Them photo fit pictures never look like the actual person wot done the crime. Where you off to then?"

"Back to my job."

"What's that.

"Junior Chartered Accountant. I don't want to be late either or I'll catch it from the boss. Well, his secretary."

He laughed again. "Ah, the trains run quite regular. You'll get one soon enough. So long as you're not arrested for being Alphonso Blink."

"It would be just my luck. That or the trains are all cancelled."

"And if they are, we'll know who's to blame! Bloomin' terrorists."

I got out at the station wanting to mop my brow. To cunningly fox those who might be on my heels, I decided to take a coach northwards. Trains had somehow lost their appeal.

By coach and buses, with a little pedestrianism thrown in, I reached the house-cloned estate where my parents lived as night descended, which assisted my furtive approach to their back door. My mother and father were in the living room, sat together on a sofa watching a television test card. When I entered the room, they froze in terror.

"Alphonso!" My mother almost screamed. "Quickly, John, phone the police!"

"Wait! Please. Mum. Dad. Don't panic. Hear what I have to say."

My father stood up and growled, "There's nothing to say. You have disgraced us. Assaulting women police officers and the French President. We can hardly step out of the house without attracting filthy stares from the neighbours. We shall have to move house."

"Phone the police!" my mother squeaked.

"Don't be alarmed either of you."

"If you had any decency," my father went on sternly wagging his finger in my face, "You'd turn yourself in."

"Well I will," I fibbed. "But I want to try one thing first and I need your help."

"You'll get no help from us my lad. We've washed our hands of you."

"Please listen. I want to legally change my name."

"We're not interested in helping you escape by establishing a false identity."

"You won't be. Can't you see? It's my name that's causing all these outrages to happen. It always has been."

"Don't be ridiculous."

"Call the police John."

"If I'd been called John, after you, or Tim, or Robert, or Harry or Jack, none of the weird things in my life would have happened."

"Nonsense."

"He's mad John. Call the police."

"It's true. I'm called after my grandfather: Alphonso Blink. The uninventor. Obviously, I'm going to be tainted by that."

"Uninventor?" my father shuddered.

I pressed on, "All I'm asking for is my birth certificate and a little money to pay the solicitor ..."

"Money?"

"I haven't a bean and the solicitor will charge me for changing my name to something like John Smith. But once I am no longer Alphonso Blink, the strange occurrences will stop. Really they will. I will move far away and become a bank manager or insurance salesman. After ten years without weirdness, I will return to thank you as a normal, loving son. Please, give me one last chance to rescue my life from calamity. If it doesn't work, I will hand myself over to the Law."

My father stood and stared at me. My mother stared at him.

"What do you think?" he asked her slowly.

"I think we should phone the police."

"He is our own son."

"It could be a trick. To get money."

"You can pay the solicitor yourself. Stand over me as I sign the documents."

At last, my father gave a grim nod. "Alright. One last chance. And if it doesn't work and you arrive here again we'll ..."

"Call the police."

And so it was at the back door, ten minutes later, my birth certificate and a hundred pounds changed hands. My father even patted my shoulder,

"Good luck Alphonso ... or, I mean, whatever your name will be next."

Almost weeping with gratitude, I slipped into drizzling darkness to embark on a new life.

Twelve *Soliciting*

Although I had an umbrella, my difficulties were still multitudinous. Where to sleep for the evening being foremost. I wanted to get as far from my parents as possible, for to be captured nearby, would worsen any social opprobrium for them. But nocturnally, a person can walk only so far across farmer's fields, in avoidance of the police. And whilst midnight hid the incriminating oddness of a man in a pinstriped suit wandering over darkened hills beneath a brolly, I could not sleep under a gamp. I needed a building around me. And in my sodden search for an isolated barn or garden shed, ruminations began dripping on future plans, so sensibly made.

For instance, my parents might feel relief at their son's impending normality, but my grandmother? How would *she* take renunciation of Alphonso Blink? After she'd lovingly sheltered me, deserting my own 'difference' would undoubtedly upset her, and I was loathe to. Aunt Esmeralda would also be vexed, especially as my name was her idea. But as she had abandoned me to its consequences and even made things worse with the kite, she could hardly complain. Still, she was fond of me I knew, and I of her, which made the entire name changing business *uncomfortable*. Much worse than any of these concerns however was the sudden realization – possibly brought on by an intensification of the rain, which began fairly hammering on my umbrella's bat like carapace, that my entire scheme might be a squib.

Clambering over a gate with me in the dark, came thoughts of solicitors blabbing about my birth certificate – for anyone of even moderate wit would be sure to notice it was that of a wanted criminal. John Smiths might abound, but there was only one Alphonso Blink. Immediately after the reading glasses went on, it would be time to summon the local constabulary. And to bribe a solicitor, even if one could be found who was reliably bent, was beyond the scope of Betty's purse. The problem seemed insoluble. Like finding sleeping quarters on a black and pouring night in the middle of a farmer's field. My only hope was to locate an incredibly stupid solicitor, for whom the contents of my birth certificate would barely register. Solicitors couldn't all be brainboxes. It was a simple matter of entering their office, asking a few unexacting questions and counting the wrong answers. I began compiling posers so straightforward that only a complete idiot could answer them incorrectly ...

Hello Mr Solicitor,

What colour shoes do you have on? Please, just answer the question.

Where do kangaroos come from? Asking me to leave merely suggests you're unsure.

Is a ballpoint pen used for a) writing, b) eating, c) gardening ...

After listing twenty or so, I stumbled on a better solution. Rather than quizzing solicitors, would it not be simpler to find one with a peculiar name? For being a fellow appellation victim they would be far more likely to sympathise with my plight. I'd be an associate of sorts. I was congratulating myself on this brilliant scheme when, as if fortune were untying all the knots in my life at once, the rain stopped and I came to a road. Not fifty yards along the tarmacadam, rose a lone and penumbral building. This proved to be derelict, so I sneaked round the back and forced my way in through a boarded-up door.

 It was darker inside than out. Drenched, I blundered around, hands fumbling the walls for a light switch. None of several found, produced a flicker of illumination. No matter, it was a ceiling over my head. After much groping of ground floor rooms, my hands eventually met with the solid outlines of a bed, or more accurately a comfortable bench complete with musty blanket. Removing my sodden garments, I lay down gratefully under a smelly cover to sleep.

 I awoke in a police cell. Sunlight streamed from a small, high window into a room completely bare but for the bench on which I lay. That I'd stumbled into a derelict police station in the small hours didn't register until I'd donned my damp clothes and wandered into another room. Light from boarded-up windows, revealed a pair of rusted handcuffs hung from a nail and an abandoned blue mug on a desk with IT'S A FAIR COP on one side and a silver-crowned insignia on the other. I raised the mug wistfully. *A Fair Cop*. That was Betty all over. A moth-eaten tunic with all the buttons removed, was hung on the back of a door.

One day, under the auspices of a new and unoriginal name, I might be able to buy and renovate such a place and live there with Betty. But for now, being still Alphonso Blink, it gave me the creeps.

My impression in the depths of night had been that the building was isolated, but not far along the adjacent road were lines of brick terraces and further still, factory chimneys. Quite likely, a walk in that direction would bring me to a shiny, new police station in a town-centre square. However, needing food, (though not a semi-masticated sandwich), and also a library, there was nothing for it but to head that way.

The library was in one of those nice, old Victorian buildings that developers so love to ball and chain. There was a reference section, complete with chairs, tables and a couple of pensioners turning over newspaper pages. At the main desk I whispered to a librarian for the loan of a biro and sheet of paper. She pushed a pen across the counter and a sheet torn from her pad, saying loudly, "You needn't return *that*."

I thanked her in tones that fell between my hushed question and her megaphone reply. How had she got the job? Was she Cox of a rowing crew in her spare time?

Returning to seat myself at a reference section table, I began a list. For a quiet half hour, I jotted down all the most ordinary surnames I could think of.

Jones. James, Williams, Davies, Brown, Gray, Johnson, Robinson, Thompson, Walker, Roberts, Clarke, Harris, Price, Wilkinson.

And then all the most appealingly commonplace forenames.

Jack, Harry, James, Joe, Thomas, Michael, Robert, Christopher, Mark, Ken, Gary, Stephen, Peter, Keith, Alan, David.

All that remained was to pair them in as unarresting a way as possible. For at this point it would still be possible to mis-step by calling myself Robert Roberts, James James, Dave Davies, Harry Harris or Tom Thompson. There were combinations of lacklustre names that put together might have belonged to a person of distinction. Christopher Gray had an elegance I wished to avoid. Peter Price a perkiness that might belong to an irritating person who was impossible to ignore. Ken Brown was appealingly dull. Keith Wilkinson so ugly it couldn't possibly belong to a man to whom excitingly surreal things happened. Michael Harris? Dave Robinson? Tom Davies? Alan Thompson? Ken Jones? Keith Johnson? Yes. Keith Johnson seemed the sort of name to belong to somebody uninspired and dull. For whom experiences that were impromptu and off the cuff were an impossibility. But no sooner had I settled on this than Tom Davies and Ken Brown complained that they were much more ordinary and I had to agree. After a tug-of-war lasting half an hour between these two, I settled finally on Ken Brown and then changed it to Tom Davies at the last moment. It was a shame that John Smith was a lost cause because Betty already knew it. It only remained to find myself a solicitor.

I searched the shelves for a solicitor's almanac and found a series of large, fat annual tomes, I took down the most recent and staggered to a table with it. Being the names and addresses of every solicitor in England, the book was a mighty read. Almost as big as England itself. Surely in a book this size, there must be a solicitor with a name as strange as my own? Turning to the first page, then the second and swiftly on to the third, I found the contents made my heart race and eyes protrude. The names of the practitioners *were all weird*. Or very nearly all at least.

Tree, Rackham and Tree.

Pillcock and Addleson.

Frogmarch, Tunc and co.

Ulvermere, Hangthorpe and Lewis.

Pozig's.

Broadwater, Trickle and Mouse.

Mutteringson and Sons.

Togglereed and Poppleton.

On and on the names went. There were so many solicitors as well. Plagues of them. Surely weird things couldn't be afflicting them all? It seemed to scotch the theory that a peculiar name was causing my own life's abnormalities. I mean, the solicitors from Frogmarch, Tunc and Co must be subject to the most harrowingly fraught experiences—to step from the office door surely provoking a shower of herrings, or stampede of lampposts. Was it some sort of a double bluff, to hide the mind-numbing circumstances of a solicitor's lot? Were outrageous names a means to offset the benumbing treadmill of the work and restore balance to atrophied lives?

For a moment I considered not changing my name and becoming a solicitor as a palliative. However, being a wanted man, a non-de-plume appeared essential. Besides, in terms of a lifelong occupation, one has to draw the line somewhere. It suggested though that in searching for a dodgy solicitor my best course might be the most normal name I could find, like Smith, Smith and Smith. Had that also not been odd. In fact from the dozens of names I saw in the directory of solicitors, I found few ordinary appellations and only one near enough to reach by bicycle.

Hall and Jenkins.

They were either brain-dead by being solicitors without the counterbalance of a weird name *or* subversive anti-solicitors masquerading as normal. In either case they would be exactly the sort of firm to enact a deed-poll transaction for the dreaded Alphonso Blink. I took down the address of *Hall and Jenkins* and closed the almanac with a thump.

Sitting on a bench beside a lake in the town park I sipped tea bought from a van before being ambushed. Four of my own selves sidled up and crammed on the bench beside me.

"You." I groaned. "What do *you* want?"

The bearded elder me, pressed thigh to thigh, spoke suspiciously, "What are you doing?"

"It's none of your business."

A me on the other side, the rainbow knitter from the carriage, disagreed. "If it's your business, it's *ipso facto* our business. We're you."

"Well perhaps it's none of my business either. Or won't be soon. It will be another person's business."

"We know what you're going to do next."

"Oh do you?"

"You're going to make a very foolish attempt to change your name by deed poll and if you succeed, we will cease to exist."

"Better and better."

"Don't hate yourself."

"Hard not to."

"Well can we just say here, you look terrible in that suit."

"But more importantly, don't deviate from our name Alphonso."

"I only want to deviate from being a deviant."

"Why when you can marry the Two Headed Girl?"

I laughed. "Even if I could find her, I don't think they'd have me. Especially Beatrice. Now if you'll excuse me, I have some urgent business."

"*Alphonso!*"

"Alphonso yourself."

"Exactly, we're all in this together. Listen …"

"I thought you liked not knowing what was going to happen?"

"That's the trouble. We do."

"Please."

"Don't do this to yourself and ourselves. All of us."

I looked up and around. "Yes. Where *are* the rest of me? There were quite few last time our paths crossed."

"In the trees behind us. Waiting to see what happens."

Dropping my paper cup into a nearby bin, I had a sudden urge to run off. After sprinting the entire length of a football pitch and then looking back over my shoulder, I saw they were still on the bench staring after me and hadn't moved. Nevertheless, I kept on running.

My arrival at the premises of *Hall and Jenkins* the next day came by way of several bus rides and after sleeping in a scorer's hut beside a town cricket pitch. The solicitor's office was in the centre of town, a smutty edifice of red brick, grand once perhaps, when the town had been. Behind iron railings, a flight of steps, guarded by two stone lions, led up to the front door. I was just patting one of these Leos on the head when a woman's voice called from behind, "Alphonso."

I turned to find Aunt Esmeralda peering at me from the front gate. "Auntie. What are you doing here?"

"What do you think?"

It seemed she'd changed little since we'd last met, some strands of grey perhaps. She slowly approached where I stood stonily as the lions.

"Don't go in there," she entreated. "Come home with me."

My heart stopped. Go to my Aunt's house? Did she mean go and *live* with her? Hide from the horrible baying bloodhounds of the Law under one of her beds? It was the most wonderful invitation I'd had in my life.

"I ...I ... didn't want to be Alphonso Blink any more," I stammered dropping down a step towards her.

"I know. But you don't have to go in there."

"Don't I?"

"No. Come live with me."

I started to cry. Sniffle anyhow.

"You are what you are."

"No I'm not."

"You are."

"I'm not. I've met me on three separate occasions and if that's what I am, I don't want to be it." And then I saw them, a crowd of me standing across the road, staring bleakly at us. "Did *they* fetch you?"

"Yes."

"Bastards."

Aunt Esmeralda looked me up and down in consternation, "Why do you hate yourself so much? You haven't done anything wrong. Except maybe wear that suit."

Again I stared across the road. A couple of selves waved. The eldest snipped off some beard as a peace offering.

"I'm going in Auntie. I'm sorry. I don't mind coming home with you afterwards as Tom Davies."

"Tom Davies?"

I nodded shamefacedly.

Her expression hardened. "There won't be anyone here when you come back out. I will have gone home. They will have gone too."

I looked at the group of men. If there was only one way to get rid of them then ...

"So be it."

She grabbed my shoulders and shook me. "Alphonso! *You're uninventing yourself!*"

"Good. I don't want to be so bizarrely strange. So different from everybody else. Somebody who causes such weird things to happen."

She stared at me angrily. "Life is magical. Life without magicality isn't worth living. Things that get in the way of magicality should be uninvented. Not you."

"Please."

I removed her hands from my shoulders. Then went up to the door and banged the brass knocker three times.

My selves booed me as I went in. Even Aunt Essie booed.

The secretary, blonde and bright and maybe late twenties, was dressed in a cream blouse, along with a pinstriped mini-skirt, pinstriped tights and pinstriped tie. If Hall and Jenkins were as sharp as she appeared, I was doomed.

"I'm looking for Mr. Hall or Mr. Jenkins? Would either of them be available to see me?"

"Good heavens no. They're long gone."

"Oh."

"Stopped practicing years ago, they became cabbages, the pair of them. No-one knew why. So my sister and I took over the firm."

"Right. And what's your name?"

"Jane Collins. She's Mary Collins."

Which was disappointing.

"Quite conventional names for the profession?"

"Yes," she laughed, "I'm presuming you need help from a solicitor?"

"To change my name by deed poll."

"That's easy enough if you've your birth cert handy. Good. Just a deed, couple of signatures and a rubber stamp. We're supposed to have a witness here who has known you ten years, but as I presume we don't ...?"

"We don't."

"Why bother?"

She smiled mischievously and before I could object, took a box of blank deeds from a shelf. I helplessly dithered. There was still time to mutter, *Sorry, I've decided to change my mind and not my name* and go leaping downstairs, two at a time, into Aunt Esmeralda's arms. But the deed poll was thrust before me with such routine nonchalance that I froze and then felt impotent to stop either a life-transforming name swap or, more likely, the clever Miss Jane finding out exactly who I was.

"Birth Cert ...?"

I limply produced it.

"So, you're changing your name to ...?"

"Tom Davies," I croaked, watching her open my birth certificate, aghast.

"From ..." she looked. There was a long pause ... "*Alphon-so Blink.*" She looked up at me in curiosity. "Really?"

My nod was abject.

"Complicated. Presumably you are *the* Alphonso Blink?"

A more abject nod.

"There can only be one, I suppose. Didn't you hit a policewoman over the head?"

"My Girlfriend."

"She was a *policewoman?*"

"Yes. *She* arrested me. And she knocked me unconscious with her truncheon on two separate occasions before I hit her. Look."

I showed her my brow.

"That's the bit the newspapers don't give us. Context. And what about the assault on the French President?"

"I did it. But I can honestly say it was an accident and that I had absolutely no control over it."

She smiled thoughtfully. "Hmmm. Perhaps then, not being up with the latest news, I filled in this deed poll without realizing Alphonso Blink was a wanted criminal needing a pseudonym?"

"But why would you do that?" I puzzled, "Mightn't you get in trouble?"

"Interesting question. Perhaps it's because, I'm about as much a solicitor as Alphonso Blink would be Tom Davies."

"*You're not a solicitor?*"

"Well, yes and no. Mary and I were secretaries when the proprietors were taken off and we had to keep the company going or lose our jobs. In truth, we'd been doing all the work anyway, because Mr. Hall and Mr. Jenkins were such leafy greens. And there's not really anything *to* soliciting once you get used to it. So legally we do everything a solicitor does, but ..."

"But I thought you needed to be qualified? Surely not just *anybody* can be a solicitor these days? Don't you need a degree in it at least?"

"Oh yes. A four-year course in charging expenses, filing cabinet skills, dressing seriously, frowning, signing things, getting other people to sign things. *Unless* you covertly take over a solicitor's office after the founding partners have been wheeled away. My sister and I have been running this place without difficulty for ten years. At least. Now if you would just sign here?"

I did.

"And here. And here."

I scribbled slowly. "I haven't really practiced the new signature yet."

"No matter. That will be seventy pounds."

Less expensive than I'd feared. I dug the money from Betty's purse. Jane let it pass.

"Thanks." She handed me the deed poll. "Very nice to meet you Mr Davies. Or might I call you Tom?"

"Tom would be fine," I said.

"Speaking without context," she confided. "I really don't like the Minister for Foreign Affairs. He would appear to be what my sister Mary would call, a stupid dickhead."

We shook hands. She smiled again. Perhaps at my shocked expression.

"Goodbye Tom. Good luck."

"Thank you so much. Goodbye."

Esmeralda wasn't there when I stepped out of *Hall and Jenkins*. And neither was Alphonso Blink. O' Brave New World that hath Tom Davies in it. Aunt Esmeralda's rejection hurt, but then it was all very well for her, she didn't have to be me. Fortunately, neither did I anymore, so long as the transformation worked. How soon would I know? Proceeding along an empty pavement, I was braced for some freakish kink in reality to occur. If it didn't, mine really was a new life, needing only a good job with a career path and pension. A mortgage would also be nice and car loan, because I needed structure. Arguing against this beautiful dream for a few strides, were fretful thoughts urging immediate flight to some far-flung hermitage, at least until the Press left off printing photo-fit pictures of Alphonso Blink. Betty's purse however, had begun to look gaunt. As only Esmeralda and Jane Smith were aware I was in the area, and being now a fully-fledged normal person, in the most ordinary of suits, it was surely safe for Tom Davies to visit the local employment centre and see what was available. After a few weeks honest labour, I'd probably have enough for a one-way trip to the Outer Hebrides.

The job centre was on the ground floor of a multi-storey car park. I found it without irregularity en-route. Inside, employment opportunities had been typed on cards and stuck behind plastic on the wall. It was depressing reading.

Cleaner. Qualifications. Degree in toilet bowl technology and hygiene. Or equivalent. Seven years' experience. Nice person preferred. £12 per hour.

Deli Assistant. We are a versatile and ambitious supermarket who are passionate about shopping with trolleys in aisles. Operating from a street corner in the centre of town we are seeking a graduate with a first degree in retail commerce to make sandwiches and fill silver trays with a varied selection of ingredients. £9.50 an hour.

Chair Tester. Must be able to sit and stand repeatedly for eight-hour shifts. £3 per hour.

Naval Recruit. Mine Disposal Unit. No qualifications needed. Swimming an advantage. Fast swimmers viewed especially favourably. Patience, two hands, and occasionally teeth essential. Knowledge of wiring and next of kin, helpful. £5 per hour.

Dog Walker. Ph.D. in Canine Studies as minimum. Candidate must be able to accompany dogs of a variety of breeds from Irish Wolfhound to Doberman/Bulldog cross for walks across demanding terrain in locations across the world. Languages preferred. Chinese, Russian and Inuit our priority. The successful candidate would have, in the interests of provision of empathetic companionship, a dislike of cats. All candidates would undergo a three-month endurance training before beginning paid work. £11.50 per hour.

Nothing seemed to fit my circumstances or qualifications very exactly. At school, exams and I had never really got on. Nor did I have any skills. What was I good at? *Nothing.* I was attractive to sheep. But A Ph. D. in shepherding would take years. Meanwhile, I hadn't the qualifications to walk a dog out of the Job Centre, never mind around Mongolia. Interestingly, I gazed down to see a hound nearby. An Alsatian. They all look the same, but this one did look particularly familiar.

"Well, fancy meeting you here," said a voice beside me.

It was ...

"Betty."

Thirteen *Toaster*

There she stood in jeans and turtle-neck sweater.

"I thought Blue was dragging me into the building because he knew I needed a job."

In surprise I whispered, "You *resigned*?"

"Sacked. For bending rules and allowing an important prisoner to escape as a result."

There was an uncomfortable moment before I indicated the surroundings apologetically. "So you need a new job?"

"Yes. But I was actually looking for you. Blue tracked you down."

I glared at the animal who stood tongue lolling and wearing the sort of lopsided grin that dogs sometimes have when they want to be friendly. There was a feeling of deja-vu. "Is this a citizen's arrest?"

"No. You were right. I was never a policewoman. Blue was sacked too. He seems to like you. We both do."

Whilst this was a relief, there was still something bothering me about our reconnection. How had Blue found me without spoor or scent? It seemed altogether too unlikely for an ordinary bloke like Tom Davies. Did it mean, my transformation hadn't worked? Or was Blue just that sort of dog? A canine Alphonso.

"So now you've found me," I spoke uneasily, "What are you going to do?"

"What are *we* going to do?"

She looked into my eyes, the soft black centres of her pupils dissolving into my heart, my guts and places even lower, naughtier.

"Even though I ..."

"Yes. Think of it this way. I hit you first. And second. Though I'm sure the once you biffed me was harder *and* you tied me up *and* gagged me. So – we could call it quits?"

Without me saying or doing anything, an agreement was reached.

She continued, "I presume you're not in here looking for me."

"I need a job."

"Me too."

But I'm unqualified. Are you qualified?"

"Only for the career I've just been sacked from. Have you got a bus fare?"

"Yes. Well, *you* have. It's your money, I stole it from your purse."

"Villain," she chided lovingly.

The purse changed hands.

"Maybe if you hit me over the head again and brought me in, they'd give you your job back?"

"The thought had crossed my mind, but ..."

"But ...?"

"I no longer have a truncheon."

"A frying pan?"

"Possibly, but not being a police officer, I no longer feel duty-bound to run in errant boyfriends."

"How's about a truce?" I asked. "You stop hitting me over the head and I become law-abiding."

She considered this a moment, then said, "Even better, I stop hitting you over the head, and you come back to my boudoir and be wicked."

The look happened again. In fact, it hadn't stopped since starting, becoming so intense that the Job Centre felt an inappropriate place to feel what I was feeling.

"It's a deal."

All the way home, holding hands on the bus, kissing on the bus, resting heads on each other's shoulders on the bus, Betty refrained from using the A and B words. For a person of discretion, they were not for public utterance. It wasn't until we reached the short garden path to her front door that my old name was aired, and then only because of a *For Sale* sign by the gate.

"You're selling up?" I gasped in surprise.

"I can't afford the mortgage, Alphonso."

"Oh."

I was about to explain that I was now Tom Davies when she breezed on.

"Unless I find another job. Something interesting. A stuntwoman, lioness tamer, blackberry-picker for a fruit pie company, a snooker player, you know, something to suit my being with you."

"*Me?*"

"Yes. So that we are living euphoniously."

"Euphoniously?"

"Well pleasing to the heart if not to the ear."

"Betty, I really don't mind what you do. How ordinary it is."

"But *I do*. My being a policewoman came between us. When we first met, you were dressed in a scarecrow's clothes. I had this crazy thought last night, that I'd like to do that as well, to run across fields with you, both of us dressed in clothes we'd stolen from scarecrows."

My mind boggled and tried to reply. No words arrived. Plenty were coming to her,

"Let's go in. Our lives have just begun. A new exciting dawn. This may seem very forward, but if this place is sold, maybe we could go and live with your grandmother in Blink Castle. There were loads of rooms and your gran did seem so very kindly."

"Did she?"

A bleak feeling spread through me.

"Yes. I realised, retrospectively, that people who are meant for each other, still need to bend a little to get on. If I'd been a bit more flexible, all that happened wouldn't have. If we lived with your gran, it would be me accepting who you really are. Because I don't want a conflict of interest or split loyalties to come between us ever again."

Crossing the front door's threshold, this did not seem to be the moment for Betty to meet Tom Davies. Obviously he would need to be introduced into our relationship a bit at a time. Most certainly after an extensive occupation of the bedroom together and when she wasn't whispering *Alphonso* lovingly in my ear.

We later adjourned to the kitchen where a newspaper lay on the table. At least I wasn't on the front page. This was reserved for a startling photograph of a new national costume.

Following the attack on the French President Monsieur Moreau, the Home Office has decided to bring in emergency measures, to combat terrorism across the country. A new public uniform is being issued which all citizens must wear as an attempt to encourage normal behaviour. A Home Office spokesperson commented: citizens will still be able to wear what they like in the home, within reason. The constabulary will be used to enforce the dress code, with powers to detain offenders or put them under a curfew.

"Did you see this new uniform that everybody has to wear?" I asked.

"I had a giggle at it this morning. Can't see many women dressing in a pinstriped skirt like that. The Union Jack tie is vile. So is the compulsory bowler hat."

"The newspaper seems very in favour."

"Well I won't be wearing it," she asserted.

"You'll have to."

"Will I? We can swap our uniforms with the scarecrows."

This didn't greatly appeal. "Wouldn't that draw attention to us? Me?"

She looked rebuffed. "I suppose."

"We'll have to stay here and keep out of sight until the hue and cry dies down."

She sighed, "But the mortgage – it's too much if we're unemployed …That's why I suggested the castle. "

I thought about this a moment. "Actually, I know where there's a stack of money, if it's still there. Enough to pay off several mortgages." I told her about the suitcase. "If we could retrace my steps from that field where we met, there's a chance I could remember my way to the barn. A long shot maybe, but …"

"It would be a day out," she enthused "And we have Blue, if we got him to sniff some money …"

"We don't want to end up in the vault of a bank."

"We won't. He's only been wrong once. That was when he went to Dover. Never could work that one out."

"If we're going to do it, we'd better hurry up. Did you read this other bit of the news?"

Insurance for walkers is being introduced next month. All pedestrians will be required to wear an up-to-date insurance disk on their public service uniform at all times to show they are covered for an accident. This will apply to every journey out of the home, whether in urban or rural surroundings. There will be on-the-spot fines for non-compliance. Repeat offences will lead to imprisonment.

"I won't be able to get insurance under my current name."

"Perhaps the insurance company won't demand it?"

"I could make one up."

She looked excited again, "Did I tell you I thought of changing *my* name?"

"Please. Don't. Betty is beautiful."

She snorted derisively. "Betty and Alphonso? *Alphonso and Betty?* They go together like chips and custard. I thought up loads. How's about: Alphonso and Caprice?" she added thoughtfully. "Alphonso and Phoebe?" There was a pause to consider this, then, "Alphonso and Guinevere. Alphonso and Ophelia? Alphonso and Rowena?"

I was holding my head in my hands. "Betty is fine."

"*Fine*? What kind of a word is *that*?"

"Alright. Betty is divinely exquisite."

"Rubbish!"

"Well *you* are. And you're called Betty. So it is. It would be miles more sensible for me to change *my* name, as I'm the one wanted by the police and who needs a pseudonym. Something that goes well with Betty. Like Tom.

"Tom!" she hooted, "*Tom!*"

"Yes. Tom and Betty. Betty and Tom. That has a certain ring, doesn't it?"

"It's *terrible*. Even John would be better than that. Come on, let's take Blue for a walk."

"Couldn't we take him out after dark? I don't want to be seen."

"It doesn't get dark till late. You could dress up in some of my clothes. Nobody will suspect it's you if you're a woman. And you have such a pretty face."

"So do you, but if you think I'm going to pull on a load of women's clothes after all that has happened to me since ..."

The dog wagged his tail, soulfully.

"It's only a dress and a pair of tights for God's sake."

"A guy called Tom would never do that."

"All the more reason *not* to change your name. Come on."

I will only say, that if you have a dog, it's cruel not to take them out for exercise.

That evening, after our excursion, I wrote a clandestine letter to my parents.

Dear Mum and Dad,

So far so good. I have changed my name by deed poll to Tom Davies and nothing abnormal has happened since. I have a girlfriend who is in the police force and we plan to get married and settle down somewhere a long way away, until it's certain I am completely ordinary. Love Tom.

I found an envelope and stamp in Betty's desk and slipped out to put the message in a post box.

The next day was a steps-retracing day. Betty thought it would be jarring and odd for me to rove the countryside dressed in a pinstriped suit because a city gent would look so out of place in such pastoral surroundings. It would be bound to make a suspicious person, more suspicious.

"Two young ladies in summer dresses going for a summer outing over the fields won't attract any attention at all."

"Betty *please*."

"You look adorable in a dress. I almost swooned over you yesterday when you were licking that ice cream so prettily. And today I can give you a parasol to twirl and protect you from the sun. It's lovely. Like having a sister."

"Do you actually have a sister?"

She grimaced. "Two. Both vile. Let's say it's like having a *nice* sister."

As we drove out to begin our search, my misgivings mounted. Surely being dressed in a dress was a sign that the deed poll was malfunctioning? For here was I about to search for a suitcase of money (harvested from a field) in a fetching frilly garment, accompanied by an Alphonso-like dog. It worried my inner Tom. On the other hand, I reminded Mr Davies, it was Betty's idea, not mine, and that truly, others would be less likely to mistake me for Alphonso Blink if disguised as a woman. Once we'd grabbed the suitcase and emigrated to some unlikely destination like Norway or Peru, I would be able to adopt fittingly masculine attire and even fill out another deed poll if Tom continued to bother Betty. Getting out of the car, with the deed poll in the pocket of my dress, I touched it as a talisman.

We kissed in the field beside the river where we'd met, which I thought would attract plenty of attention if anyone were to see us. But I couldn't help myself, and neither could she. *Herself* that is. Or me either, for that matter. We met the scarecrow, whose wardrobe had not been refurbished by the farmer. I apologised profusely for what I'd done and promised to return at some point in the future with a brand-new suit. I'm not sure my apology was accepted, but Betty donated a scarf. From there I was able to locate the tree in the woods that had hidden me from Betty and Blue when we had first *not* met, and I clambered up it again to perch on the very same bough. They sat below, re-enacting the scene and eating a sandwich (not beef), before I told them to look up and they did, though as Betty said, more up my dress than the tree. She realized half-way through a sandwich that it was mine. I declined to finish it, but didn't half take a bite out of one of hers.

From there, the journey was more difficult. I found the road easily enough, then the sloping meadow I'd slumbered in surrounded by adoring flocks. But after that all the fields looked the same, even though they were all different.

"I'm not sure where to go next," I confessed at a stile.

"Blue will know."

"How could he?"

"Just look into his eyes and say what you want him to find."

"He's a dog. He doesn't speak English."

"But he understands it. Like sit, stay, or where's Alphonso? Go on, what other option is there?"

I knelt, trying not to get grass stains on my frock and looked into the dog's gentle trusting eyes. "Blue. Hello. Find the suitcase orchard."

And he trotted off immediately with an assurance I was not quite able to share. Not that it mattered, I was enjoying the excursion so much. It is a lovely and poignant thing to live through in pleasure what you have once had to experience in pain. Betty and I held hands. Smiled at each other. Kissed over the top of gates. Just once, in the far distance I saw a flock of sheep being led up a hill by a shepherdess, crook in hand, skipping – not angrily, but with a carefree abandon. In joy.

And then Blue brought me to a hillside full of large rocks and I recognised the place where the Horton's had fallen beneath my spell. There was plenty of dung on the grass but no actual sheep in evidence.

"That dog is amazing. This field is near the orchard of suitcases. He's on the right track."

"Of course he is."

"Lead on, hound of hounds, dog of dogs, Alsatian of Alsatians. We shall never be lost whilst such four paws and a nose exist."

Blue gave his cock-eyed grin.

Unbelievably, when we reached the orchard, the windfall was still there.

"Incredible," I breathed.

Betty gazed up and around at the trees. There were several suitcases still hanging on boughs. Meanwhile I opened the case and found the clothes once foolishly exchanged for a shepherdess costume. Jeans. Shirt. Jumper. Socks.

Betty was beside me in a moment and wrested them from my hands, pressing the bundle to her cheek. "Alphonso's clothes. Oh my! How adorably wonderful."

"The jeans have a hole in the knee," I pointed out, to provide a little perspective.

"Even better. The jumper has a hole as well. But not the shirt. Nor the socks." She hugged my ex-attire lovingly to her chest. "We must take these home with us."

"Really?"

"We can't leave them to rot in this wood."

"We could."

"We *couldn't*. We're not." She folded them reverentially and patted them down into the case, then picked it up. "It's just made a perfect day more perfect. Shall we go home?"

"It's not *that* suitcase I've come to rescue. There's a barn somewhere on the top of a nearby hill. I left another suitcase there. The one stuffed with money."

"Does it matter Alphonso?" she said softly. Trees gently swayed overhead. Dappled green light played across her face. "We don't need loads of money. We just need each other."

"We might as well get it now we're here. The mortgage. And we might need it to escape from, well, everyone."

"I suppose so. But why didn't you take it the first time?"

We began walking through the orchard. Many of the suitcases it seemed had been picked. One or two lay on the floor looking bruised. There was no impulse inside me to investigate their contents.

"I didn't need it. That day, what was in the case seemed like a symbol of something ... I don't know what."

"And now ..."

"It's *needed*."

We began puffing up a steep slope, a bit too out of breath for further conversation. And then, at the hill's crest a dark outline appeared.

"The Barn."

I ran the rest of the way, Blue galloping by my side. There was no time to gaze at the Constable view. The bales were still stacked just as I remembered them. I clambered up bristly oblongs to the corner where I'd slept and where Blue was already enthusiastically snuffling. Under a thin layer of straw was the abandoned suitcase. I snapped the clasps open, threw the lid back and sighed in relief. It was stuffed with bundles and bundles of cash, still fresh presumably. Enough to keep a billionaire happy for an hour. There was a rustling behind me and Betty panted to my side then dropped to her knees.

"Wow."

"A lot." I said with grim satisfaction. "Enough to buy every house on your street."

"What would we do with twenty crap houses?"

As if in answer, I slammed the lid down and pressed the clasps shut.

"We could knock them down, I suppose," she continued, "And build a nice castle."

It wasn't what I wanted to hear. We crept out of the barn and back the way we came.

For some reason, even though I was exultant, finding the case put a dampener on the day. It might have been because we were no longer two young ladies out walking a dog. We had become a conspicuously odd couple of young ladies *carrying suitcases* across fields accompanied by a dog, which could hardly be dismissed as an everyday occurrence and would be bound to bring a second look and questioning thoughts in anyone we met. It made me want to skulk. But we didn't meet anyone. Though we *did* encounter at the rocks, a couple of Hortons.

"Don't look at them," I panicked, dreading recognition.

And indeed, one of them gave me a most penetrating yellow stare. But Blue trotted over and the woollen ninnies fled with many a bleated baa.

To the disappointment of myself and possibly the scarecrow as well, Betty firmly squashed the notion of dressing the naked decoy in my old attire.

"Absolutely *not*."

In fact, once back in Betty's house, almost the first thing she did was dump the case on her kitchen table, throw back the lid and lift out my folded garments.

"You're safe in here, so you can put them back on."

My ex-jeans were waggled not-very-enticingly in the air.

"I'd sooner not."

"But I want to see the original, authentic Alphonso Blink."

"He wasn't much to look at, honestly. Especially his clothes."

"You're not getting too attached to mine?"

"Don't be ridiculous."

Though they *were* nice.

She gave me an uncharacteristically hard stare. "What is wrong with you? Something has changed since your arrest. It's like you are running from something."

"Yes, the Police."

"No. From yourself."

I winced.

She continued, "I'm wondering if my clubbing you so often has damaged your brain."

And so I told her. "The thing is Betty, I'm no longer Alphonso Blink."

"Now *you're* being ridiculous."

"No really, I decided I wanted to stop being him because his name was causing all the terrible things to happen to me."

"Your name?" she sounded incredulous. "How can a name cause trouble?"

"I don't know. It just does."

"But *how*?"

"In all truth Betty, my name is at the root of all my travails."

"It is not."

"So I changed it to Tom Davies."

"Please."

"And now I'm him, the catastrophes that occur without me even knowing I'm causing them, will stop and nobody need ever know I was once a terrible person."

"But you never were. You said so yourself. You never did anything wrong. You were just different."

"I hit you over the head."

"I hit you first. Twice."

"I made the Foreign Minister's hair attack the French President."

"That was hilarious."

"It caused a major international incident."

"It was a storm in a hair-dresser's teacup."

"I jumped off a train I'd been put on breaking my sentence."

"You should never have been on it."

"I stole your clothes."

"And I bet you looked pretty hot in them."

"And your purse."

"I DON'T CARE!"

"But I do. And if I'm called Tom Davies, the weirdnesses that have dogged my life since birth will stop."

"They really won't."

"How could you know what it's like to be called by some incredibly insane name, when you're called something totally reasonable like Betty ... Betty ... Betty ....?

"Smith."

"Smith?" My mind reeled.

"Smith." She affirmed. "Betty Blink would be ever so much nicer."

"Well tough, because I'm not Alphonso Blink any more. I changed my name by deed poll."

I ripped the document from the pocket of my dress and flourished it in her face. Betty snatched it from my hand and gazed in horror at what was written there.

"Oh my God. Oh my *God!* Tom Davies! *TOM DAVIES!* I don't want to go out with any old Tom fucking Davies!" And in one swift movement, she crumpled the deed, turned, stuffed it in the toaster and slammed the lever down. *"Tom Davies is a dickhead!"*

I screamed, "Betty! No!" and rushed towards the toaster only to find her blocking the way – forcibly. "My deed poll!"

She wrestled me back whilst over her shoulder I saw the deed combust, flames shooting up from the toaster along with several large puffs of smoke.

"Nooooooooo! *Tom.* Tom come back!"

By the time I'd wriggled from her grasp, the conflagration had died down.

I shouted into Betty's face, "What have you done, you idiot!" Then upended the toaster and shook it. Black fragments of ash sailed downwards to the floor. My innards exploded in fury, "You stupid, stupid woman! How dare you burn something that was so important to me?"

"Aren't *I* important to you?"

"Not any more."

"So your name is more important to you than I am?"

"Yes! A hundred times more important. A thousand times more important. You're not important to me *in the slightest.*"

"Well, if being called Tom Davies for the rest of your life is more important than I am, you can go!"

"I will!" I sneered, "Betty *Smith!*"

She made a surging growl, "If I only had a truncheon, I'd hit you with it so many times!"

I laughed cynically,

"I know and turn me in! Because I was wrong, you're a policewoman through and through and you always will be."

"Get out!" she shrieked, "Get out before I *do* call the police!"

So I did, Blue wagging his tail sadly as I went past and slammed the front door.

Fourteen   *Excurse*

I stalked from the house almost spontaneously combusting into ashy silhouettes along with the deed poll. Cremating it was unforgivable! A despicable crime! Were I a judge, Betty would have been on a train of infinite duration with only the toaster for company and Blue dispatched to equally endless kennels, if that were mathematically possible. And why had I barged out of the house forgetting the suitcase of money and my former clothes? It was impossible to ask for them back. I couldn't lose that much face. To exit in such belligerent loftiness then return on all fours in whimpering humiliation was not going to happen. Anyhow at that very moment, she would be summoning the police to shop me and reapply for her job. Infuriatingly, I had now in all likelihood, reverted to Alphonso Blink and if so, it was all despicable Betty's fault! By the side of a road that led away from town, I had a minor tantrum—clenching my fists, stamping my feet, and calling her every word in the rudeness dictionary.

My one hope was that the deed-poll copy in Jane Collins' possession would be sufficient to retain my new identity. In which case, were it still valid, what would Tom Davies do? Of course, he wouldn't be standing at the edge of town in a nice dress, penniless, and on the run from the police. But just say he was? Say I was in his shoes and not

Betty's. Without question my current circumstances would freak Tom inside out. He'd want to rip the clothes off, but nakedness was worse. In truth the hopeless bastard wouldn't have the foggiest notion what to do, because there *was* no normal way to proceed. He'd turn round and round and round in circles on the spot in horror at the aberrant kookiness of the situation; and give me my due, I tried this for a whole half minute until I was dizzy, then realised a man walking his dog had seen me. He hurried on, obviously disturbed by my gyrations because he was probably called Tom Davies as well. Maybe if I followed him home and asked how a normal person might cope with such desperate circumstances, he'd tell me what I'd do. But he wouldn't. He'd fetch the police. The real answer then was that Tom Davies would fetch the police to arrest himself. Almost weeping at this conundrum, I acknowledged there was nothing for it, but to do what Alphonso Blink would have done instead, for he had been here before. Not exactly where I was standing, but places like it. The only course open was to walk on as an unobtrusive young woman taking an evening stroll, until something happened and accept I was crap at being Tom Davies.

So, I traipsed along until reaching a stile. Taking this as an invitation and surmounting the rickety wooden steps and bar, I followed a public footpath into more Constable-daubed countryside, telling myself that it was as yet early days with Tom, and that we probably just needed practice. A weirdo couldn't expect to become conventional overnight. It was obviously something that perseverance would handsomely reward. For instance, Resolution One: never wear women's clothes. Resolution Two: always keep important documents in a safe place – ie not a pocket of your dress, (see Resolution One.) Resolution Three: Never ...

In this way, I wended my way through landscapes executed in the romantic tradition, over hill and stile, past a village or two, until dusk began to gather in the day. Negotiating the footpath's rascally ways in failing light failing to appeal, I stopped in a churchyard and peered from behind a crypt, at a hamlet of posh cottages, in the hope of sighting a back garden shed. With the day petering out, I was forced to sidle some hundred yards down a lane for a closer look and in doing so passed an open gate with a sign saying:

STATION.

Flackton Branch line (connecting).

Though my love for locomotive transport had uncoupled somewhat since our last outing, I could not help but wonder if the platform came complete with a waiting room and unlocked door. By a dim and inadequate light mounted on the ticket office exterior, I spied a red-brick, Victorian sanctuary next-door and was heading for it, when a train approached.

I dived into the waiting room which mercifully had not been locked, and groped my way to a bench. Heart amplified in my ears, I sat in the gloom, looking from a window at the greater gloom of the platform where a steam train and carriages were shuddering to a stop. For several minutes, nothing happened. No stationmaster emerged to shout or peep a whistle. There was no egress from any of the carriages, which were dark and seemingly uninhabited. Then, all creaks and groans, the locomotive left. Which was a relief.

Whilst the bench I was seated upon was slatted and not suited to a night's repose in a thin dress, it still felt better than the floor of a garden shed, so I lay down. Why couldn't they provide comfortable sofas and armchairs in such places? I was just trying to accommodate my shoulders on the slats, when another train arrived. This had me sitting upright in alarm, but again nothing whatsoever occurred. No doors slammed. No voices called. No footsteps approached or receded. Once more the train, utterly benighted, looked bereft of life. I had a vague urge to creep out onto the platform to peek in at a carriage window before the train, like the one before it, chuffed away. Again I slumped onto the bench, cursing that I had not even a scarf to make a pillow. Inevitably, only minutes later a third train drew in. This was getting ridiculous. How could I sleep with all these steam-hissing interruptions? The pillowless rigidity of the bench was bad enough. At which my thoughts fell to contemplation of the lengthy cushioned seats a traveller might outstretch upon in the vacant carriages outside. Where were the trains bound? Northwards for sure. Scotland. Maybe even further. The Orkneys? Iceland even? Whatever, they would bring me swiftly from Betty's orbit in more shelter and comfort than a load of stiles and muddy footpaths. So long as the carriages were not full of

Alphonso Blinks in various stages of their development, boarding might be the best option. Anyhow, I might still be Tom Davies, in which case, what would *he* do? What would dear, old down-to-earth Tom's reaction be to a train rolling in where he was waiting on a platform? He'd get on it.

However, by the time I'd had all these thoughts, the train juddered, hissed and with a succession of painstaking groans, like a ninety-year-old getting out of a chair, departed. Typical. *Typical!* There is no more difficult tightrope to walk in life than that of indecision. There's being impulsive and jumping on a train which might be bound in the wrong direction and full of people a person doesn't want to meet, and then there's cautious consideration in a tiny window of seconds to mull over the reasons why boarding might not be wise. And by the time you've done this, three trains that might have given a delightful spin have vanished and a fourth one never appears, so the potential passenger completely misses their opportunity for an excursion. Be impulsive and lose or ponderous and lose. *Unless you're lucky.* Then impulsiveness can win or overthinking triumph. It is impossible to know which to do when, and its purely chance whether a person gets it right. So for a person to kick themselves repeatedly for missing the third and last train, or for boarding it only to encounter a carriage of arresting constables, is absurd, because in neither situation could the person know what was a sensible course of action to pursue. For a good long while I sat on hard slats of wood waiting for a fourth train to trundle into the station, but it didn't.

Eventually, I lay down and kicked myself despondently to sleep.

If any further trains arrived in the night, they didn't rouse me. I woke in the back-to-front dusk of dawn, to hear a slowing puff, puff, puff, puff and decrescendo of clanks before something outside hissed to a standstill. As if from a jack-in-a-box I jerked up to see carriages in the turquoise light, looking dark and deserted as those of the previous eve. Slipping from the waiting room, I crossed the platform stealthily and tried to peek in a carriage window. It was too high. There was nothing for it: with exaggerated circumspection, so that no passenger or official might heed my boarding, I opened a door and stepped up inside. Though train compartment doors are designed to be slammed noisily, I shut it softly, noiselessly, as if the outside world were a sleeping baby's room.

Moments later, with a jolt and some laboured tugs, the train resumed its breathy panting towards some unknown and (hopefully) distant terminus. Staggering slightly, I turned to find the compartment occupied. There, outstretched on a long, cushioned seat and sleeping like an enchanted princess, was the Two Headed Girl. Almost toppling onto the couch opposite, then leaning back to assimilate the shock, I found myself studying her in the murky light. They lay slightly on their side, one head resting on the other with the intimacy of two loving sisters sharing a bed. One of the heads, Celeste I thought, was snoring barely perceptible, ladylike, snores.

For a long while I fondly admired the dreaming nymph, and wondered how she came to be there, before my attention wandered to the windows, where scenery was now rushing by in the opposite direction to myself, as if late for an important meeting with some other scenery, Windermere say or Glencoe. I tried to imagine two different bits of scenery meeting in a café over cups of tea. It was quite difficult. For one thing the café would have to be absolutely huge. I looked back at my companion and saw the eyes of Beatrice glittering at me. Her gaze met mine with the force of a collision, just as Celeste's eyes fluttered open.

"You," Beatrice breathed venomously.

"Yes."

Celeste gaped. "Alphonso."

Beatrice grimly spelled it out, "Alphonso Blink."

I nodded. It didn't seem the moment to split nomenclatural hairs. They sat up. Beatrice continued, every word burning, "How did you get in here?"

"The door."

The two heads swivelled to quizz each other with a look, then swivelled back to me.

"It stopped? The train?"

I nodded again. "Yes."

"And you got on?"

"Seemingly."

"Through *this* door?"

They walked over to try the handle.

"Yes. Does it matter?"

"It's locked!"

Disbelievingly I went to try it for myself. They moved pointedly aside, as if I stank. The handle wouldn't turn nor the window pull down. Puzzling.

Almost beside herself, Beatrice shouted, *"So why didn't you wake us when you had it open?"*

"I didn't know you were here when I closed it," I shrugged. "Or that it would lock. When I saw you lying there, looking so lovely, everything else went out of my head."

Beatrice erupted into an anguished howl. "You imbecile! You village idiot of village idiots. You pebble-witted dunce!"

I felt unable to refute these charges.

"Come on Cel, let's leave this treacherous cur with the contents of a bin for an intellect and find another carriage. He's stunk out this compartment with the decomposition of his brain."

Celeste, who had been regarding me all this time with a stricken look, cried, "And why are you still wearing women's clothes?"

I looked down at my dress and tights and could manage only a feeble smile.

With contempt, the Two-Headed Girl swept out into the corridor and banged the sliding door shut. A lesser man than myself might here, in a reductionist simplification of this and other vexations of recent days, have spluttered, "*Women!*" To my great credit, I did not stoop to this utterance, only thought it, and then but fleetingly, for my being in a dress somewhat undermined things. Suddenly alone in the compartment, I sat trying to piece together what Beatrice's outbursts had meant. If she and Celeste couldn't get off, how had I got on? At last, the puzzle could no longer compete with my stomach's grumbling complaints and I went in search of breakfast.

After negotiating several swaying corridors, peering into compartment after empty compartment and finding not a single guard, nor ticket collector, nor restaurant car steward, it was clear that I had boarded a locomotive version of the *Marie Celeste*. But for Celeste being on it. Presuming the restaurant car was therefore self-service, I raided the galley kitchen, rustling some cornflakes into a bowl and brewing tea.

After breakfast, searching for Beatrice and Celeste, I heard animated voices and peered in a window of the rearmost compartment of the train to see the Two-Headed Girl. Suddenly aware of me through the glass, they broke off talking to themselves and aggressively 'V' signed with both hands. Returning a tepid wave, I then trudged away to a distant carriage.

For two days Celeste and Beatrice shunned me. At my arrival in the restaurant car, their conversation would abruptly stop, knife and fork clattering onto a plate in a sudden silence. They would rise immediately and, heads snootily high, retire. Meeting in a corridor they turned instantly about at the sight of me sooner than endure the proximity of my passing.

Several times I called out to them, "If this is about my monstering the Foreign Minister's hair, can I just say that it was completely unintentional and I'm sorry if somehow it led to your arrest and ..."

But my words seemed to break on their retreating back and fall to the floor unheard. On the evening of the second day, hearing a guitar and soulful accompaniment, I knocked on their compartment door to mouth 'sorry' through the window. This changed the song immediately to chopped cords and a yelled lyric:

"One-headed bastard with a traitorous tongue,
We're singing your song that should never be sung,
for the chorus just repeats one four letter word,
The one that people think is the worst they've ever heard."

Though I didn't wait to hear it, the word pursued me back up the corridor.

On the morning of the third day, after breakfasting in the restaurant car, I returned to the carriage I had selected as my bower and outstretched glumly. One thing was for sure, when the train next stopped, as it must at some point, Tom Davies was hopping off. Not least to find new clothes, for my frock had begun to look crumpled. I was smoothing out persistent creases when, with a bang, the door slid back. The two-headed girl entered abruptly, and I sat upright. Crashing the door shut behind them, they gave me a four-eyed glare. The heads then fell into conversation with each other.

"If we have to share this train with him ..." Beatrice began.

"And unfortunately, it seems we do."

"Then a temporary ceasefire is necessitated, so that we may announce our grievances, punish him and get answers to a number of pressing questions?"

"Do you wish to tell him this or shall I?"

"He's just the sort of miserable worm to listen in to a private conversation and already know."

"The cad," said Celeste.

"The bounder."

"It's enough to make me eat our white flag."

"Do we even want a truce with him after the brazen way he has deliberately overheard us, to the point of you choking yourself on tasteless white cloth?"

"What a brute he is."

"Or she."

This entrance and subsequent exchange left me utterly charmed.

"To tell the truth," I lied, "I have not been listening to single word that you've said about my eavesdropping on your conversation. I regard that sort of thing as ill-mannered. But I'm glad you're both here as I was going to suggest a temporary ceasefire."

Beatrice turned to Celeste dismissively. "What a stupid idea!"

"Absurd notion."

"As if we could ever have a temporary ceasefire with such a guttersnipe?"

Celeste looked thoughtful. "I suppose however, we should hear his terms and conditions?"

Beatrice shook her head adamantly. "I personally wouldn't draw up a seat at the negotiating table for less than complete surrender."

"That is magnanimous of you," Celeste replied. "I would, furthermore, demand the kissing of our boots."

"Yes. That would be fair."

"And also the writing of a canto of verses, begging forgiveness for whatever charges we accuse him of, even if they are patently false and trumped up."

"Agreed. The renunciation of women's clothes might also help."

Celeste looked doubtful. "Alas, on that point I fear we shall stumble into deadlock. Would stopping the train and opening the doors do instead?"

Beatrice nodded approvingly. "There, negotiations, which notionally had stalled, might achieve a breakthrough. Let us proceed. We are in a strong position. The cards in our hands and up our sleeves are abundantly aces. But we must keep these close to our chest, until we see what he is after, the cunning beast."

"Shall we begin?"

"Certainly."

They seated themselves opposite.

"Who shall we leave the talking to?" Beatrice enquired. "Yourself or mine?"

"I think both of us, but I should start."

"As you like it."

"He *is* a reverse Ganymede."

During this conversation, I had affected to stare out of the window at a passing panorama of moorland and mountains. When the conversation between them closed, Beatrice barked, "You! *Blink.*"

My head turned to meet two forbidding frowns.

"Yes?" I nonchalantly enquired. "What do you want? You barge into my private chambers and then ignore me for five minutes by indulging in an exclusive conversation that I would have been forced to listen to if I had not been so well brought up."

The heads raised a single eyebrow at each other. Celeste then returned her gaze to mine. "Do you surrender?"

I gave a look of surprise.

"Of course. You have hundreds of aces up your sleeves and are therefore irresistible."

"Unconditionally?"

"It's the only sort of surrender I know."

Celeste looked faintly pleased. "He does at least have a modicum of taste and discernment. To find us irresistible I mean."

"Shh," Beatrice warned, "If he discovers how susceptible we are to flattery, all is lost." Looking unimpressed and ominous, she continued, "Having surrendered, unconditionally, you must submit to interrogation."

"Of course, and because you are so infinitely irresistible, I will tell you everything. Especially that I am sorry for what happened with the Foreign Minister's Hair."

For the first time, Celeste spoke as if this wasn't all a game. "Why on earth did you do it?"

"*How* on earth did you do it?" added Beatrice in mystification.

My shoulders shrugged. "I wasn't aware at any moment that I had."

"Ridiculous."

"Absurd."

"How could you make a Foreign Minister's coiffure enwrap the French President and know nothing about it," Beatrice seethed.

I shook my head sorrowfully.

"The truth is, if I hang around anywhere long enough, something odd will occur, but obviously not, of its own accord." I gave them some examples from my childhood.

The heads listened and said in unison, "*Preposterous.*"

I shrugged yet again. *"Sorry."*

"You realise," Beatrice scolded, "that as a result of your aberrant behaviour we have been deported on this train for being 'different'? With only our own selves for company."

I groaned, "Nightmarish."

"We can't escape each other," Beatrice stropped, "and have been going slowly mad. Moreover, your actions have trashed our musical career ..."

"And worst of all," Celeste looked miserable, "our father must also have been deported and we shall never see him again."

Beatrice was unrelenting. "We have every reason to break our guitar over your head."

"It's a common feeling women have towards me," I replied wretchedly.

"But our guitar, though cheap, in fact we got it free, is worth more than your head."

I began to feel a person can only unconditionally surrender so far.

"From a wealthy admirer," Celeste explained, with more leniency, "who splashed out. So it's probably worth more than all our heads."

There was a momentary pause.

"Perhaps at this point I could kiss your boots, write a long poem of apology, and weave some men's clothing?"

Beatrice eyed me moodily. "First, how did you stop the train to board it and open the door?"

Again my shoulders went up and down like a coat hanger being hooked onto a rail.

"I haven't a clue."

The Two-Headed Girl threw up her arms in frustration.

"If he has a personality flaw …" Celeste began.

"And he *does*. I believe many," Beatrice agreed.

"It is a tendency at times to repetition."

Beatrice addressed me once more. "So the train stopped for no reason other than your being in the vicinity, and you had no inkling it was going to happen?"

"Yes."

"Then couldn't it stop now? You're in the vicinity I believe. Couldn't be more in it."

My reply was anguished. "It doesn't work like that. I have no conscious control over what happens."

"Then what earthly use is such a trait?" Beatrice expostulated.

"None!" I cried, "It's horrendous. And as a result, I have forsworn strangeness."

I felt suddenly woebegone.

"How?" said Celeste, curiously. She laughed, "Surely not by surrendering to a person with two heads?"

This wrongfooted me, for surrendering to them was a strangeness I would not have forgone for the world. Silence fell. There was a ceasefire in fact, during which the Two-Headed Girl sat on the seat opposite.

"*Now* you can kiss our boots," Beatrice consented.

In obedience, I slipped to my knees and bent to kiss their shoes, though two didn't seem quite enough somehow. I felt there should have been at least four, minimum. And it must have been that which prompted me to remove their shoes and socks to kiss their bare feet.

"That tickles."

"But I liked it," Celeste purred approvingly. "Now surrendered prisoner, kiss our knees."

The jeans were rather dry and uninteresting to kiss, but I did as I was told.

"Would you mind so very much," Celeste asked Beatrice, "If as an apology for all he has done wrong, I made him kiss my lips?"

"I don't suppose I would. It's quite dull on this train, and there might be some vicarious sensations, almost pleasant, from the experience."

I was hauled onto the couch beside Celeste and given a mesmeric smile.

"Well then Blink, to atone for your terrible misdeeds, kiss me."

Backed into a corner thus, I had little option but to comply.

After a minute or so of this, Celeste paused for breath and said softly, "I still don't think he has atoned enough. Do you?"

"Like I say it's quite dull on this train, even being a gooseberry is better than nothing."

"So can I kiss him again? I do feel he might eventually make up for what he did."

"I suppose. If you must. Punishment comes in many fantastical forms."

The second kiss went on a little longer. Celeste gasped to Beatrice in the aftermath, "Do you want a go?" There was a silence. "There's a lot to be said for oscular reparation. It certainly passes the time."

Beatrice looked at me and her beautiful eyes darkened with an interest, previously unavowed. "We do have a lot of it on our hands. Come here prisoner."

I went round to Beatrice's side and sat. For a heart-stopping moment we looked at each other, then remunerations began and went on for some considerable time. When we drew apart, I was shaking. So was the two-headed girl.

"Well *that* turned you on," Celeste observed.

"A bit," Beatrice blushed.

"A lot."

"Nonsense, that was the residue from your own kiss."

"Liar."

"But I feel he is still very much in our debt."

"Without question."

"And if he's going to kick this ridiculous habit of wearing women's clothes, he should do so now."

And with that, the dress was shockingly dragged up over my head to leave me clad in only black tights. Another kiss with Beatrice immediately followed, which became so amorous that my hands couldn't help sliding up beneath their jumper to find no bra, at which I lost my head and they both theirs. Dragged to the floor on top of them, and being kissed on the neck and lips simultaneously, I felt hands slowly pushing the black tights down in further atonement for my sins. In this way, one thing led to another until an inevitable conclusion was reached: that perhaps being Alphonso Blink wasn't so very terrible after all.

Fifteen   *Training*

There followed a Golden Age of railway travel. Countless hours in a rushing metal tube, not caring where we were headed because we had already reached our destination. Time stopped, or at least—like scenery through the windows—we ceased to notice it passing. The train carriages became a self-contained parallel universe.

The first action of the Two Headed Girl, was to confiscate the dress and replace it with a pair of their own jeans and t-shirt.

"A little too tight," Beatrice frowned, assessing my new outfit, "And still, technically women's clothes,"

"But then, nobody will know except us." Celeste pointed out.

"There's nobody *but* us on the train."

"Even better. We can take them all back off the prisoner whenever we feel he shouldn't be wearing women's clothes."

"That's virtually all the time."

"Exactly."

Days rolled rhythmically by and apart from sex, sex and more sex, we explored our increasingly delightful prison. Whilst at first we wished to escape the train, which halted only at night, presumably to change drivers and replenish the kitchen, (the restaurant car abutted the engine and was locked only during these stops), we soon gave up on doors and windows that refused to open and, for several weeks, abandoned ourselves to the delight of each other's company. Not least, they would compose for fun—two heads with one heart, they were as attuned as the strings their fingers plucked. Lifting their guitar, a song would appear with startling speed, Beatrice doing most of the lyrical work, and Celeste the music, but each contributing some of both. Sprawled on a compartment seat, listening to songs emerge as if they'd always existed and had just been taken down from a platonic shelf and dusted off, a wand passed over me. A spell cast by two angelic voices harmonically entwined.

I was baffled at first by the turbulently intellectual Beatrice bothering with me, then realised the attraction was my outré identity: Alphonso Blink—who rode a square-wheeled bicycle, fired arrows from a fallen weather-vane, escaped prison dressed as a policewoman and even messed with a politician's 'public hair', (her words). She asked many times about past aberrations and guffawed at my school experiences with the desks and headmaster's car.

"And you really didn't know it was going to occur? Wonderful."

They were awestruck by Esmeralda pinning a kite to the sky and loved to hear of Blink Castle and my grandfather's inventions.

For Beatrice and the gentle divinity of Celeste to embrace my abnormal self was like a miracle. I had been waiting for our relationship all my life. So had they. And my being the first man they had ever simultaneously found desirable and thus an outlet for all their pent-up eroticism, well – no wonder we fell so deeply in love. Who cared about the train? Let it roll on and on and on forever.

"Oh amazing Alphonso we love you." Celeste enthused as she and Beatrice left lipstick marks all over my bare chest. "You've made us happy. For the first time in our lives, we are in accord."

"We could always sing in harmony, but never live in it. Until you kissed our feet."

"Your surrender deserves a Nobel Peace Prize."

One night, stargazing from a carriage window whilst Celeste and Beatrice softly snored, I found myself thanking every constellation that was winking down at me for the love of a Two Headed Girl. With an inner whisper I also blessed Betty. She had been right about one thing – I was not Tom Davies and never could be. Had she not incinerated the deed poll so that I ran off in a dudgeon, the phoenix of my true self might never have risen from the toaster. I would never have strayed into a rural waiting room and boarded the train to find myself in the arms of Celeste and Beatrice. It was a thought to snuff every star from the sky.

Somewhere inside me, I knew that all journeys must hit a buffer eventually, yet I desperately wanted this to be many many miles over the horizon. One night however, as the Two-Headed Girl sat in a compartment making up a song, they stopped in mid-composition on an unresolved chord and the sentence,

"... if you don't know what you want,
　how can you get it ...?
and we want to get off with you."

Beatrice paused, looked at Celeste who smiled encouragingly and took a deep breath. "Alphonso, this orgy on a train is all very well ..."

"In fact" Celeste added, "It's the best thing that has ever happened to Beatrice and I."

"Easily. Better than digging sandcastles by the sea when we were six. Which was the last time we ever agreed about anything important. But for two reasons, we now need to escape these carriages."

"Firstly," Celeste explained, "to find out what happened to father. We're worried about him."

I felt Maxime would be perfectly happy, even in prison, so long as a razor and strop were to hand, but kept mum.

"The other reason," Beatrice's voice hesitated, "is ... well, how do we broach this with the poor unsuspecting man? Who before falling into our hands led the innocent life of a convict, sheep messiah and bicycle-thieving social outcast?"

"He is but green in years, though I have *this* to waft before his face should he pass out with shock." Celeste waved a lace handkerchief.

"A baby?" I hazarded.

They went off into helpless snorting mirth.

"Not yet," Beatrice managed to say after half a minute. "Is he warm?"

Celeste had barely recovered. "Which of us should tell him?"

"Surely both."

"Then let us say it together. One, two, three ..."

"Marry us."

I started slightly. *"Marriage?"*

Amusingly, they nodded in unison, but I smiled at something else. "To me?"

"Of course," Beatrice laughed. "I know, it's sudden and we haven't bent at the knee or bought you a ring, but we concur—and that's amazing—we were tearing ourselves down the middle until you arrived. We're now one two-headed woman instead of two one-headed women badly stitched together. So despite our many orgasms, we feel this incredible experience and the train need to stop. We want to be Celeste and Beatrice Blink."

I was dumbstruck.

"Oh. Do *you* want to marry *us* incidentally?" Celeste asked.

"Of course," I replied, though winded. "I want to kiss your bare feet every day for the rest of my life."

"And we'll try our best to wash them each morning."

"I don't care if they're filthy."

Beatrice looked suddenly doubtful, "Should we marry such a reprobate?"

A hand outstretched and pulled me close.

"Yes," whispered Celeste, "Sooner than is possible, if possible. The only question is how?"

After a pre-marital embrace, Beatrice became businesslike. "We tried pulling the communication cord several times pre-Alphonso, and nothing happened. We could try again."

So we did with the same result, post-Alphonso. Over cups of tea in the restaurant car, we considered our options.

"We can't help feeling dear fiancé, that if you once managed to stop the train, open the carriage door and step aboard, you must somehow be able to do it again."

I sighed. "The odd occurrences that dog me, never arrive because I want them to. Quite the reverse."

"Ah." Beatrice looked thoughtful, "So you must want *not* to get off."

"Well, except to get married, I *don't*."

"Then why doesn't it stop the train?"

My hands gestured emptily. "Ask it."

Beatrice, grabbed my head and stared into my eyes, as if my head were a crystal ball. Her gaze explored deep inside me and she intoned,

"Alphonso Blink's psyche, why don't you stop the train like a good little unconscious?" Her dark eyes peered mesmerically into my own, despite which, the train hurtled on. "Wow, I can see right past his kneecaps down to his toenails.

Celeste snorted. "Can you see his unconscious?"

"It's hiding. Around the bend of his elbow." Then she closed her eyes and kissed me.

"Hey! That's not looking for his unconscious!" Celeste protested.

"Sorry," Beatrice apologised with a sigh, "looking in his eyes was a turn-on."

"I know. Though surely not when surveying his toenails?"

"I was looking less far down than that. Besides the unconscious wasn't showing up."

"Wonderfully pleasant though this is," I breathed, Beatrice releasing my head, "You have to understand that my unconscious is wilfully disobedient and wants only to get me into trouble."

"Nonsense. Why would it want to do that?" Beatrice asked.

"Because it hates me and I hate it."

Celeste gently pulled my head round to look at hers. "Give me a go. No wonder it won't do what you want if you hate it." From point blank range, she also stared into my eyes, but softly. "Hello? Hello in there?"

Beatrice and I both laughed.

"Ignore them. I don't know what you want to do, though I'm sure it wouldn't be bringing trouble to dear Alphonso. If you don't want to stop the train, you must have reasons and I'm sure they're very good ones. But if you want to tell me why, I'll listen. So speak amazing psyche, tell me." Nothing happened. The train if anything sped up. She then also kissed me, breaking off after a few moments to say, "It obviously needs more concerted persuasion."

Their optimism was difficult to share. "I don't wish to be a stick-in-the mud, but surely self-control, if it were possible, would have manifested itself by now?"

Beatrice however was determined to solve me. "From what you've said, it's a connoisseur of strange. Convince it the train is terrifyingly conventional. All the seats are the same. The carriages follow each other with unquestioning obedience and without any personality of their own. This train, like thousands of trains all over the world, probably hasn't had an original thought in its life. It's *so* stuffy. Doesn't even have a name. Just a number. It trundles along, wherever it's told, sticking to the rails."

"It would kill us if it came off."

"Why should it care? It should show George Stephenson that trains of independent spirit can go anywhere they like!"

"Let us remind our fiancé's psyche furthermore," Celeste chimed in, "that the tickets are also uniform."

"The uniforms are uniform. Porters. Stationmasters. Ticket collectors."

"The repetitive noise of the rails."

"Rhythmically unimaginative."

"Okay, okay. I can *consciously* think of the train like that. But it's my *unconscious* that's in charge."

For a moment the two heads looked stumped.

"Then we need to plant things in your unconscious when it isn't aware," Beatrice mused, "You know how dreams grab hold of random stuff that happens in the day? Autosuggestion. So …"

"Yes!" Celeste broke in excitedly, "So if he wants the train to stop, he needs to stop things symbolically. Stop eating dinner in mid-forkful. Stop talking to us in mid-sentence and we'll stop doing ..." she paused, "Like that."

Next thing, we were walking the corridors together and suddenly becoming statues.

"Stop for enough time to get off a train," said Beatrice. "At least two minutes, just in case. Then we can walk and stop again. After a whole afternoon, it's bound to go in. We should also ..." she paused.

"... definitely converse like ..." Celeste replied.

"... I think ...?"

"... makes total sense if ..." they replied.

"Yes, yes, yes." Beatrice, cried, eyes flashing in excitement, "We also need to open things, like the door. No good if the train stops and the door's stuck. Open things Alphonso. Like your mouth."

I obeyed, letting it gape for a few moments.

"We must open everything."

"Our legs," giggled Celeste. The Two-Headed Girl lay and splayed her legs, waggling them in the air, much to their own hilarity. "If that doesn't open a few doors, I don't know what will."

In this way, and others, we spent several days trying to master my unconscious. However, the train never did slow down in daylight hours, until one morning ...

I woke late to find the view from our carriage window was no longer English. Unfamiliar landscapes went by like an endless Monet moving beside a stationary train. There was an outbreak of excitement beside me.

"We're in France!" shrieked Celeste.

"We've gone through the tunnel by mistake!" Beatrice yahooed.

They lapsed into animated incomprehensibility. It was hard not to feel left out.

"I hope we don't stop here, I don't know the language."

"Mime," said Beatrice.

And then it happened – chugs of the engine growing further apart, squeals from the brakes, steam blowing out its cheeks.

"We're stopping!" I peered from the window in shock. "We're coming to a station."

The Two-Headed Girl knelt on the window seat to look.

"Try the door," said Beatrice. "It must be your unconscious—the Alphonso effect."

"It's not," I wailed. "There's people on the platform."

Two lovely heads turned to each other in concern.

"Better hide, Alphonso."

"Where? The luggage rack?"

"The bathroom," Celeste flapped. "That cupboard full of paper towels."

"Will I fit in there?"

"Hurry we're stopping," she moaned. "There's Gendarmes and ... oh my!

"What?" I panicked.

"Hide! It's him. *Him!* "

"Who?"

"The English Foreign Minister," Beatrice hissed. "Martin Pitt."

It didn't seem likely.

"What's he doing in France?"

"Shut up! He's getting on. Alphonso, into the corridor. He mustn't see you."

With only the briefest glimpse of a suit, some shoulders, slicked black hair and an overfed face, I ducked out of the compartment and slid the door shut. Nearly.

The train juddered to a standstill and exhaled loudly. I heard an outside door swing open, then slam closed. The train remained still. There were no shouts or whistles suggesting departure. A man's voice spoke.

"Beatrice, Celeste. I wished for a private word. I hope you don't mind." The voice was fruity and deep, like a plum cake speaking from the bottom of a mine shaft. There was no immediate reply. "Come, come, you're surely not angry with *me*, your greatest fan?"

Beatrice's voice replied, "What are *you* doing here?"

"A diplomatic mission to smooth over an unfortunate incident that recently took place between myself and the French President."

"It had nothing to do with us."

"I'm certain of it."

"But you put us on this train nonetheless."

"Not me personally. But it has to be said that there was a backlash in the cabinet with regards to people who are—let us say—*not usual*, as a result of the incident, and in the context of what happened with all the locks and tresses, being the daughter of my hairdresser and possessed of two heads made you an obvious scapegoat, especially when the real culprit escaped justice."

Celeste spoke for the first time, "Not our father?"

"Goodness no. Mr. Blink."

"And what have you done with Father?"

"Me? Nothing."

"You, the government, anybody?"

"As far as I am aware, he is at large in the wide world snipping hair and shaving clients, though not at his old premises. He eluded the police—obviously Maxime was wanted for questioning. A warrant was sent out for his arrest, but nobody has come forward with any information."

"How do we know you're telling the truth?" came Beatrice's voice.

"You don't, but it's the facts all the same."

"You still haven't told us why you're here."

"As I said, a diplomatic mission which I accomplished this morning. It happened that I was made aware of this train passing within reach. So I thought it would be pleasant to pay my respects."

Beatrice rumbled on, "Scant respect we've been shown. If we're innocent, we should not be on this train. So presumably we can get off?"

"In many people's eyes—not my own—you are *not* innocent of being a freak and therefore a threat to society."

A dangerous note crept into Beatrice's voice, "We'll never be as much of a freak nor so threatening to society as you."

"Perhaps. But that is not how the rest of society see it. I happen to believe you are a great artist and would dearly like to see you rehabilitated, if that were possible."

"You've just said it isn't."

"There might be a way."

"Ah."

"Yes." After a careful pause the Minister went on, "I'm sure you will not immediately value this solution, but I'll offer it anyhow."

"Go on."

"Marry me."

There was a long silence before Beatrice with something of a choke in her windpipe replied. "No."

Celeste spoke next. "Never."

For myself, I was close to bursting through the door and bawling, 'NOOOOOOOOO!'

"You?" Beatrice sneered.

"Why not. I have long been an admirer of your performances and recordings. I can honestly say I am in love with you."

"How flattering. And just how would being married to you make us acceptable to those who would persecute us for being a freak?"

"I am a respected and conventional public figure. Your being my wife would to some extent normalise your public persona. And I would naturally campaign assiduously to argue that exceptions have to be made for great artists and always have. They are always unconventional. That is the price for masterpieces. You would be free to be yourself in the marriage and pursue your career without interference from me."

"How kind he is," said Beatrice sarcastically to Celeste.

"And how very thoughtful."

"But unfortunately Mr. Pitt, we must turn down your benevolent offer, because we are already engaged to be married to someone else."

A surprised silence fell. A least the silence *felt* surprised from outside in the corridor.

"Engaged?"

"Yes."

"To whom, may I ask?"

"You may not ask. Therefore we may not tell."

Another silence. This one possibly dejected. For there was a sigh.

"Then ladies, I will interrupt your travels no further. A shame, for your genius really should be more widely appreciated and now I regret it probably never will be."

"It might, when we eventually get off this train."

"You won't."

"You could order it."

"Not possible I'm afraid."

"Unless we stick your dirty ring on our finger?"

"I'm sorry you see it that way. You must acknowledge though, that were you to disembark here and now, my conventionality and good name could give no protection. I would also be condemned for liberating a freak and potential terrorist. Were you not my wife, grave personal and political repercussions would result for both of us. I implore you to break this engagement and so let your work, with all its originality and genius, astonish the wide world. Marry me for your own and the public good, for goodness sake."

I own without qualms, that where women are concerned I can be petulant and rash, (perhaps Blinkian traits) and that what happened next was no great testament to my wits. But his plum-pudding voice sounded so convincingly sincere, so reasonable—even though it wasn't—I felt a bolt of anxiety that Celeste and Beatrice might just fall for his blandishments. Yanking the sliding door aside with a hot-headed howl, I shouted,

"*You!* Get out! Get out of here, before I kick you out!"

Which was absurd, given I punched well below my weight. My sudden furious appearance did however cause the Minister's features to look like they'd been hit by an invisible custard pie.

"Who is this?" he spluttered.

"I'm Alphonso Blink!" I spluttered back, "THE Alphonso Blink!"

"Our fiancé," Beatrice smirked.

Celeste just looked worried.

"Then he will be arrested," Minister Pitt spat, rising from where he'd been seated across from the Two Headed Girl.

"He won't!" Celeste uncharacteristically snarled.

And before the man could yell for help, she and Beatrice leapt at him, their hands pressed over his mouth in a desperate attempt to stop him summoning assistance.

"Alphonso, grab him! Hold him down!"

Martin Pitt would undoubtedly have been brawny enough to overwhelm both of us had a wrestling match ensued. But it never came to that. My unconscious had everything under control, except itself. As Beatrice said afterwards, 'it was like his head ejaculated hair.' Without prompting, a voluminous mane gushed from the minister's crown in all directions as if from a fountain and fell writhing about the compartment. The Two-Headed Girl and I stepped back in shock, and quite possibly, had Pitt not gasped hugely at the behaviour of his sprouting coiffure, there might have been time to yelp for the Gendarmes. In the moments after Celeste and Beatrice's hand left his mouth however, a thick rope of black locks wound tightly about his mouth as a gag. At lightning speed, and with the Two-Headed Girl and I goggle-eyed in astonishment, the minister was wrapped—in fact, well-nigh mummified—in a Gordian entanglement of his own dark hair.

As if that weren't extraordinary enough, the eruptions from Pitt's head accelerated from the gushings of a hydrant to blowing his top as if his pate had struck oil. Black curls exploded against the ceiling. Stood in the middle of the compartment we clung to each other and watched locks fall tumbling about us in hordes. Suddenly, we were in a shrinking room. Hair rose animatedly knee-high, waist-high, then shoulder high with an alacrity which had Beatrice and Celeste screaming,

"Alphonso! Stop it!"

"I'm trying!"

My hands were on the minister's barely visible head, attempting to stem the flow, but I couldn't hold it down for a second and spluttered as it sprayed my face. Such was the volume of the Minister's mane, and the speed of its production, that I looked round to see my fiancé almost obliterated by a churning black mass.

"Alphonso! Help!"

The compartment was being stuffed like a cushion. Realising it might become impossible to move and we would be suffocated in a compressed bouffant, I made for the door to alleviate the pressure. But thick, matted filaments had me struggling like a fly in a web, I panicked. Beatrice and Celeste were trying to reach me, screaming my name. Buried in tresses and whimpering breathlessly, I squirmed my hand into solid bolts of hair, feeling desperately for a handle. Where was Maxime with a pair of scissors when you needed him? By stretching and shouldering I eventually touched cold metal and thrust this down. The immense buildup in the carriage burst over two astonished Gendarmes on the platform, who stumbled back beneath a gigantic wave of hair hurled violently from the door. Like hirsute projectile vomit, a torrent of dark locks followed, blurting from the compartment in impossible amounts, with myself, borne helplessly on top. In a dizzied, upside-down moment, carried as if by a whirling ocean current, I saw entangled Gendarmes and rail staff attempting a hasty withdrawal. Dumped amidst burgeoning coils on the platform and spitting the taste of shampoo from my mouth, I heard the yells of Celeste and Beatrice being borne likewise from the carriage on several more bulldozing surges. Their wailing body fetched up nearby whilst the minister's once carefully-combed locks continued hurtling from the carriage door, engulfing the station platform in a dark and tumbling lava. Gigantic bushels of black hair churned over everything in sight. It was like experiencing an earthquake or tsunami, an unnatural disaster of heart-pounding enormity. Would the Minister's out-of-control barnet consume everything for miles?

On their hands and knees, Beatrice and Celeste negotiated monstrous curls, to help free me from knots and tangles.

"*Alphonso! Tell it to keep growing.*"

"What?" I yelled.

"Then it will stop!"

"It's nothing to do with me!" I gasped staggering knee-deep in black strands.

"Except that it completely and utterly IS!" Beatrice shouted back, whilst she and Celeste hauled me out of a wardrobe-sized quiff. Some distance off, a Gendarme was grappling with hairy bondage as if with the tentacles of a giant octopus.

Dragging each other, hand in hand, the Two-Headed Girl and I stumbled mewling past smothered cars towards the station exit. Hair was everywhere. I felt like a nit on a giant's head. My last glimpse of the Gendarmes and officials was of them piling into a ticket office and trying to shut the door. Reaching the road, we stole one last look at the blanketing curls in our wake. Every carriage of the train was plaited in humungous knots. Surely I couldn't have caused something so *big*? But then losing the Two-Headed Girl would have been bigger.

"Look!" Celeste cried pointing at a sign.

Gare d'Ifs

"Why me?" I wailed, before my hand was tugged and we were gone, pelting down a French country road, leaving an epic surrealist calamity at our heels. My only prayer was that Minister Pitt's rug would not engulf the entirety of France, because the little I'd seen looked nice.

Sixteen   *Plums*

Not having had much practice at long-distance running, the Two-Headed Girl was breathless less than a mile from the scenes of follicular devastation.

"The whole world will descend on this place once news leaks out," Beatrice wheezed, "and we'll never get far enough away on foot."

"Behind that farmhouse there's a horse," I observed a little desperately.

"Even better," said Celeste, "There's a 2CV in the yard."

I didn't see how that could help us.

"It's pink." Beatrice objected.

Under normal circumstances, *so she said*, Celeste wasn't the sort to hotwire a 2CV, but as we sped along on the wrong but right side of the road, an explanation followed.

"I forgot to say," said Beatrice dryly, "that after giving up on being a policewoman, she wanted to be a mechanic."

"I don't know why I was so interested in it."

"Me neither,"

"That was before I learned the guitar. I wanted to be good at *something*. You were always so amazing at everything."

"I wasn't amazing at standing by a car whilst my body was commandeered by a garage hand. But then show me someone who is."

"Anyhow," Celeste went on, "Maxime bought a CV2 and together we dismantled the engine whilst he explained what was what, then reassembled it."

"About as much fun as it sounds."

"You could have learned too."

"Yes, if it hadn't been incredibly boring and messy. There was oil all over my hands and I wasn't even doing it. Celeste got black smudges of oil *everywhere*."

"We were wearing dungarees."

"Not on my nose."

"You touched it, not me."

"*We* touched it. A big smear that wouldn't come off."

Celeste winced at the memory. "There was a 'falling out', so I had to learn about pistons and carburetors from books. If Beatrice was in a really good mood, she'd let me tinker under a bonnet for half an hour. I hotwired our 2CV a few times after reading how. Connect a positive wire from the starter to the coil ..."

"Okay, okay. You are to be commended dear fellow-head for commandeering this vehicle," Beatrice remarked, "and I am proud to be sharing the same body with one of such resource and daring ..."

"However?"

"Keep your eyes on the road ..."

"*You're* driving as well."

"Not really, I always leave that to you, with your interest in the minutiae of automobile propulsion. Do you realise incidentally that we are driving on the French side of the road but that your head is on the English side of our body?"

"Shall we get back to 'however'?"

"However, do you know where we are?"

"France."

"Quite a big place by all accounts. And whereabouts in it are we heading?"

"*Le Chateau Sans Passe.*"

"So do you know how to get there?"

"No, but dearest fellow head, I felt our first concern was to get extremely far from the train with a toupee. Once at a safe distance, we can find a map book, work out our co-ordinates and plot a route to the chateau."

"Just to look at the finer details: where will we get the map book as we possess not a centime?"

"Steal one from a map book shop? It seems a natural next step."

"Would not a two-headed thief be conspicuous?"

"Yes."

"And Alphonso can hardly march into a map book emporium and shove a Michelin guide up his shirt without a smattering of the language."

"You don't have to speak French to be a thief."

"True, but suppose he is seen pilfering the book and has to bluff his way out of the situation with only the gibberish of his native tongue? Moreover, we are driving a stolen vehicle. The authorities will doubtless soon put two and two together when a car is reported missing from nearby a certain railway station. By morning, this pink CV2, and its numberplate will be on a 'wanted' poster. And having not a sou, what will we eat?"

"Your point being?"

"That having no map book, no legal transport and no money, we are fucked."

Celeste nodded. "Yes. But it's not my fault."

"No. It's bloody Alphonso's."

"Sorry."

"But we can't blame him because we love him so much and the hairy carnage he caused was undoubtedly his unconscious barging in to save us. I mean, did you do it deliberately?"

"No!" I cried from the passenger seat. "I did nothing. Least of all long for his head to spout copious amounts of hair."

"Fascinating. But deep inside, you did want us to escape from Minister Pitt and the train."

"I suppose."

"Might it be then, the first instance of your unconscious doing something you wanted in conscious life?"

"Maybe."

"Then perhaps all the training on the train, worked after all."

I doubted it.

"Where are we going now?" Beatrice asked Celeste who was steering the car onto a narrow track.

"I'm thinking that if we follow minor, minor roads, there will be more chance of finding an abandoned ruin where we can hide until the predicament our adorable fiancé has landed us in is resolved."

"We can't complain," Beatrice reflected, "It was the most awe-inspiring event I've ever witnessed. We shall tell our two-headed children, that once upon a time daddy covered an entire train in hair." She smiled, "Fancy being engaged to someone even weirder than we are, Celeste."

"I really never did think it would happen."

We motored on through the headlit night, rejecting any number of derelict buildings, for being too derelict in their dereliction or for having underelict neighbours. Only in the first blushes of dawn did the pink CV2 bump unsteadily past a signpost saying *la-Haut* and, taking a road with a grassy Mohican, come to a profusion of ivy with a roof. We pulled into a cobbled yard of weeds.

"Voila."

In some countries a ruined house can look unsightly and depressing, but in France dilapidation is invariably charming, the very place you'd want to stay for a weekend to watch rain dripping in through the roof. Here, the chimney was wonky, shutters rotten, and an iron railing had come loose from a balcony wall and leaned away in precarious suspension.

The front door being surprisingly stout and locked, I clambered through a broken window into a kitchen of lawless brambles, nettles and ivy. Upstairs was better. There was a bedroom, dry but for where a broken skylight had rotted floorboards to make a perilous trapdoor into the room below. For some reason, there were three antique sewing machines in one corner, but also a cast iron bed and upon it a mattress with protruding springs.

"Perfect," sighed Beatrice.

I knew what she meant.

Whilst the car was secreted in a sunken-roofed barn (a collapsed souffle of stone and corrugated iron), I covered our wheel tracks into the yard. It felt like the ruin was on its knees praying for a new owner to scatter cash in handfuls and grow a new farm. We then returned to the bedroom and fell on the bed, exhausted.

When I woke, it must have been mid-afternoon, and the Two-Headed Girl was standing beside the bed, the hem of her jumper lifted to form a bulging pouch.

Beatrice spoke with mocking reverence, "Good morrow Alphonso Blink, fiancé extraordinaire, afflicter of Foreign Minister's follicles, King of Weirdness, it is your Queen, bearing a late breakfast."

"Plums."

A plum was dropped onto my midriff.

"Plums. Plums. Plums."

Several more were lobbed onto the same place.

"And furthermore, plums."

They let the rest of their jumper-full, cascade onto the bed beside me.

"From a tree outside the barn," Beatrice explained.

I examined and bit into one of the fruit.

Celeste added, "A plum tree we think."

"Or an apple tree that's just very, very confused."

"Mmmm." They were sweet and succulent.

My fiancé perched on the bed with only twenty plums separating us.

"We have sat upon the back doorstep, spitting out stones in deep rumination of our next move and Beatrice thinks you should learn French."

I looked doubtful.

The dark-haired one explained, "You could then Alphonso, walk amongst normal people without suspicion to buy bread and cheese and map books."

"But," Celeste frowned, "I think there are only so many plums on the tree and that we will starve to death long before you become fluent enough for the market. Even if we had some money, which we don't."

"He could sell plums. And I've heard of people learning French in a weekend."

"Preposterous. Five years of weekends maybe."

"Alphonso might be a natural linguist. His extraordinary unconscious might decide to learn the entire French language in an hour. And Celeste, you do not have a better plan."

"No."

"We're in complete limbo here until we at least steal a map book. We can't ask a local where we are. We've got two heads and Alphonso's a monoglot. If we don't give him French lessons, what else can we do except eat plums and have sex?"

"We've had the plums."

Their methods were unorthodox but hard to forget, which is, *fin de journée* all one really requires of a French teacher. So, after some basic study, ie *Je cherche une carte de France,* we progressed to a point-and-speak type of instruction, "*Fesses. Teton. Seins.*"

I repeated this, but added, "My question here as a zealous student, would be to learn under what circumstances, on entering a shop to purchase a map, I would need to know the word for buttocks, nipple or breast?"

There *were* other approaches to learning.

CELESTE: Repeat, *Celeste est la femme la plus belle et la plus intelligente du monde.* It doesn't really matter what it means so long as you know it by heart.

BEATRICE: And also this, although it's bad French, *Mais, pas aussi belle et intelligente que Béatrice, car elle est hors de ce monde.*

Worryingly, progress was escargot-like.

"What's French for 'Definitely not enough plums?'"

We cleared the kitchen of briars to find a range with cracked hobs and a broken oven door. There was also an armchair and table coated in white dust like flour. Behind the house, there lay a gloomy pond where *la peche* were rising, but as we lacked a pole, line and hook they were unable to join us for dinner. Doubtless they would have tasted dismal as their watery habitat. Our evening meal was a plum, sorrel and dandelion-leaf salad instead. Eaten in troubled silence.

Next morning I was turning on an uncomfortable mattress when the Two-Headed Girl appeared breathless at the doorway.

"Alphonso, come quickly," Beatrice gasped. "See what your clever wife-to-be has discovered,"

"What?"

"He means *dites moi.*"

"Follow your clever wife-to-be ..."

"Or future epouse ..."

" ... into the great outdoors and be amazed. Etonne! Ravi!"

"Must I?"

Two hands yanked me up.

"Oui!"

They danced across the courtyard and led me behind the barn to a patch of waist-high, disordered weeds, enclosed by four ancient walls.

"The old kitchen garden. We found herbs: bay, sage, marjoram, thyme."

"There's a peach tree trained up this wall. The fruit isn't ripe yet though."

"Some rogue leeks over here."

I followed them along a path they'd beaten with a stick.

"But best of all, down in this corner ... *See!*"

And there, where regiments of nettles had been hacked aside, nestled a small crop of suitcases. Wild luggage obviously.

"We thought you'd better pick them."

"There's six."

"Seven."

"Oh yes. But three of them are only small."

"Perhaps not ripe."

"The biggest one at the back is practically a trunk though."

I scrutinized the plants which were larger-leaved than those I had met in England. A continental variety obviously. The handle of the nearest was even embossed with: *modèles portables*. Kneeling before the unharvested produce, I smoothed dirt from the leather sides of the nearest case and snapped it from a stalk that was thick and hairy. Like a courgette's.

"Please don't let it be a shepherdess costume inside," Beatrice begged.

I ignored her, sprang the clasps and lifted the lid. The interior was filled with half-eaten croissants, rolls of masking tape, seven used wine corks and a photograph of the Pompidou Centre.

"Weird," Celeste breathed, then recoiled from a proffered croissant. "Urgh."

"It's okay," I reassured and tore into the pastry. "That's just how they grow. Delicious. So fresh. Still warm."

"Mmmm." Beatrice agreed. "I'll eat for both of us Celeste. Fill you up."

There was no resisting the promise of the trunk. Its hinges squealed when I pushed the lid back to look eagerly inside. Inevitably it was empty except for a large spider at the bottom. "Oh."

We were completely deflated.

"Hardly worth growing."

"Like a pod with no peas in it."

"Huh. It's disappointing that the largest one has nothing in it."

"Though that's often the way."

I hastily moved on to another case. This was at least packed with clothes. A long brown dress and an apron ...

"No!" Celeste asserted, snatching them away.

"Urgh." Beatrice held the dress at arm's length. "We're not wearing it either."

Apart from a moth-eaten bonnet, there were also filthy trousers, an old collarless shirt, flea-bitten jacket, barely serviceable boots, long johns and a cap. After some moments of further deflation, I recognized a French farmer's outfit for what it was. *"Men's clothes*! If they fit." For I still stood in garb sourced from my fiancé's wardrobe.

Disinterested in watching me size fetid garments against myself, they investigated another case.

"Matches! That's at least useful," beamed Beatrice.

"More croissants."

The rest looked like miscellaneous junk. A stone. A flowerpot. Numerous rusty cans of spray paint."

"Twelve cans. All green."

Finally a book written in French on caring for sheep.

"It's okay," Celeste reassured, "You won't be able to read it for years."

"I was hoping for a few million francs," Beatrice grumbled.

The next case was the smallest but it didn't matter, they lifted a three-inch book from the interior.

"Maps of France!"

"The print's miniscule."

"Harvested prematurely."

"Just about legible. Wonderful what you can grow in this climate."

Beatrice laughed delightedly, "It IS your unconscious Alphonso. It's trying to help. You know when you can't solve a problem and then you sleep on it and in the morning the answer just comes to you. This is your answer."

"What is?"

"I don't know. Something in the cases. At least if we squint, we might find out where we are. There's two left."

"It's like Christmas." Celeste breathed excitedly, "Open the smallest first."

"Ow!" they both yelled.

Beatrice rubbed their arm, "Fucking nettle."

The second last, no larger than a vanity case was delved into. It might just as well have been empty for there was only a handful of centimes inside.

Beatrice groaned, "Left to ripen, it might have grown into wads of one-thousand franc notes."

"One left."

"I guess if it's empty it means my unconscious is as clueless as the rest of me."

"*It will be the answer,*" Beatrice maintained.

The case contained a pot of white enamel paint and a pot of black. And a small brush. Celeste grew suddenly excited.

"*The paints!*"

I shrugged, "Yes?"

"It's a car disguise kit."

"*What?* Oh no." Beatrice sighed, guessing her future. "Drat your unconscious Alphonso."

For the rest of that day, we worked on the car's new identity and my own. The clothes were washed, wrung out and draped on a wall to dry, then the Citroen's windows, mirrors, trim and door handles were masked for spraying. The number plates were whited over and counterfeit numerals neatly painted in in black. On a break from these labours Celeste and Beatrice studied the midget map book.

"It would help if it said somewhere – *you are here.*"

"You can't expect a poor plant to think of everything," I pointed out.

"We know the station," Celeste mumbled. "That's clearly marked. And we know what the signpost said on the road which pointed us this way."

"We picked the suitcase too soon." Beatrice pored over the map. "Another couple of days and it would have been big enough to read properly. What's that place in red?"

"According to my calculations we must be in about this radius, if Alphonso's map book is honest."

"It's nothing to do with me."

"You keep saying that," Beatrice observed, "and it always is. But look Cel, that hill is called *tu est ici*."

"It's just a place called *you are here*."

"So why is it in red?"

"Surely that's a bit much even for Alphonso? Anyhow we can't be only thirty odd miles from the station. We drove for ages."

"In circles probably."

Celeste looked thoughtful. "I suppose it's the book's location even more than ours – it *was* grown here. So maybe we shouldn't be surprised if …" A few minutes later she was pointing at a tiny page. "Look, we're about a hundred and fifty miles from the *Chateau Sans Passe*. More if we have to dodge a few towns to get there. Still, we could do it in a night. If we drive during the day, motorists coming in the opposite direction would probably notice our surplus head."

"Yours."

"*Yours.*"

"Please don't argue."

"We're not," Beatrice replied, "We're agreeing that we have a surplus head."

"If we leave the car out in the sun to dry now, we could go tonight."

For our evening meal, we chanced a fire in the crocked range and made, amidst clouds of smoke, a soup of leeks, herbs, nettles and plums with croissant croutons. Then, when daylight began to slowly abandon the house, so did we, in a not-pink *deux-chevaux*.

Seventeen *Aunts*

It took longer to reach the *Chateau Sans Passe* than anticipated, partly because we used minor roads to avoid detection, but also our miniature map could not be read by the interior light which necessitated frequent stops to use one of the car's bulbous-eyed headlamps. Otherwise, our journey was uneventful and mercifully gendarme-free. By the time we reached the chateau's poplar-lined driveway, sunbeams were brimming over the horizon. Temporarily blinded, it was a few moments before we noticed a man in a garish cyclist costume, pedaling along the avenue of trees ahead of us, on a square wheeled bike.

At our approach the rider pulled over and dismounted to stare at us. There came a scream of recognition from Celeste and the car skidded to a halt. The Two-Headed Girl leapt out and ran to Maxime almost knocking him down with their relieved embrace.

"Oh daddy, daddy, daddy daddy, daddy!" wept Celeste. "You're okay!"

"My dears!" The man staggered. "Alphonso," he gasped. "Hello again, would you please hold my bike so I can ..."

He needed two hands to contain the enthusiastic hugs of his daughter. But it was at this moment that something niggled me about Maxime. Though his moustache and centre-parted hair were jet-black as before, the cycling costume, revealed hairs on his legs that were grey. Even white. This little vanity might not have discombobulated me had he lain the bicycle on the grass verge without care to receive his daughter's attentions. Instead, he called it 'his bike' and gripped the handlebars preciously until I took over. Old square wheels was *my bike* wasn't it? Or at least, if not mine, then ... And then I knew. Watching the joyous family reunion, the truth went through me like a thunderbolt through Frankenstein. I was struck by the blindingly obvious: Maxime was not Maxime at all. *He was my grandfather* – Alphonso Blink. The Great Alphonso, riding the bike he had himself invented. In which case (here I fumbled and almost dropped his contraption), the Two-Headed Girl was my Auntie.

My mind boggled. I must have stood for several seconds gaping and making incoherent noises to myself. The situation was surely impossible? Alphonso knew who I was. *They* knew who I was. Did they not know who *he* was? It was the sort of imbroglio that could only happen to me. Calm departed, slamming every door as it ran off incoherently babbling. I needed to talk to the man because ... because ... because their embrace was disentangling itself as father and daughter remembered I was there and Celeste was breaking our catastrophic news,

"Daddy, you'll never guess. We're going to marry Alphonso! We're engaged!"

To my astonishment, his face lit up.

"Because he's even weirder than we are," Beatrice explained sardonically.

Maxime, or whoever he was, took my free hand in both his and beamed, "That's wonderful. Absolutely wonderful. Of all news this is the best. I've been reading about your exploits in *Le Monde* my boy. You're the ideal husband for my girl. You'll make a perfect trio."

What was he talking about? He must have known we could never be married under the circumstances. Unbelievably they seemed not to notice I was dazed.

"Just why are you wearing that absurd outfit daddy?" Beatrice asked.

"I'm in training for the Tour. I'll tell you all about it over a brioche or two."

Somehow, I'd have to try to act normally—hard enough at the best of times—and then corner the Great Alphonso to find out what on earth was going on. Until then, I could only try to rewind my life to a point before Maxime's exposure. Being in the *Le Chateau Sans Passe* would hardly help.

"Get back in your car and drive up to the house. Georges and I have been expecting you, he'll be delighted to see the girls again, and also to meet Alphonso. I'll tag along behind and we'll meet up on the terrace for breakfast."

The *Chateau Sans Passe* was not as its name suggested, a gothic monstrosity in need of exorcism. In fact, the drive rounded a corner to bisect geometrical gardens leading up to a small country house of straw-blonde stone and roofs of red tile. At each corner of the building were squared towers with yellow shuttered windows. The effect was of a residence with nothing to hide, rejoicing in a sunny and innocent architectural aesthetic.

Hearing the car pull up, Georges Dupont emerged to meet us, hugging Celeste and Beatrice, who had visited previously on holidays. He was in his early forties with a wiry, cyclist's build and features chiselled from something softer than granite. My discomfort deepened when he shook my hand, the one that had once felt the top of his wife's thigh at the Umbrella Club. We were led round to a terrace where Georges seated us at a table. He was teasing out our story over breakfast, when Maxime or Alphonso or whoever he was, joined us, garbed once more in a suit.

"There you are," welcomed Georges, "I've heard congratulations are in order." He popped the cork from a bottle of champagne.

I half expected Maxime to confess all then and there, but he only lifted a glass of fizz and smiled, "To a long and happy marriage."

"Don't you drink?" Georges asked, noticing my inaction during the toast.

I took a gulp.

"Poor Alphonso," Celeste sympathised, "He's only taken one bite from his croissant. Are you worried about being in hot water with the gendarmes?"

"I suppose our getting married here, might draw the unwanted attention of the authorities onto us," I improvised feebly.

Maxime chuckled. "Not at all. The government are delighted with you. Listen to this from the front page of yesterday's *Le Monde*:

Another Bad Hair Day for the British Foreign Minister.

The English Foreign Minister handed in his resignation today after his hair once again went out-of-control in the presence of something Gallic. Deported by the French government, opposition parties in his own country denounced him as the weirdest person in England and possibly the world, and an embarrassment to a government that was clamping down in the name of patriotism on people being 'different'. It goes on to say that whilst the Minister blamed what had happened on Alphonso Blink's mysterious appearance and that of a deported Two-Headed Girl, the Gendarmes and rail staff present noticed that these two people appeared to be just as terrified as everyone else by the Minister's erupting hair and were therefore unlikely to have caused it. It does go on to suggest however that you stole a pink Citroen 2CV. But that's a peccadillo."

This had the small comfort of leaping from a frying pan into the inferno of marrying my Aunt. What would Beatrice and Celeste say when they found out? I wanted to crawl off under the table, snatch the square wheeled bicycle and ride and ride and ride not stopping till I reached the Pyrenees.

"So you need not worry Alphonso, providing nobody discovers the car,"

"And even that was me," Celeste reassured.

"You will find yourself celebrated rather than pilloried by the French. They found the entire affair hilarious. Now, you must regale us with your side of the story. We are agog."

Beatrice frowned, "Father, I don't wish to be rude ..."

"But to break the habits of a lifetime, deeply ingrained ..."

"Well, I just wanted to ask, before we tell you everything, if perhaps you aren't a bit old to enter the tour unless there's a middle-aged section?"

"How sensitively you put it. Don't blame me, my girl, blame the contraption itself. Though I met the Great Alphonso only infrequently, I know from your fiancé here that the square-wheeled bicycle was designed to win the Tour de-France. Meeting it in the salon I realised this sentient velocipede had been left in a shed for years pining to accomplish what it had been fabricated for. I gave our Alphonso here this address, in the hope that Georges might help the bicycle find a rider and achieve its ambition. The first episode of the Minister's hair intervened. Forewarned of my impending arrest as the culprit, I drove to the Umbrella Club to whisk you away to safety. It never occurred to me that Alphonso would be implicated."

"I betrayed him," said Beatrice, "for getting you into trouble. And ourselves."

"Arriving at the club, I found police entering the building and, too late to help, was forced to dodge into the park to escape detection. There, hiding in the bushes, I found the bike and escaped on it, intending to wage a legal battle for your release from France. On that journey I discovered the bicycle was of such a revolutionary design, that even someone of my advanced years might compete at the highest level, a least to the point of winning a stage or time trial. My enquiries on arrival here, revealed that Alphonso had escaped and that you my dearest ones had been deported on a train of indefinite duration. In which case there was nothing I could do but mourn and hope you might escape by your own irrepressible wits. Partly to take my mind off it all, I started to train for the Tour, getting my entry processed with Georges' help. Then the news exploded with the second story of the Foreign Minister's hair. Now it's your turn."

And so the breakfast went interminably on. I just about managed to finish the croissant, chewing it as enthusiastically as cardboard. Celeste and Beatrice gave an abridged and thankfully censored account of our adventures and then at last the meeting was adjourned and Georges took us inside.

"I suppose if they are to be married, they can share a room," he said jovially to Maxime.

"Of course, this is no time for prudishness."

We were shown into a bedroom of gentle simplicity, which like the rest of chateau interior was of pale stone, exposed throughout. Moments later, my fiancé and myself were alone.

"What's wrong?" asked Beatrice, dark eyes deeply concerned. "Something's bothering you."

Two faces searched my own.

Having worked out that they couldn't possibly know their father was my grandfather, I felt it imperative to speak to him first. "I can't say."

Celeste looked worried. "Something really *is* wrong. Tell us Alphonso."

They took my hand in theirs.

"I have to speak to your father about something, that's all."

Beatrice spoke comfortingly, "He's really happy about our engagement. We can tell."

"I know."

"So?"

"I'm sorry. Just at this moment …"

Celeste kissed my cheek tenderly, at which being on the verge of tears, I helplessly said what I couldn't say,

"Your father is my grandfather."

They looked at me like *I* had two heads.

"What?"

"Maxime? Your *grandfather*?" Beatrice snorted.

"He's not Maxime. He's Alphonso Blink. The Great Alphonso. An inventor."

The two heads laughed.

"How could he be?" Celeste reassured, "He's been Maxime all our lives."

"He's right," came a voice from the door. "Sorry, I should have knocked, but I couldn't help overhearing as I approached."

"Daddy?" said two voices in unison.

He gravely entered, "Yes and no." He seated himself on the bed. "Celeste and Beatrice, forgive me." He rubbed his brow awkwardly. "Alphonso has guessed my real identity. I am indeed his grandfather Alphonso Blink and also your adoptive father."

The two-headed girl looked like she was going to keel over into my arms.

"This really *is* weird," gasped Celeste.

"Then who is our *real* father?" Beatrice asked, stunned.

"Maxime. He was arrested and immediately deported for using an uninventing machine borrowed from me outside a nuclear processing plant. He was a passionate supporter of CND and was trying to disinvent the splitting of the atom. As a result he was put on a train of infinite duration. He didn't know at the time that your mother was pregnant, otherwise he might have been less rash. He pretended to be Alphonso Blink in an attempt to protect me, so the authorities would believe the threat I posed to the state with uninventing, had gone forever. And in a way, also I think, he wanted to let me be Maxime."

"Why?"

"Because he was my best friend. And because I had fallen in love with Georgetta and Bryony and they with me." There was a horrible silence. "It was a love quadrangle and in the most ridiculous way, he stood aside. The Two-Headed Woman and I lived almost happily for a few years. But Maxime's loss wore away at us both. Ironically, his sacrifice undermined our love. Georgetta and Bryony continually argued with each other about which of them was responsible for what happened. Eventually, she went in search of Maxime's train, fully expecting to return, for she, like myself, was devoted to you both. I woke one morning to find a note on the table asking me to look after you while she was gone. But she never came back. Leaving me to bring you up."

"Couldn't Grandmother have helped?" I asked.

"We separated acrimoniously. I was honest about my love for Georgetta and Bryony."

There was just enough pause for a dustpan and brush.

"So, if my fiancé is not my aunt then ..."

Beatrice laughed, "... the Law cannot prohibit us finishing your sentences in a state of holy matrimony."

Which was a relief. Maxime meanwhile resumed, "I'm sorry, Celeste and Beatrice, I didn't tell you before. When was the right moment? When she left and you were barely a toddler? When you were seven or eight or mid-teens? I was always bothered about how it might affect the delicate balance between you. It has come out now. So perhaps this is the right moment."

"Perhaps it is," said Beatrice.

There was a long but not difficult silence.

"The thing is," my grandfather said eventually, "to continue as the uninventing Alphonso would not have been safe for us, I might easily have been caught, deported and then who would look after you? Also a very ignoble part of me hoped Bryony and Georgetta might return without

Maxime so we could all live together, for being your father, and your mother's lover, was and still is, the great adventure of my life. So continuing as Maxime the hairdresser, seemed the sensible thing to do, not rocking the boat. The thought of anything happening to you has long been my greatest nightmare. I would have fought the police to rescue you, in the Umbrella Club, had I not met first, Alphonsos of assorted vintage messing about in a park playground on my square-wheeled bike. They assured me everything was going to turn out okay."

"They're not allowed to do that!" I burst out indignantly, "Did they tell you what was going to happen?"

"They said only that I need not fear it, not least because I'd then not appreciate all the other amazing things that would occur and that I might as well pedal off to Dover. Being reunited with the bike, I was able to make amends for abandoning it for so long in a Blink Castle workshop. I realised it was owed another shot at the Tour. That brought me here to this moment of truth."

The Two-Headed Girl went and sat beside him on the bed.

"Daddy," Celeste bit her lip, "Thank you for telling us all that."

They took his hand in theirs and squeezed it.

Beatrice said, "You've been Maxime our father for so long now, it seems silly to stop just because you didn't provide one titchy little sperm to start us off. You did everything else."

At which point, I got up and quietly left the room.

Our engagement did not last long, wedding bells cut it drastically short. And if Maxime's confession (the name was kept to avoid confusions) disturbed Celeste and Beatrice, they did not show it. Worrying, obviously, was not their longest suit. For instance, it never once occurred to them to question if marriage to me was sensible?

We were sitting in our bedroom, the date set, with me trying to write an invitation to my mum and dad, when Beatrice said, "By the way, we're keeping the 2CV. We might need it for the honeymoon. We can pay the owners back when some money arrives from somewhere."

Which left me fretting, "Like where? Have you actually thought through," I asked, "how hopeless I am? No qualifications. No skills. No income. No savings. About as useful as soap that doesn't lather."

"No." Beatrice replied.

"When I went to the job centre in England," I continued, "there was not a single vacancy I could fill. How am I going to support you?"

"By coming to our gigs."

"What gigs?"

"If you carry on learning the language, we can stay in France. We're not unwelcome here. Celeste and myself can write songs in French and perform them. We don't want to stop composing and playing music."

"You could be our roadie," Celeste suggested. "If you developed some muscles."

"Chip in with the occasional suitcase full of centimes and half-eaten patisseries."

"We're fine with it if you are."

Worryingly, I was and returned to my missive.

Dear Mum and Dad,

This letter is to invite you to my wedding which will be in France. Quite short notice, I know, but it wasn't me who set the date, it was my fiancé. The letter before this may have given the impression that I was going to marry a policewoman and make a go of normal life under the pseudonym of Tom Davies. None of which happened. In fact, that attempt to stop being Alphonso Blink failed miserably. But then you know that already, as you will have read the news about my covering a train in France with the Foreign Minister's hair. In the course of that adventure I met and fell in love with a young woman with two heads. It is she, Beatrice and Celeste, that I am going to marry, and if you would like to attend the ceremony, please see the invitation card attached. I will understand if you do not wish to come. At some date in the future I will try to refund the money you loaned to me to change my name, but only after paying for a car we stole.

Much love and best wishes. Alphonso.

They didn't respond.

My grandfather was training hard, but we still found time to catch up. He wasn't at all bothered about having to flee the country on account of my hair-raising misdeeds. Seated together on a garden bench one evening, I spoke of our first meeting,

"So you knew all the time who I was?"

"Of course. The moment I saw Square Wheels. Besides, you look so Blinkian. I couldn't let you go without knowing what you and the bicycle were cooking up. It was hard not to laugh shaving your legs."

"Hmph."

"But I didn't expect Beatrice and Celeste to come in. Nor that you would fall for each other."

I spoke to him of my days at the Castle, of his inventions everywhere, gathering dust.

"She hasn't got rid of them at least," he mused, massaging a calf.

"Gran seemed very proud to show them off."

"I'd like to go back one day," he confided glum-faced, "if she'd let me in. I can't blame her for chucking a chamber pot over me. We had children of ten and twelve when I left. I did *try* to return, admittedly after Georgetta and Bryony were gone, but she pulled the drawbridge up in my face. The terrible thing is, if I travelled back in time, I'd do almost exactly the same again. Because the Two-Headed Woman was the most astonishing person I ever met and for two years we were in love. Her daughter is just as astonishing. How can I regret spending my life with them? It was selfish hurting your grandmother, John and Esmeralda, I know. The truth is I'm just an extremely selfish man."

He moved onto the other calf.

"I'd like Grannie to come to the wedding though, if you don't mind," I said.

The massage stopped. "To see you married to the daughter of the woman I left her for?" he snorted. "She won't come."

"Why not?"

"Because what I did was unforgivable."

She did.

But the owner of the Umbrella Club arrived first. Jacqueline sat next to me at dinner and to my relief didn't say *so what happened to your first wife*? Nor place my hand on her bare thigh. Doubtless due to her husband being seated opposite. In fact, she behaved as if we'd never met.

"So you actually visited my club the night of the police raid, when Celeste and Beatrice were arrested?" she asked mischievously.

"Yes, it was an amazing show."

"Wonderful. That you visited, I mean, not that you were all handcuffed and taken away. I hope the staff made you feel welcome."

"They did. Especially the bouncer."

"He didn't make the police welcome. He punched several of them. It's very drab at the Umbrella Club without your fiancés performing," she lamented,

"And I don't think we can return any time soon," I sighed, "My actions seem to have caused an avalanche of legislation to stamp out 'difference'."

"I wouldn't worry about it," Maxime remarked, "By the law of unintended consequences, any action, especially an extreme one, will eventually provoke the very opposite of what it first set out to achieve."

"And you became engaged on a train of indefinite duration?" Jacqueline continued, "How romantic. Better than the Orient Express."

The day before the nuptials, Grandma Blink arrived in an open-topped car driven by Aunt Esmeralda who parped the horn until I came galloping down the Chateau steps to envelop them both in my arms.

"Hello Grannie, Grannie, Grannie, Grannie,"

"Hello Alphonso."

"Auntie, Auntie, Auntie, Auntie."

"My dear nephew, we meet again."

"Thank you for coming so far."

"We thought we'd drop by." Aunt Esmeralda fitted a broad-brimmed hat of many plumes onto her head. "We only live next door. Nationally speaking. And here is father."

Maxime came down the steps and went straight to my grandmother. "Welcome Imogen, I'm delighted to see you." He reached out tentatively with both hands and gratefully received both hers.

"Hello Maxime."

There was a slight grimace, before he replied. "Only to avoid confusion with our grandson."

Which brought a small look of confusion to my grandmother's face. She looked at me searchingly for a moment, just as we were joined by the Two-Headed Girl, Jacqueline and Georges. There were more welcomes and introductions.

"This is the bride-to-be, Beatrice and Celeste. Beatrice and Celeste: Imogen. Alphonso's Grandmother and so, my wife."

Again, my grandmother looked taken aback. She stammered brittle *bon-bons* before we were led through the house and onto the terrace for lunch. Here, Maxime, Jacqueline and Georges enquired of Imogen about the rigours of the journey, whilst some feet away Beatrice whispered to Esmeralda,

"Last time we met, you were our Auntie, but we should tell you that quite recently you've become more a step-sister."

Esmeralda looked surprised. "Oh. Then a certain feline is out of a certain sack?"

"A few days ago, our fiancé guessed what we didn't know ourselves."

"I see." Esmeralda shot a glance at me and then my grandmother who, looking stiff, was at that very moment leading Maxime down some steps and around a bush into the garden. "This information was omitted from the invitation. The situation is therefore a little delicate. I'm now here to see a step-sister wedded to my nephew. How wonderfully odd. But I wonder if my mother will see it quite that way. Oh dear Alphonso."

"Perhaps I should go and tell her that it was me putting two and two together—the bicycle and his grey-haired legs."

Esmeralda looked thoughtful. "Go. She might stay calm if you're there."

Celeste frowned, "It's an unfortunate accident that's all. You see, myself and Beatrice insisted on sending out the invites."

Esmeralda nodded, "Perhaps though, he could have foreseen ...."

"He did, and we told him not to worry."

"Oh. Very well. Even so he could have waited to tell her what had happened, before introducing her as his wife."

"But then you two wouldn't have known all we now know when we were introduced." Beatrice argued. "That wouldn't have been comfortable either, retrospectively. It's a good thing that it's all out in the open. We *are* in Le Chateau Sans Passe. Anyhow ..."

Their conversation drifted out of earshot because I had hurried, in as casual a manner possible, to the terrace steps and down into the garden. Behind a boxwood hedge there were already raised voices.

"... but can't you see that in their eyes I'm arriving not as Alphonso's nice little old grannie, but the wife you jilted for their mother and all the dynamite that situation contains for each of us. Especially me."

"Imogen, I'm sorry, so sorry. The timing was incredibly unfortunate. But Celeste and Beatrice are wonderful, they won't see you in relation to their own mother ..."

"I could see Mrs. Second Best in their eyes the moment we were introduced. Obviously they know their mother could not have been anything but anathema to me, and that you abandoned our children for a child made in her own image who is now marrying another Alphonso Blink I love."

Here, stepping round the hedge, I intervened. "Grannie, please, it's my fault.

"It is *not*."

She glared formidably.

"But I guessed accidentally that Maxime was my grandfather and couldn't hide my upset to Beatrice and Celeste, as it would have meant the marriage was off. When I could barely kiss them, they dragged it out of me."

"I bet they did."

"So grandfather *had* to tell them and you weren't forewarned because ..."

Hands on hips she fumed, "Because there was no forewarning when he ran off with their mother either. We were due to go on a European Tour the next day. Forewarning is not your grandfather's forte. Perhaps he should have told them what a skunk he was, years earlier and we wouldn't be in this situation now."

"Imogen *please*," Maxime whispered. "Calm down,"

"I won't calm down. Calming down is for doormats. And you are not going to wipe your feet on me all over again. I've had enough of your revolting company and I've only been here half an hour. I should never have let Esmeralda persuade me to come." And with that she turned abruptly and strode back towards the terrace.

"Grannie!"

She walked on without looking round. "I'm sorry Alphonso."

Maxime and I followed haplessly towards the Chateau.

"What are you doing?" I wailed.

"I'm going. Esmeralda can drive me home."

Five people looked down the terrace steps in horror as my Grandmother stamped up them.

"Mother ..." Esmeralda began.

"Back in the car!"

Maxime ran in front of her. "Imogen please. For Alphonso's sake."

"Which Alphonso? *You* as always! Get out of my way."

"We all desperately want you to be at the wedding."

"And I just as desperately don't want to be there!"

"Please calm down!"

"Arrrrgghhh. I won't!" She shoved him back, and then spying food on the table, began pelting him with patisseries and fruit.

"Grannie!"

"Mum!"

We tried to grab her arms.

Celeste looked furious, "What are you doing?"

"Pelting your not-father."

"He *is* our father!"

"He isn't. He's your stepfather and still my husband and as such, I have the right to pelt him with bread and oranges. Get *off* my arms."

Beatrice looked even more furious. Her dark eyes filled with menace. "Well if you pelt him with food, we will pelt you."

"Fine. About what I would expect from the child of such a mother."

"Imogen!" My grandfather spoke angrily.

"Let's go," Esmeralda groaned.

"So it's okay for you and her mother to misbehave, but I mustn't is that it?"

"You stupid old woman!" Beatrice snapped.

"You two-faced monster!"

Maxime fell to his knees clutching his head.

"Stop her Alphonso!" begged Celeste, "shut her up!"

"Yes, shut me up!" my Grandmother vehemently replied. "Shut up all the years of separation and rejection and hurt. How many years? Twenty. That's one..." she threw a roll at Maxime, "Two ..." and another, "Three ..." then an apple. Then an orange.

"Imogen!" he gasped, arms shielding his head.

Tears streaming, my Grandmother smashed a plate on seven. Celeste screamed and Beatrice let a poised brioche fall.

Jacqueline stepped forward and yelled, "This is ridiculous, please!"

"*Stop.*"

It was Esmeralda who spoke. She said the word quietly, but somehow, colours all around us transformed kaleidoscopically. Trees went red, the clouds green, our own selves purple. It wasn't a kite being nailed to the sky, or a Foreign Minister's hair mummifying a train, nor a grove of trees pendulous with suitcases, but it was from the same place, and somehow even bigger, more hyper-real. The moment was shattering, like the entire world had ended. Birds ceased chirruping in the trees. The only sounds were my Grandmother and Celeste weeping. Nothing else happened until the colours returned to normal.

Then Maxime rose from his knees and went to embrace my Grandmother. "I'm sorry Imogen."

She sniffled into his neck, "You horrible man. It's because I still love you."

"I'm glad, because I love you, you horrible woman."

"I *was* just horrible, wasn't I?"

"You stopped short of exchanging missiles with your Grandson's fiancé."

"But I said a terrible thing."

"In the heat of a very hot moment."

"If you had invented a time-machine, I would travel backwards in it and unsay that very terrible thing."

To me, Beatrice was always an unbelievably magical being, but never more so than when she summoned the grace to say, "We don't need a time machine. We can just unsay things now. I'm really sorry I called you a stupid old woman."

My grandmother raised her face from Maxime's shoulder with a crumpled smile.

"You spoke the truth though," she sniffled. "I didn't. You are *not* a two-faced monster."

"We *do* have two faces," Celeste pointed out helpfully, "It was just the monster bit."

Maxime who had been holding my Gran as if she had cracked in half, unwrapped his arms, so she could approach the Two-Headed Girl and recant.

"I spoke cruelly because of an antagonism to this marriage. To roll up my fishwife's tongue and shove it back where it came from, with all unsaid so we could be friends, is all I might ask. For I can see you are a courageous, loyal, intelligent and impossibly beautiful person with two heads. As far from a monster as can be. Forgive me for blabbermouthing otherwise if ever you can."

The two women embraced and unaccountably, *I* burst into tears.

Eighteen   *Visits*

On the eve of my wedding night, for reasons of space and—absurdly—keeping the bride-and-groom-to-be apart, I was dispatched to a cottage in the Chateau grounds. Here I bookwormed in an armchair until Aunt Esmeralda dropped by wearing a lengthy scarlet dress and occupying a chaise lounge with her unfathomably mysterious presence.

"I came in part, to say that there are vacancies in the Chateau after all because, and this will shock your young ears into dropping off onto the carpet, Mr. and Mrs. Blink have decided to share a room!"

"Really?"

The Three Musketeers (in French) dropped to the carpet instead.

"So there's a spare bedroom spare."

"I'm fine here."

"I thought you would be. But ..." she tutted, "*Parents.*"

My Aunt being less easy to read than untranslated Dumas, I asked, "Aren't you pleased?"

"As a cow with a dish and a spoon. It's your wedding present to me."

Still, her smile was tight.

"And Beatrice," I enthused, "wasn't she ...?"

"Amazing." Esmeralda agreed, "You've changed her. Pacified her."

"Not I."

"I'm my mother's daughter. For years I thought, why did Alphonso throw me over for a thrower of two-headed tantrums? And then demand I be her Auntie?"

"Ouch."

She laughed abruptly. "Though I was a better Auntie to them than I was to you."

"*Ouch*. Ouch."

"I was more welcome at the salon. Brother John and I are a two-person war."

"All this stuff going on that I never dreamed of."

"Wouldn't have been a pleasant dream if you had." Then as if vexed with herself for tarnishing the eve of my wedding, she concluded, "At least all is well that has ended well."

Which reminded me. "I'm embarrassed now about that stupid deed poll. You were so right to upbraid me outside the solicitor's office. Fortunately, the document didn't interfere at all with who I am."

Aunt Esmeralda laughed. "Though had I not gone in immediately you left and persuaded Jane to destroy her side of the paperwork, we might not now be sitting where we're sat."

It took me a few seconds to assimilate this. Then, for the umpteenth time, I silently hugged Betty's toaster which had brought me The Two-Headed Girl and shoved Tom Davies into oblivion. I might have ended up a chartered accountant! Except .... and here I suddenly stared at Aunt Esmeralda ... wasn't that what she was? With a frown of concern I asked, "Aunt Es, are you really a ... you know, chartered accountant?"

She thought about it, "Yes and no."

"What does that mean?"

"Like your grandfather once wrote, money can impoverish, so I help people get rich by other means. I'm a chartered accountant of a different sort of abundance. You might say I help people manage their inner wealth by avoidance of taxes on the fortune inside them."

It sounded weird. "How?"

"All kinds of ways. Once I hammered a kite to the sky?"

"I remember vividly."

"And will you ever forget it?"

"No. How did you do it?"

She looked at me as if this were obvious. "The same way you made a Minister's hair grow."

"But I don't know how I did that."

"I don't know how I nailed the kite to the sky. I just did it because I'm me. You're you."

Her palms gestured: *simple.*

"You can control it though."

"Maybe. Sometimes."

"And you don't get into trouble." My voice sounded aggrieved. "You don't set a foreign Minister's hair on the French President."

"No. I must say, that was impressive. Be-wigging the train even more so."

"That doesn't happen to you."

"If only," she marvelled.

"Why?"

"Because we're completely different people," my Aunt gently reiterated,

"Wouldn't it bother you that somehow, not of your own volition, the Foreign Minister's hair attacked a President?"

"No. But then we don't know that somewhere inside you, *you* didn't want it."

This seemed ridiculous. "Why would I?"

"I don't know. Maybe there's something about politicians you don't like?"

"I know nothing about politics. Well, except …"

"Except …?"

"Except what I read in Grandfather's book. But I don't care about all that stuff."

"Really?" My Aunt looked skeptical. "All that *normality* in your childhood persecuting you for years? You're indifferent to being made to feel like scum for being 'different?' Laws being made against you?"

"No."

"I bet you're pretty angry."

And I realised I was.

"You know," she confessed, with enigmatic deliberation, "I always wondered if Bryony and Georgetta leaving Maxime and her daughter was to do with me."

Again, it took me several moments to absorb this. "Wouldn't you know?"

She shrugged as if to emphasise the point. "Maybe not."

"Because you wanted your mum and dad to get back together?"

"I was angry. Not in control. All sorts of strange things happen when a person is not in control of their psyche."

"But Alphonso and Imogen didn't get back together."

"No. Until now."

I woke next morning to pattering rain on the shutters and blissful anticipation of marrying the Two-Headed Girl. Did I care if it poured on my wedding day? So long as the church didn't leak, no—though it did seem thoughtless of the weather. Still, if the heavens were grey, my hired suit was sky blue, set off by a white-spotted orange bow-tie and unmatching, flowery socks.

Grandma Blink came to help me prepare, straightening my dicky bow and making breakfast. "Are you nervous?" she asked, pouring tea.

"Only of my unconscious smashing stained-glass windows in mid-ceremony. Apart from that, no. To marry somebody so amazingly unique is like a miracle. I won't be an outsider any more desperately wanting to be somebody I'm not." I told her of my deed poll misdeeds.

"A narrow escape," she mused, "Tom Davies' existence, poor man, would be crushingly drab, I'm sure."

Over croissants came a question of my own, "So have you made it up with Grandpa?"

Her face wrestled itself. "I'm torn down the middle because I still love him enormously whilst my pride is just as enormously hurt. Imagine Love and Pride in boxing gloves punching each other. I have opted for Love with a nose dribbling blood."

"I guess that's why you didn't tell me you were separated?"

"It was a way of punishing him. I felt he didn't deserve to know you, at least not through me. I was very conflicted. Another part of me didn't want to denounce him as the villain he undoubtedly was to his own grandson and sound like the bitter twisted old woman that I undoubtedly am."

"You *did* say he'd been killed," I half-laughed.

"He behaved very badly. Sometimes I felt that was what he deserved. But at the same time, he's a really lovable extraordinary man. And anyone can behave badly, especially after getting up on the wrong side of the marital bed."

"You got up on the wrong side in a very spectacular way."

"Good. I did warn you I threw things."

"Your aim spoke of much practice."

"I think to truly forgive, you need first to throw a few rolls, oranges, apples and bits of crockery."

There was a bijou chapel belonging to the chateau estate with a private approach through the grounds, so Grandma Blink and I walked there – fittingly, beneath an umbrella – and arrived early. Built for the private worship of those who now occupied the outside of the chapel rather than the inside, the place was tiny, but then so was the guest list. Inside, a white-robed priest waited in candlelit silence, along with Georges (my best man) and, seated on a pew, Jacqueline with a local friend who had been roped into playing the wedding march on piano accordion. After what seemed an age, but was probably only half an hour, Esmeralda arrived with news of an imminent bride. Several bars of wheezing Mendelssohn later, Beatrice and Celeste drifted up beside me, resplendent in white and both veiled.

"How magnificent you look," I murmured.

Beatrice laughed, "We thought you might turn up in a white dress and veil yourself. Congratulations for controlling the urge to arrive in drag."

"I shall not let that offensive remark blight the happiest day of my life. Though to be scrupulously honest, I arrived holding a woman's umbrella."

"Then all is as it should be," Celeste sighed. "Let us begin as we mean to go on."

My grandfather, holding the Two Headed Girl's arm to give them away and looking crisp and dapper as on the first morning I'd seen him, tried hard not to laugh.

Nothing happened at the altar during the ceremony other, of course, than our tying a knot, which was a most unexpected relief. So after I'd said *je le veux* and they, *nous le voulons*, and exchanged rings, it only remained to kiss the bride, and here there *was* a slight hiccough.

"He remembered the words," said Celeste. "We should kiss him as a reward."

"But who first?" Beatrice replied gravely.

"B comes before C in the alphabet, but C comes before B in *Count your Blessings.*"

In the end I tossed a centime. "Beatrice, you call."

"Heads of course."

Heads it was. Lifting back the white gauze, I kissed her exquisite face and divinely upturned lip. Then did it all over again with the equally ravishing Celeste.

A person ought not to feel much different after some rehearsed mumbles, ring swapping and kisses in a church. There's nothing in any of these activities that, scientifically speaking, need alter a groom's physiology or consciousness. Yet that is exactly what *did* happen. On exiting the chapel to find the rain had stopped, I felt like Alphonso Blink always should have felt but never had. I was SO *me*.

We paused for a few photographs and were just about to traipse back to the chateau when I saw, beneath the shelter of dripping sycamores nearby, a motley congregation of men and recognised them immediately. I apologised to the bride and co, "Your forbearance everyone, I need a moment with my selves."

They understood.

Approaching the rabble of me's, freshly married as I was, there was no trace of my former aversion. "Greetings gentlemen."

A number of them raised hats, one or two saluted, every one of them looked pleased.

"You're soaking," I observed.

"Well, we weren't sure how packing ourselves into the chapel like steaming sardines would be received," said a not-much-older version of myself.

"With some consternation, I'm sure."

"Exactly. Better then to be stood dripping here with the trees."

"It's warm rain at least," another affirmed.

"It went well," said yet another.

"Yes."

Then I realised it wasn't a question and they were looking at me with calm expectation.

"Gentlemen," I fondly declared, "despite the chapel being not quite appropriate for a reunion, I'd like to thank you all for coming to my wedding day. You could muster on the chateau terrace for a toast with the ..."

Another me interrupted me. "We wanted to give our best wishes to you and the bride. It's very nostalgic our being here."

There were murmurs of assent.

"And I almost messed it all up with my dunderheaded deed poll."

There were some laughs, head-shaking and groans. A middle-aged Alphonso, looking not unlike Maxime, recalled, "We vanished entirely for half an hour. Peculiar experience we all agreed."

Further murmurs of assent followed.

"Sorry. Still, as a result I've grown to very much like being Alphonso Blink," I beamed.

"That's us lot you know?" said a serious-looking me.

"Indeed. Each and every one of you has become dear to my heart."

There was a smattering of applause, a little muffled by the sodden trees and landscape. Then, one by one, they stepped forward to embrace me, somewhat moistening my suit.

"Scarf," said one and draped me in a rainbow-coloured boa constrictor.

The eldest came last. "You lost my beard hairs, didn't you?"

I nodded guiltily. "Don't be offended, but could I ask *why* you snipped them off for me in the first place?"

"Wedding present."

"Bit of a strange gift wasn't it?"

"Yes, but we're impulsive we Alphonso Blinks. Look ..." He took some scissors from a pocket and snipped another lock of hair from his grey beard. "Presents should be really memorable on your wedding day and she won't forget this."

"I'd say not,"

He tucked the wiry lock in the breast pocket of my suit and grinned. "Don't lose the hairs again. The supply isn't infinite you know."

"I do."

He shook my hand. "Goodbye me."

"Will we meet again?"

"Who knows?"

"I thought you lot did."

"Ah, but we don't always agree."

And with that he turned and sauntered after the others, leaving me strangely upset and alone.

Back along the chapel laneway I trudged, wondering why everything about my life was always so deeply incomprehensible. Wanting to rejoin the main party, especially my wife, I launched into the first few steps of a jog, but was halted by a voice from shadowy laurels that lined that section of the path.

"Tom."

I looked round and saw Betty emerge in a red-spotted plastic mac, with the hood up.

"You? *Here!* "

The Universe reeled.

"I saw you coming out of church with that two-headed woman."

"My wife, Beatrice and Celeste. But how did you find me here of all places?"

She pulled the hood back and shook her hair. "Something old, something new, something borrowed, something ..."

"Of course ..."

At Betty's feet, he wagged his tail, sorrowful-eyed.

"I might have known."

"But we've come too late haven't we, Blue and I?"

This was awkward. "To be honest, weeks earlier wouldn't have made any difference."

She looked crestfallen. "Really?"

I struggled to explain, "It's nothing to do with toasting the deed poll, thank goodness you did, but ... well, Celeste and Beatrice are more like me. Equally weird. You're ... you're a lovely, lovely normal person."

"Well at least I'm not a policewoman any more."

"But you're not a lioness tamer are you?"

She laughed sadly. "No. I'm a cleaner. I realised with my degree and other qualifications, I only needed to do a short course to get my Bleaching and Scrubbing certificate."

I was shocked, "You didn't have to do that. What about all the money in the case?"

"I took it back to the barn with Blue and buried it in the bales of straw."

The past clawed painfully at the present.

"Never mind. Didn't belong to me anyhow. Belonged to some weirdo called Tom Davies."

"You'll laugh, but one of the guys on the Bleaching course was called Tom Davies and he asked me out. I said 'no'. Maybe next time he asks ..."

I reflected that one life was insufficient to follow all the amazing threads that came to hand.

"Betty, I know this sounds like a meaningless cliché, maybe it is, but can we still be friends, good friends?"

She thought about it for a moment, then shook her head, "Probably not."

There was a moment between us. The sort that only we had, but which I couldn't have any more, especially on my wedding day. *Because life only has one thread.*

"I'd ask you to stay for a drink but …"

"Come on Blue. Time to go. Good boy."

She went off briskly in the opposite direction to the chapel and myself.

After a toast on the terrace, I presented my bride with the hairs from my top pocket which they received with puzzled distaste.

"If this is what he's going to be like when he's older, dear Celeste, I believe we have made a most terrible mistake."

Our honeymoon, naturally, was in Paris. I was dead against this, but it was two heads against one. I thought it inconceivable that we would not be recognised, arrested and shoved ungently by Gendarmes back through the Channel Tunnel. And could my psyche be trusted with an iconic structure like the Eiffel Tower? Surely not. I was paranoid it might walk off on those giant legs and plant itself somewhere extremely inappropriate like, well, England. It didn't bear thinking about. But we drove there in the green 2CV anyway with French lessons the whole journey. As a wedding present, the Duponts had compensated the original owners of our car with a newer pinker 2CV, so that apart from false numberplates and a few other 'trivialities', as Beatrice called them, log books and so forth, we were all but legal.

Honeymooning in Paris with my bride was actually more romantic than stressful. They attracted stares, it is true, but their beauty was always going to turn more heads than their own. We were stopped any number of times by excited citizens wishing to know if we were the couple who had made the Foreign Minister's hair go crazy. But Celeste and Beatrice only looked bored and replied in perfect french that no, those people were English and therefore a different Two Headed Girl; then (to me) would sigh, 'come on Camille.'

We stayed three nights in a plush hotel, and by day, alternated buying clothes with sightseeing. I got on well with the Eiffel Tower and no paintings were rearranged in the Louvre, but when Celeste averred that chic Parisian clothes for men were actually very feminine, our shopping bags weighed more heavily. My French improved so much that if people spoke slowly and spelled things out, I felt the day would eventually come when I'd be able to understand what was being said.

By night we explored clubs with live music, to 'spy on the competition'.

"Jacqueline wants to start an Umbrella Club in Paris for us," Beatrice divulged. *"Club Parapluie."*

On our final evening, two disappointing venues and their acts had us retiring to the hotel early. Too early for bed. So Beatrice and Celeste threw together the omelette of a honeymoon song,

"Post wedding day they say,
you should go quite far away
and do all the things that were forbidden to you
before the knot was tied,

But we'd done them already so many times
and did them again to make sure
and then were left wanting that little bit more
must a honeymoon be a bore
if you've already done what a honeymoon is for?
  should you walk hand-in-hand and wonder
if you've both made a terrible blunder
I'd say that's getting it wrong
all you need is a burst of this song
  Let's go to the top of the Eiffel Tower and jump off together
  (we're in love we'd probably survive)
  Let's take off our clothes in the rain, dive into the Seine
  and complain of wet weather
  (it's polluted but we'd get out alive)
  Let's find the most expensive and posh epicure
  and eat far too much and throw up on the floor
  Cos if you were naughty before you were wed
  for suuuuuuuuure,
  on your honeymoon all you can do
  is those things you've never attempted to
  before."

We were singing the chorus lustily and laughing, when there was a knock. I opened the door to find two Gendarmes and a man in a suit who offered his hand.

"Alphonso Blink?"

He was not intimidating enough for a denial so I nodded and shook it.

"You may not recognise me. I am Andre Moreau. The President of France. Might I come in."

"Of course."

It was his country after all. He signaled for the Gendarmes to stay put.

"Ah, your two headed companion."

"We're married," said Celeste.

"I won't take up much of your time. May I sit down?"

"Please," Beatrice mischievously smiled, "You're the first President we've entertained today."

He smiled also. "So you are the Blinks?"

"Yes," Celeste answered, "Married four days ago. We're on our honeymoon."

"I hope your stay has been memorable."

"Well, we won't forget this!" laughed Beatrice, and he laughed a little with her.

"Forgive my intrusion. Your presence in the city Madame, has not gone unnoticed. There are not many two-headed women in the world. It was presumed that the man accompanying you was the notorious Alphonso Blink and learning of your whereabouts, I could not resist a visit. Believe me, both of you, I come in amity, but curious to my very bones." He gave me a courteous look, "I have a question for you Alphonso. With regard to the English Foreign Minister, I only wish to know, why on earth did you do what you did?"

For the next hour, I explained why. He listened attentively, astonished when I recounted waking in the police station and knowing nothing of what had happened.

"You mean somebody else did it?"

I tried to explain the quirks of my unconscious. When it came to our affair on the train, the engagement and our account of Martin Pitt's proposal in the carriage culminating in my outraged response and a second scene of hairy pandemonium, the President actually giggled. He giggled helplessly for half a minute and could barely stop himself.

"Enough," he wiped his eyes, "please, enough!"
Celeste and Beatrice filled in the rest of our story. After which, he stood, slowly mastering himself.

"I thank you both for entertaining me this evening and for your patience with my curiosity. Enjoy the rest of your honeymoon. You are welcome in Paris. Welcome in France." He shook our hands warmly. "Bon Nuit."

Nineteen *Wheels*

We arrived back at the *Chateau Sans Passe* to find Maxime and Imogen gone.

Georges explained, "Alphonso kept his word to her. They packed some bags and set out on a European tour as he'd promised long ago."

"Venice, Rome, Bucharest, Berlin, Athens," said Jacqueline dreamily.

"Wonderful," breathed Celeste.

"But the race?" I frowned.

Georges grimaced. "I know, I know, we talked through this at great length. A difficult decision. He knew it would be five weeks away from Imogen from now to the Champs Elysee. Too much when they'd only just been reunited. He was desperate to make good his promise to her after all these years."

"Fancy," Beatrice smiled, "Daddy, a romantic after all."

"But the bicycle?" I asked.

Georges shook his head. "It's hard on *Roues Carrées*."

"You could find another rider."

"I've tried myself, but it just bumps and rears. So I've decided on a substitute with a conventional machine.

There's always next year's race and it will give Alphonso more time to train."

"It's waited years and years."

"Imogen too," Jacqueline reminded, adding artfully, "Alphonso wondered if you might ride it."

"Me?" The suggestion was preposterous. "I'm no cyclist."

"You're fitter than Daddy," said Beatrice.

"And you know how to ride *Roues Carrées*," Georges persuaded.

I spluttered speechless.

"Yes, I know," he laughed.

But there was excitement building in the eyes of Beatrice and Celeste.

"Why not Alphonso?"

They bounced up and down on the spot.

"What else are you going to do?" Beatrice enthused. "We are going to arrange a tour of gigs with Jacqueline. We'll have to write a set of French songs and for a few weeks won't be very – *available*. You can train whilst we write. Then do *the* Tour whilst we do *ours*."

"Imagine if you won!" Celeste stared into space imagining it.

"I wouldn't."

"You might," Georges said, "The machine *is* a revolutionary design. Even your grandfather was pedalling at incredible speeds. Over seventy kilometres an hour."

I was appalled. "But it starts in two weeks."

"Time enough to do what has to be done. After all, your grandfather said, winning isn't the important thing. It was taking part that mattered to Square Wheels. Go for the ride."

"And I'm a wanted man."

"Not here and you would be riding under an assumed name." Georges cajoled.

"I honestly don't think ..."

"Oh Alphonso!" The Girl with Two Heads wailed at my timidity.

"Alright." I began to slide. "Maybe. Perhaps. Let me ..."

"Imagine making love to him in *Le maillot jaune*." The two heads looked at each other and rolled their eyeballs moonily.

Georges handed me an envelope. "Here. From your grandfather."

I took the missive to the bedroom for privacy and opened it moodily, none too pleased with my elder namesake.

Dearest Alphonso,

Huh.

I am sorry to have missed you on your return. By now, I am sure Georges will have apprised you as to the likely contents of this letter. The thing is, I feel guilty about the bike and guilty about your grandmother and I can't keep both happy, unless you help me. You can't take your grandmother on our second honeymoon around Europe, but you could ride Square Wheels on the Tour. I've thought of other riders. But you're the only one who is right. You have an affinity. Nobody else does. I don't wish to lumber you with a task that is utterly onerous. I could ride the bicycle in next year's Tour, maybe. But that's a long wait for a velocipede that has already had a long wait. Don't worry if it's impossible. I will see you on our return from visiting every country in Europe.

Your grandmother sends her love, and of course, so do I.

The Other Alphonso.

I sat grumpily on the bed. I really did not feel equal to it. But then what did I feel equal to? Hiding under the bed clothes. The last thing I wanted in the world was to be in the public eye. Make love to me in *Le maillot jaune?* They could just buy a yellow jumper. Yet ... yet ... *yet* ... it would *so* please my beloved wife. And how could Beatrice or Celeste love and respect a husband who spent his life curled beneath a feather duvet? Albeit metaphorically. They were an extraordinary person. The only extraordinary thing about me was some inner poltergeist that I had little or no control over. I recalled their astonishing performance in the Umbrella Club. How could I live up to that? Be a fitting partner for such a person? Old Square Wheels was revolutionary. Imagine if I *did* win the Tour de France? At least then I could skulk under the Two Headed Girl's bedlinen with some distinction.

I went downstairs to the hallway where Square Wheels was propped against a wall. Was it ridiculous to imagine a relationship between us? *No.* Was it angry about

Alphonso's second abandonment? That's what I felt on touching the handlebars and ancient leather seat. Ridiculous. It crossed my mind that the machine was not sentient, only subject to the workings of my inner self. Or maybe I was merely feeling that anthropomorphism, multiplied tenfold, with which people fondly imbue heirlooms or sentimentalised objects? Touching the handlebars again I received a tingling shock. The metal *was* aggrieved. There could be no question what the bicycle was asking of me—and I didn't want to do it. Yet if Square Wheels hadn't brought me to the Salon I'd never have met The Two-Headed Girl. My resistance crumbled.

"Okay. I'll do it."

Honestly, the bike glowed.

"I promise you now. I will do it."

"Yes!" Beatrice and Celeste erupted together behind me.

I yelped in fright and turned to see them jumping up and down on the spot and clapping their hands, "Bravo! Bravo! Bravo!"

Georges appeared from behind them and said, "Excellent."

The Two-Headed Girl embraced me tightly.

"You won't miss much." Beatrice kissed me hard on the cheek. "Because our gigs will be all in French and your French is still a turd that *so* needs brushing up."

"You'll win." Celeste cried, "I know you will. That would be wonderful multiplied by wonderful! And we'll make love to you in the yellow jersey!"

"We'll take it off. Put it back on and take it off again. And then put it back on and take it back off."

"Georges, save me please."

Everybody was laughing. Even the bicycle it seemed.

"We're in luck." Georges informed me, "The Tour used to be held in July for three weeks, but organizational chaos in the last decade has led to it being pushed back. Each year it gets later because everything is so scrambled. For a while it was August. Now it's September."

"But how can you enter me so late in the proceedings?" I fretted.

"You will take the pseudonym Maxime was going to use, John Smith."

Spoken without flinching.

"I'll never win with that name."

"It does not matter." Georges shrugged, "You are there to take part, for *Roues Carrée*."

I nodded. "But isn't it cheating?"

He laughed. "The entire history of the Tour has been cheating. It has never been more than a means of transporting dishonesty from A to B. Take the problem with pins ..."

"*Pins?*"

"Yes. For some years, each rider has been assigned a personal pin and they've been caught sticking them in each other's tyres."

"Terrible."

"It's all part of a structural chaos that began when the organisers set up systems which riders had to use to sign up for the tour. It was done to streamline operations, make them more efficient and cost effective and of course stop cheating. A series of menus and recorded messages were set out in a room in Paris. To ensure impartiality, each menu was hung round the neck of one of five dummies. A rider would go into a room, press the tape recorder and be given five different options. For instance: *if you would like information about the route for this year's tour, press one. If you would like to book your bicycle in for its pre-tour checkup, press two,* etc etc. You would then press a dummy in its midriff and they would have a taped message inside them, rather like a doll that talks when you pull a string. But often none of the menu numbers would have what the rider wished. For instance, one of the specified requirements for entering the tour this year was that competitors should officially sign up with a User-name to authorise the sending of a code which they could then write down and present to officials at the start of the race to prove who they were. The sign-up details should have been on a menu but were omitted by mistake. Last year's winner was disqualified for smashing the tape recorders to bits and beating up the dummies whilst screaming, *I just want to talk to a real person!!!* A shame because he is a brilliant cyclist. So the corruption and disorganisation has only increased, with authorisation codes being sent 'accidentally' to Paraguay and Madagascar. Teams given verbal passwords to remember sometimes forgot to write them down or lost the books they were written in because rivals slipped amnesia pills in their drink. Fortunately, in your case, we have managed to set up all that side of it already."

Within a day, I was whisked off to train with 'the team', who already knew about Square Wheels. If French was a steep learning curve, learning to ride co-operatively in the Tour de France was an even tougher ascent. So many musts and must-nots. Although Square Wheels acquitted itself well in training sessions and needed only a fraction of the effort riders of a conventional bike would need, at the end of each day, I could do little more than flake on a bed and miss my wife. In this way, two weeks flashed by the way a train does travelling in the opposite direction to the one you're on.

"You will enter as a domestique—one who serves the team leader," Georges told me at the beginning, "That way there's no pressure. After all, it doesn't really matter how Square Wheels performs. But if all goes well, and the machine goes *zoooom*, it could become possible for you to lead instead. It happens."

The evening before the race, coming to my hotel room, Georges once more delivered a letter, "From them," he smiled, handing me a yellow envelope. Inside, on yellow notepaper, but inked in blue, were the words,

Dearest Fellow Blink, this is to wish you luck with winning the race. We know you will, but shall not count our chickpeas before they sprout. Don't fear disappointing us. We will love you whatever the colour of your jersey.

Our French songs and set are almost written. We have twelve, having written one a day, and Jacqueline has set up a tour for us just as Georges has set one up for you. Are they not lovely? There will still be half a dozen shows left to perform after the race is over, so you won't miss our set completely, and we will definitely be on the Champs Elysee screaming for you on the final day. And remember, it's not cheating to train your unconscious to win. Even if it was, it's the Tour.

All our love over and over and over. See you soon.
the Two-Headed Wife.

And then there was the race itself. Twenty-one stages, twenty-four days, three-thousand kilometres. The lowest cumulative time to win.

What struck me most about the tour was the unbelievably violent passion of those involved – especially the spectators. They cared so much: shouting, exhorting, screaming, hopping beside us, bawling obscenities into rider's faces, their own contorted by a rage and emotional inflammation. It was weirder than I by far and a few times had me wanting to pull over and shout: *What is wrong? It is just men riding bicycles along roads and up mountains. It is something that happens every day, a lot. A postman riding his bicycle on a round does not have hundreds of people running alongside him to scream: 'keep going Kevin, only twenty-seven more letterboxes to go!'* Why no tribalism for postal deliveries? Which was missing the point, I know. Because the Tour was also dazzlingly tumultuous in its way.

There was laughter and derision from crowds, fellow competitors, even Gendarmes at the sight of Square Wheels lining up. Children pointed and jumped up and down. How could a bike with square wheels be racing the Tour de France? Except there was nothing in the rules to say it couldn't. It was investigated by officials with nitpicking scrupulousness beforehand. Much to their irritation, I sensed, they could find no lawful objection to the machine.

At *Le Grande Departe*, the kaleidoscopic crowds, and festive hullaballoo had me shrinking in my cycling shoes. A minnow hoiked from the Seine and swung to an angler's palm to gawp and mouth at the horrifying world of dry land would doubtless feel as I did in the palm of the Tour that first day: gills gasping for irretrievable breaths, non-stop. From the prologue to the end of the first stage, I was surrounded by world-class athletes, masters of all the ups and downs and flats the landscape could throw at them, in a whirl of unfamiliar commotion. My fraudulent attempts to compete on a square-wheeled machine seemed fatuous, though, we did keep up, in spite of my inadequacies —the bicycle was of such revolutionary design. And after day one, little improved. We were tested for drugs and tested for drugs and tested for drugs. Several times Square Wheels was taken to bits completely then reassembled in attempts to find an engine that didn't exist. I'm sure if officials could have disassembled me, they would have done so, and found even less.

The shooting speeds, whizzing blurrily down mountain slopes and around hairpin bends brought neither fear nor exhilaration—I trusted Square Wheels unconditionally. We were also buffeted several times by riders from other teams in a way that might have derailed a lesser machine (there couldn't have been a lesser rider than myself). Whilst I had to expend a fraction of the effort of other competitors it was all exhausting and mentally depleting. And though for half the race we did nothing spectacular, our rivals were surly and unpleasant. So were their fans and followers I had to pedal through, especially on the ascents. I would snatch a glimpse of some mountainside ahead and see it pouring human lava, spectators urging some on, cursing others. The fact that I was riding a square-wheeled bicycle did at least attract *some* supporters along the way, and they shouted encouragement. Oddly however, their spurring my side only increased the misery. Speeding along hour after hour, learning in the saddle, my one good fortune was to be riding a thoroughbred where the rest of the peloton were mounted —comparatively—on nags.

By the halfway stage, my cumulative time was also middling. About what you would expect from a John Smith in fact. A ride that was quite beige under the circumstances. It was in the last ten stages that Square Wheels suddenly accelerated. We won eight of them which was not so beige. More a rainbow-coloured scarf wound around the cycling world to elicit spluttering, indignant fury. The other teams, their fans, sponsors, and friends in the press all denounced us as cheats. After winning the first three of those eight stages, there were calls for Square Wheels to be disqualified for being too 'different' from the rest of the bicycles. After the eighth win during which we had been roughly shoved by a number of spectators during a climb and I was wearing a yellow jersey, there was an outcry that the Tour was being won by a freak. Such was the amount of rabid spittle sprayed at me from quadrophobic fans, I feared for my life. By the end of the nineteenth stage, which we won comfortably, large press headlines were denouncing John Smith. Was he bogus, this cyclist from nowhere? Fortunately, the Tour's systems of authentication were so obscure, nothing defamatory could be unearthed. But arriving at a Saint Malo hotel to boos and hisses from a crowd, left me desperate to leave the Tour. Surely if I rode up the Champs Elysee in the *Maillot Jaunne*, there would be riots and I would be guillotined along with my cheering wife. Then there was a rumour in one of the papers that I was not John Smith but Alphonso Blink! It was only Georges pointing to a report that the President had intervened which persuaded me to carry on:

If something is different and makes them better and faster and they win, it's not cheating, they are just ahead. Those behind must go faster, that is all.

This mollified me somewhat.

Georges watched me pace back and forth across the hotel room carpet and spoke calmly, "One more ride Alphonso. One more day and it's done. You are winner of the Tour de France and everybody will love you. The

President has intervened on your behalf. The bike has captured the public imagination. It's a sensation. You are striking a blow for difference the world over."

"Oui." I stopped pacing to sigh, "Vive la Alphonso".

I set out on stage twenty of twenty-one in the yellow jersey. Most spectators lining the streets *were* cheering me on and it seemed only a minority were hostile to a square-wheeled machine leading the race. Oddly, and for the first time during the entire Tour, I felt exhilarated. Our ride was a national sensation and would end at the Champs-Élysées in a mass celebration of difference—the Two-Headed Girl and I embracing over glasses of champagne.

"Vive les Blinks!"

Unfortunately for this beautiful bubble, not many miles down the designated route, Square Wheels, of its own accord, suddenly veered off through a gap between two hoardings. Past astonished onlookers we sped, over a car park, rodeo bumping on kerbs and other obstructions before speeding across a field. We headed out of the Tour de France as if we had crashed.

"What are you doing?" I screamed, knowing better than to squeeze the brakes.

It didn't stop, scattering a herd of cattle, slaloming between trees in a park and finding an earthen ramp to leap and land on a minor road. Evidently, my race was run. Quite why Square Wheels had taken a funny turn was beyond me. It hurtled on as if still competing for the Tour.

Though to be unexpectedly torn from the madding crowds was a relief—no more leg-pumping John Smith, no more faces snarling into my own, no more deafening exhortations—I was confounded by this swerving off the route for deserted country lanes. Our winning the Tour would have been a formality. Was knowing that enough for the machine? Or had it capitulated to save me all the horrible razzmatazz of winning, which I'd never wanted. If so, it was a noble gesture and I never felt more at one with Square Wheels than on our Grande Departe from the Tour de France. I didn't much care where we were headed, hopefully the *Chateau Sans Passe* where I could hide in a wardrobe until somebody else winning the race became bigger news than my throwing it away. There *was* an uneasiness around that. What possible explanation could I offer to Georges? Sorry lovely, generous spirited man, whose wife has a tremendous inner thigh, on the brink of victory I turned tail and trashed your tour. And Grandfather Alphonso: Well, the miraculous machine you invented to win the race could easily have done but didn't. And my dear excited wife? I could see stars falling from their eyes when they heard we'd dropped out when so far ahead. For although Georges and my grandfather had said winning was irrelevant and it was all about Square Wheels taking part, we'd got far too close to Paris in a yellow jersey for it not to matter. *To them.*

On the other hand, as the bike whirred and spun along roads mercifully uncrowded but for my own guilty thoughts, I couldn't help but feel that losing was wonderful.

And besides, it had been Square Wheel's decision to dump the race, not mine and if this was to shield me from the unremitting limelight of a *Maillon Jaunne,* then bless the machine's iron soul. Knowing it could have won a race it had been invented to win was probably enough. If old Square Wheels didn't need some hysterical coronation in Paris we should all applaud it.

Though we saw virtually nobody on the roads, the yellow jersey began to bother me. I was tempted to remove the conspicuous garment and cycle bare-chested. How had a situation arisen yet again, in which a change of clothes, probably stolen, would be required? I mentioned this to my companion. "I know you don't wear clothes, but ..."

We bumped up a roadside verge into a wood where Square Wheels manoeuvred slowly between large and venerable oaks for several hundred yards. It stopped suddenly and I dismounted to lean the bicycle against a tree.

"Now what?"

The rear wheel began to spin, showering earth into the air behind the machine. It was like a dog digging at a rabbit hole. For some minutes I stood frowning at this performance. It was only when the rear wheel stopped and I examined the site of its excavations that an earthy pungency arose and I saw the aromatic truffle of a suitcase had been revealed. Of course! It was that time of year! Misty, moist September. Grabbing a filthy handle, I yanked the case out and laid it before me, springing the clasps. My hopes for neatly folded garments of becoming virility were soon dashed. Not wanting to seem ungrateful, I didn't weep, or repeatedly slap my brow, but removed the damning costume of a tour leader for a long, green-patterned dress, green tights, a straw hat and pretty flat shoes. Also emerald. A potato sack would have been as acceptable to me, perhaps more so. Still, I thanked Square Wheels and stuffed the yellow jersey (because it didn't belong to me and they might want it back) into a handbag provided and hung this on the handlebars. Pausing to tie the straw hat's green ribbon beneath my chin, I then remounted and on we went.

Some time later, at the sort of sedate pace befitting a young woman in a dress and a straw hat, we arrived in a large town, garnering scant attention. *Roues Carrées* came bowling to a halt below steps leading up to a double glass door bearing a poster:

Ce soir 21h La Fille à Deux Têtes

My French was good enough to read that. The blessed bicycle had delivered me to a gig! The town Hall clock said seven. Beatrice and Celeste might be already warming up in the dressing room. Should I go and hug them immediately, pulling the yellow jersey from my handbag as a gift? Then again, to blunder in and confess what had happened, might undermine their performance. It would surely be better to meet after the encores. Unless ... *unless* they had already heard of my disappearance and were too worried to play. It was impossible to know beforehand which my beloveds would prefer. *There is no more difficult tightrope to walk in life than that of indecision.* And there being no answer to the conundrum, I posed as the sister of the Two-Headed Girl on a surprise visit to dupe the door staff, and was led to the dressing room corridor by a kindly usher. Thereafter, I took a deep breath and pulled the yellow jersey from my bag. I wanted Beatrice and Celeste to see that I had at least worn it once, even if, after my disqualification, they would never want to repeatedly take it on and off my torso. They'd be disappointed at best. Fuming at worst. It couldn't be helped.

I paused outside the door and dithered whether to knock or turn the handle, fearing my entrance might be a defining moment in our relationship. What stopped my hand was a strangled noise from within. Frowning, I pressed my ear to the door, only to eavesdrop on the noisy eruption of a double, multiple *petite-mort*. Shocked and disconcerted by the screams, I immediately barged in to see a couch on which a naked Two-Headed Girl lay sprawled beneath a Two Headed Boy, equally bereft of clothes. The arms of my wife were clasped passionately around their paramour's back. At this abrupt and theatrical entrance of a cuckolded husband, there were gasps of shock. Both heads of the Two Headed Boy twisted round to stare at me wide eyed.

"Mademoiselle," he panted, "s'il te plaît, frappe."

"Ce n'est pas une Mademoiselle," Beatrice wailed, "C'est mon mari!"

"Alphonso," squeaked Celeste.

The naked pair tried to disentangle themselves. My wife sat up in guilty shock holding a cushion to her breasts.

"Alphonso!" Beatrice repeated breathlessly, "What are you doing here?"

I just stared, speechless, watching their Two Headed Lover struggle into underwear and jeans.

"We're sorry." Celeste wept. "We only meant to kiss him once, to see what it was like. Our dream since forever."

Absurdly, all I could think was that both his two heads seemed better looking than me, with firmer more masculine chins and lots of stubble.

After an exchange of dismayed looks, Celeste said miserably, "They came to every gig. And...well, *he has two heads.*" She stutteringly sobbed, "C ... C ...Can you b ... b ... blame us?"

And looking at the distraught faces of my wife, both tear-streaked and exquisitely beautiful, I couldn't. Because, though overwrought myself, I somehow completely and utterly understood.

"No," my annihilated self whispered, "I can't blame you at all."

And I meant it. Seeing the bare-chested Two-Headed Boy hurriedly struggling to turn his shirt the right way out, I gave a weird laugh and threw him the *Maillot Jaunne,* "Here." My smile wobbled. "You won."

"Alphonso!" my wife cried despairingly with both voices, *"We're sorry!"*

But I pulled the door shut on their words. In a thunderous silence, I ran headlong down the corridor like a child, because my world had ended.

My world had ended.

My world had ended.
My world had ended.
My world had ended.
My world had ended.
My world had ended.
My world had ended.
My world had ended.
My world had ended.
My world had ended.
My world had ended.
My world had ended.

Taking Square Wheels from the foyer where it had been propped, waiting patiently, against a wall, I led us both out into the street and allowed the machine a miserable, "Merci."

Twenty   *Blink*

There's not much more to add. I remounted Square Wheels and peddled off. It mattered little where, though I did say aloud, "Not the *Chateau Sans Passe*, please."

Some minutes later, heading out of town, I confided miserably to the bicycle. "If they'd been fornicating with a *one*-headed boy, I'd have trashed the room. But a French Two-Headed Boy? How could Beatrice and Celeste possibly forgo a kiss? And during a kiss, the hands can go anywhere. You touch this place that tingles or that one and who can then stop themselves, married or not? Imagine if all the world were two-headed but for me and then I met a one-headed girl? Would I be able to walk away from an embrace? I know what you are thinking Square Wheels, dear friend – that I should go back and fight for her. Punch both her lover's noses. Make their stubble grow crazily long and tie them in knots. But for my wife, they are obviously a *perfect fit*. Not least, this Two-Headed Boy could stride confidently into a map book shop and demand an atlas of the entire republic, any time of the day or night. Moreover, being French, they would be better lovers." I tried pedalling faster as if that would help leave the memory of what I had witnessed behind. "I don't want to be selfish and insist on my conjugal rights. I have to let go. Like Imogen did. But, dear velocipede, it is hard. Have you ever fallen in love with another bicycle? A tandem perhaps?" By this point I was weeping blindly, and unable to see the road. "It is hard because my wife, who I adore, is irretrievably lost unless I grow another head."

Fortunately, the bike seemed to know where we were going. We ended up before dawn, on the coast, in a small fishing village and there, with the aid of a bundle of francs from a purse in my handbag, I bribed a fisherman to drop me at an equally small English fishing village over the channel. The crossing was flat and calm and grey. And so was I.

Smuggled back into England, like a consignment of cognac, and bumping Square Wheels onto a quay unnoticed, I was glad of my feminine greenery, for returning home meant also a return to being a wanted man. Having snoozed a little on the boat, and guessing our destination was Blink Castle, it seemed safest to pedal by night until dawn and I did so. When light came spearing over the horizon, I opted wearily and warily to doze for the day on a haystack in a field. Before drifting off to sleep in a fine drizzle, I wondered at all that had happened to me and grieved sorely over the betrayal of Beatrice and Celeste. At one point, Grandpa Alphonso's book came into my mind. Without the Two-Headed Girl, I was definitely poorer, almost destitute, bereft of meaning in life, and on a farmer's haystack without food or cover to boot. On the other hand, I was also richer beyond belief for any of it having happened at all. *Wasn't I?* If only I could grasp that incredible fortune in my two hands. But it was fugitive as my dreams.

I woke, a little damp and craving a half-eaten sandwich (having lost all hope of ever finding unsampled fare). Clambering down from the stack where Square Wheels was leaning against the bales, dripping patiently, I pulled straws from my hair and wisps from the dress, only to look up and see a weather-beaten farmer eyeing us from over a gate by the road. I thought perhaps he was aggrieved about my fluffing up his hay but no, as Square Wheels and I approached he frowned.

"You can't be wearing those clothes, lady."

I gazed down at my garments. Were my tights laddered? "Why ever not?"

"Against the law. Get a fine for all that green."

I snorted, "What nonsense."

He pointed proudly to his own clothes, a somewhat muddied pinstriped jacket and trousers, with union-jack waistcoat. "The new civilian-issue uniform. Everyone has to wear it. Women as well as men. There's fines even for odd socks. Police can spot-check you in your home and arrest or fine you depending on the severity of the offence."

All of which seemed to meet with his approval, so I said humbly, I'd buy a new outfit forthwith.

"By the way," he added thoughtfully, in case I hadn't noticed. "Your bike has square wheels."

"Goodness," I said with feigned surprise. "So it does. Fancy that. Goodbye."

With the day almost done, I pedalled off, doubly reluctant to be out gallivanting in broad daylight if a green dress and tights were grounds for prosecution. That, *and* I was riding a bike with square wheels without insurance. Fortunately, we were mere miles from our destination and in the mauve of early evening, I saw a signpost saying:

Blink Castle. Quite near.

I dismounted to take the river path in case the grounds were still under surveillance. It was the route I had walked as a scarecrow, after first meeting a policewoman and her dog. Nearing the back gates, I waited to let dusk darken and so assist an approach to the castle unseen. Home. A round bedroom. I'd have to scale the battlements and break in, but I knew Grandma Imogen wouldn't mind. She *would* mind that I was now single. Might my Grandparents fall out over what had happened? Given Maxime's allegiance to Beatrice and Celeste, it seemed inevitable. I groaned to think of my Blinkian forbears splitting up all over again. In which case, it would be best to be gone before they returned. *Where* though? I was stuck in a land where my very soul was outlawed. My parents? Impossible. France and the *Chateau Sans Passe?* Even more so. Betty, if her house had not already been sold, would slam the door in my face. In any case, I doubted somehow that scrubbing toilets would pay the mortgage. Unless (and this was a nauseating thought), the Tom Davies, she had met on the cleaning course, had now, freshly qualified, moved in to help with the bills. And here my dismal imagination saw Betty in the arms of a pasty-faced, featureless man wearing government-issue clothes and murmuring softly in her ear, "I'd like many of these outfits. One for each day of the week. All identical. By which I mean, exactly the same. Carbon-copied clothing, put plainly. And also my darling, matching nylon pyjamas to wear in bed beside you."

Imagining Betty nuzzled up against this hunk of mundanity and savouring his reek of disinfectant, wrung a lugubrious sigh from my being. The river close by, gurgled as if stifling a laugh. Doubtless, if I'd thrown myself in, it would have been no more than ankle deep. It seemed Square Wheels' intuitive sixth-sense had become sufficiently attuned to my woe to actually make a noise, for I heard it sniffle. Or at least snuffle. And then realised a dog was nosily investigating myself and the bike. A voice called softly in the twilight.

"Blue? *Blu - ue?* Here boy."

Was that hound destined to find me anywhere on earth?

"Betty?" I called incredulously.

I saw her shadow approach. *"Alphonso?* In women's clothes again. I thought you'd stopped all that?"

"Well look at *your* clothes. You're wearing that ridiculous civilian uniform."

"I have to. It's the law. And an insurance disc to walk Blue. You've only yourself to blame."

"Me?"

"I'm sure it was that president's hair episode which brought in a load of laws to suppress difference."

"Rubbish." I parked Square Wheels against a stone wall. "Anyhow, what on earth are you doing here?"

"Well, ditto."

"I asked first."

"We weren't looking for *you*. We'd just gone walkies."

"Round here?"

Her head fell to one side. "Your Gran didn't tell you she'd hired me?"

"No."

There was just enough light to see her surprise. "When I was leaving the grounds of that Chateau on your wedding day, she recognised me. I'd interviewed her as a policewoman in Blink Castle before you absconded. She and your grandfather had been discussing going away for a couple of months, and one of her doubts had been the castle and who would look after it. I remembered you'd said she couldn't get a cleaner for the place and told her about my qualification and volunteered. She gave me the keys to look after it until they returned. So here I am. She probably felt sorry for me. How about you?"

By the time I finished recounting my disastrous adventures, owls were hooting.

"So the Universe got it right for Beatrice and Celeste in the end," I sighed, "just a shame the timing was star-crossed. I mean, it might have been easier if the Two-Headed Girl had met the Two-Headed Boy, *before* meeting me." I paused, and looked at the dark shape of Betty silhouetted against the sky.

"But they didn't," said her shadow, I thought somewhat brutally.

"No." There was another, longer pause, before I continued, "Or maybe my unconscious made me manifest a Two-Headed Boy so I could be with someone else?"

Which elicited a derisive snort. "But unfortunately," and she underscored this point as if with red pen, "you're married now."

"True." I straightened my dress in resignation. "The Universe for some reason, fucked up. The constellations and planets are undoubtedly to blame."

Neither of us spoke. It seemed the past had been swept up into a bin and there could be no future. Except ...

"I was actually coming back here to stay for a while. I've nowhere else to go."

"Okay," she grunted in reply, "but don't make a mess."

"Fine."

Then, as if abashed by her own harshness, Betty's voice softened,

"*Though* ... if there *were* another woman you were attracted to ..."

The river gurgled again.

"And there *is* ..." I admitted, "... if she could forgive me ..."

Another deliberation.

"Depends on how hard-hearted she is ..."

"Not very, I think."

"Some soppy little fool I bet."

"Who knocks people unconscious with truncheons."

"Perhaps then you should avoid her."

"I can't. Her dog keeps tracking me down."

At this, she came closer and pulled me towards her by my dress, confiding, "You know, I don't want you to go off with this truncheon-wielding harpy. I would be jealous. Stay here with me and share my bed."

I couldn't see into her eyes. But it seemed all the surrounding night was the black of her pupils and I was falling, helpless as ever, into their infinity.

"Are you suggesting an extra marital affair?" I asked, hands finding her waist.

"What's sauce for the geese ..." she breathed.

"I suppose this affair could go on and on and on for years."

Her arms tightened around my back. "Or you could just make me Mrs Blink and be a bigamist. I really don't mind so long as we're together."

I didn't either, so she kissed me and it couldn't be denied that Betty was the best kisser in the world.

"I wonder what will happen to England?" I said, apropos of nothing, when the kiss finally came to an end.

"Yes." She spoke softly. "I wonder." And kissed me again.

Acknowledgements

Some thanks to those who helped me with this book, especially those who read it and responded: so Matthew Geden, Chris Beaumont, Bill Liao, Belinda Wild please accept a bouquet of appreciation for your time and insights. Also I'd like to pay tribute to Ed Handyside for his truly educational feedback in so many areas of the manuscript. Jane Debanne, two infant Wilds and Rachel Allen must be thanked for their not inconsiderable assistance. Morgan and Eimile Ni Shearraigh too must accept a bow for their sharp eyes and wits. Anne Caldwell and Clem Cairns both so wonderful in their amazing selves have my gratitude forever. Though, fair enough, they had that before the book was even thought of. Special thanks to Willow Liao for her wonderful and generous engagement with the text and cover.

Printed in Dunstable, United Kingdom